Westward retrieved his case and paused at the door.

"One more thing, Brian."

"What's that?"

"The club has never had a motto, has it?"

Chambers paused and frowned pensively. "No, it hasn't, come to think of it."

"Now we do – 'Per Unitatum Vis'. Look it up – it is the key to the club's success.

****

THREE MINUTES

THREE MINUTES

———————————

A novel

by

Ben C. Lawes

Matador
9 Priory Business Park,
Wistow Road, Kibworth Beauchamp,
Leicestershire. LE8 0RX
Tel: 0116 279 2299
Email: books@troubador.co.uk
Web: www.troubador.co.uk/matador
Twitter: @matadorbooks

ISBN 978 1788039 598

British Library Cataloguing in Publication Data.
A catalogue record for this book is available from the British Library.

Printed and bound by CPI Group (UK) Ltd, Croydon, CR0 4YY
Typeset in 11pt Minion Pro Regular

Matador is an imprint of Troubador Publishing Ltd

For my Saviour, Jesus Christ.

Acknowledgements

To my wonderful wife who offered so many thoughtful, humorous and invaluable insights into the female psyche.

To my children for their reading and re-reading of various drafts and their unceasing encouragement

To Stallion Arts and Media for the excellent cover art work. Your creativity is, as always, beyond bounds!

To everyone else who has contributed positively, please take the credit. For any errors, I will take the blame!

"Competitive? Ha! That's an understatement!"

Gerald Masters,
Company director,
Masters Computing Services,
Woodmouth.

Chapter 1

*I*t's *exhausting being me,* Jordan Westward mused, *let's hurry up and get this over with.* An uncomfortable silence descended in the board room as James Nelson stood up at the head of the table. He quietly mumbled a 'good morning' as he rustled around in his briefcase. The majority of the responses from those present amounted to little more than a casual nod.

As he clicked his case closed he scanned the handsome room, wood panelling covering three walls and the huge window on the adjacent side which overlooked a large car park in front of the stadium. He waited a few moments as the secretary left a tray of china for tea and coffee at the centre of the table.

Present were Marcus Leworthy, a local solicitor known for his unscrupulous methods of achieving results, more often than not stretching laws to almost breaking them himself. He had longed for an opportunity to reap havoc in Westward's life.

To his left was John Wilson, a frail, retired race horse owner and Christopher Hemmings, a quiet man in his thirties, grandson of Fred Hemmings, scorer of 37 goals in a season, still the Woodmouth Albion record. Hemmings owned several farms within a twenty mile radius of Woodmouth. Finally, Charles Monaghan, a trader of classic cars, who enjoyed a generous reputation for opening his collection for public viewing during summers in the town.

"Gentlemen, thank you for turning out at such short notice," Nelson began as he passed around copies of a document concealed in plain, brown A4 envelopes. "I will officially open the meeting now; there are no outstanding business carried over from the previous meeting, so I guess we can get straight to the issue in hand. I think we all know each other well enough to skip the introductions so let us commence. I will, as always, keep this brief and to the point."

He sat down again before continuing. "I am sure that you are aware that the club's financial status is, shall we say, less than healthy. The Inland Revenue are breathing down our necks for last year's tax – and who knows where we'll get this year's from when it becomes due. They have given us until the end of this week or else the only way forward, if indeed it is forward, will be bankruptcy for the club. That will mean instant demotion to League Two – and almost certainly the end of the club. Now, I am sure you are all well aware of the financial facilities available to this gentleman," Nelson gestured for Westward to join him at the head of the table, "he has an offer which he wishes to expound on. I hand things over to you, Mr. Westward." Buttoning his double-breasted jacket, Westward strode confidently around to the head of the table.

Just another sales pitch, he thought to himself, *no different to any other. You can do this.*

"Thank you, Mr. Chairman. I probably do not need to introduce myself. I am sure that each of you is already aware of the presence of my company in the town and as Mr. Nelson has already commented on: the respectable status of my finances." He paused and cleared his throat. "Perhaps we could start by opening the envelope in front of you. It contains the finer details of a plan to save the club, which I will go over with you."

The room filled with the scratchy tearing of the envelopes. One or two eye brows were raised as they read the title of the document. Westward briefly flicked his lengthy blond hair over his jacket collar before placing his hands behind his back as he waited for a hush to return before continuing.

"I understand that the debt as it stands is around £40 million. I have also been made aware that there is also the aforementioned outstanding tax bill of another £3 million. With my plan, I would buy the club, lock, stock and barrel, which obviously includes the debts. The club would in effect cease to exist as an individual concern, but would become a subsidiary of my company. I won't bore you with the legal bit, only to say that the share price I have offered is still fair when you consider that if liquidation is a reality and that no further cash injection materialises, there may be no alternative for the club in the time-scales to hand. To be honest, I could have waited a few weeks and got the club for much less, but," he smiled coyly, "I just wanted to show that I'm a fair man and, dare I say, I'm really not in it for the money."

Charles Monaghan raised a hand. "I bought my shares during a re-issue five years ago. Paid up shares were a pound each. What do I stand to get for the shares now?" he asked in soft, Irish tones

"Current value, according to the market and club conditions is £3.60. I am willing to pay, as you can see on page three, the sum of £4. In effect, you'll quadruple your money."

Westward could tell by Monaghan's silent whistle that the Irishman had been won over as Hemmings joined the proceedings. "I told my grandfather that I would always act according to the best interests of the club. One question though - if I don't sell and the club does go into liquidation, what do you estimate the shares being worth?"

Westward began slowly pacing around, his shoes silent on the sumptuous carpet. "It's a difficult one to answer with any accuracy, to be honest. Nevertheless it is a question that seriously needs addressing, so I am very glad that someone bought it up. I spoke to my accountant who has dealt with similar situations, not in the football arena it must be said, but to do with winding up orders all the same. He estimates that the shares would probably drop drastically once liquidation is suspected. This could be as low as two pounds, maybe one-fifty, perhaps even lower," he gave a sigh and shrugged his shoulders in uncertainty, "Who knows? OK, it still gives you gentlemen a profit whichever way you look at it, but with my plan, the club continues and you make some money."

Hemmings leaned over to Monaghan and whispered to him behind a hand. Monaghan nodded to whatever was said.

Too easy, Westward thought to himself, *that's two in the bag. Now let's give them the boring bit of how to close and re-open the club.*

Marcus Leworthy, however, in the past having made his dislike for the visiting speaker well known, was not as keen to progress. "Before we jump for joy at what some would hail a 'saviour,'" he sarcastically spat as he pushed his over-sized glasses further up his nose, "we have a few days. I vote we use the time that we have to see if other options show up." He smirked in a self-satisfying but very unfriendly manner as he folded his arms. Westward hid his frown and continued his presentation in the hope that Leworthy could be swayed.

"As a solicitor in your capacity, Mr. Leworthy, I don't suppose that you have come across this kind of scenario. Let me explain what happens. The vast majority of winding up orders are placed when debts are unable to be met within the acceptable time frame set by the debtors. The club is now seriously in arrears to the Inland Revenue. I take it that you are aware who they are?" he sarcastically asked. "There is also the embarrassing situation where there may not be money available to pay the player's wages. Yes, there is an option of seeing what might be in the wings. However, this could be disastrous, especially, should another prospective buyer uncover, say....some misuse of club funds? fraudulent trading?" he browsed the room for any change of expression, "plus, it must be said that if another prospective buyer decides not to conclude the purchase, my offer would not be re-tabled at the current value. Liquidation would then be the only road available. Bear in mind also that any costs of administering the liquidation would come out of the club assets........."

Westward was abruptly cut short.

From outside there was heard the muffled crunch of the impact of car metal and the unbridled repetition of a car alarm.

Moments later, Kayley Porter knocked and peeked her face around the door without entering the room. "Who owns a Jaguar here? I think you need to get downstairs!" Leworthy shot up and ran out as if a bomb was about to explode.

"He sure loves his car!" Hemmings joked as Leworthy dashed down the stairs.

Silence fell once again for a few awkward moments as each man looked around the walls without really observing anything. All of a sudden, James Nelson broke in with some excitement. "Gentlemen, between us all, what is the overall percentage of shares that we own?" A quick mental calculation between the men came to 80%.

"Well, while Mr. Unworthy, I mean Leworthy, is absent: off the record, what do you think of our guest's offer?"

Each looked at each other and nodded in agreement that they accepted its generosity.

"Well, I don't know about you but good riddance to the chap and I have a way to seal the deal while he is not here. Let me read you a passage from the Memorandum of Articles and Association of the club, and I quote: section 3 paragraph 2 says 'Should a proposal for sale of shares amounting to more than 75% be offered, and directors present at the tabling own more than 75% of shares, only those present may be eligible to vote for or against such sale. Any director not present will not be eligible to vote for or against such a sale.' Gentlemen, I believe we can conclude business by casting a vote. All those in favour say 'aye'." He looked around the room as Monaghan and Hemmings raised their hands. "And all those not in favour of sale of the shares say 'nay'." Once again he looked around the room. He slapped both hands on the desk, stood and held a hand out to the man.

"Well, congratulations, young man, you've just bought yourself a football club." Westward looked over to present club manager Brian Chambers who held up both hands in a boxer's stance acknowledging victory.

Immediately, Westward sent a short text to a colleague in the USA confirming the conclusion of the meeting. All men made their reasons for leaving and departed as Westward along with Chambers followed them down the stairs to the car park. Outside stood a most upset Marcus Leworthy examining the extensive damage caused to the offside front wing of his car by a very new to the road learner driver.

"I'll be up in a moment, gentlemen, nearly finished," he

muttered, first rubbing his forehead in exasperation and then straightening his tie, trying to retain a professional manner.

Nelson patted his shoulder. "Meeting's over, old boy!"

Leworthy's face dropped. "What?"

"Club's sold now!"

Leworthy looked aghast. "What do you mean? How? I didn't cast a vote!" he retorted.

"Do you remember back a couple of years you asked for an amendment to the club's papers about presence at EGM's?"

The blood drained from Leworthy's face as his mind took him back to a meeting where his proposal was tabled. He saw that this may have been to his advantage should he be present and certain others not. He had never even conceived that it would have worked against him. Fuming and speechless, Leworthy could just watch as Westward smirked, self-satisfied, and tapped his forehead with a two-finger salute. He climbed into his WRX, started the engine and allowed himself a grin as he drove slowly past a fiery faced Marcus Leworthy. As Westward approached the exit top the car park, he recalled his first attendance at the ground many years prior and the conversation that he had had with his father. At eight years old, Jordan Westward's words had hung in the heavenlies for nearly thirty years.

He could scarcely believe that they were speedily moving towards a fulfilment.

****

Thirty years earlier

The eight year old boy, thrilled to be at a professional level game for the very first time, stood huddled against his father. He was just tall enough to enjoy the activities around him as he leant with his slender arms on top of the short wall separating the fans from the pitch. The lad stood in awe at the colours of the teams, accentuated by the floodlights, mesmerised by the sounds of the crowd and the heavy breathing of players as they approached him to retrieve the match ball for a throw-in, vapour exhaling from their mouths. Despite his being tired, hungry and cold, he gazed in wonderment – any regular night, he would already be asleep at home.

His team were being rewarded for their endeavours two weeks earlier when they succeeded in holding their opponents to a shock 1-1 draw away from home, only a last gasp equaliser denying them a famous victory. The team and its fans had been boosted by this result as it had been on the back of a run of three straight defeats while their adversaries had enjoyed six consecutive victories.

The opportunity for the home team to prove their worth had not been lost on the media as national TV coverage was showing the country a prime example of how the F.A. Cup offered the potential for dramatic upsets. The boy looked about him, wide-eyed, at the continuous changing expressions on the people's faces. One moment a look of excited expectation on the supporter next to him. Clenched fists and gritted teeth, a short but loud cheer, followed by an upturned head with closed eyes, and pained, frustrated expression. The low crossed ball rolled agonisingly past the outstretched leg of the home side's star striker, and off out of play for a goal kick.

The man on the other side of him was accidentally bumped into by a passing middle-aged lady, causing him to spill a few drops of his hot tea onto the boy's coat. The old man's flat cap, thinning hair and discoloured teeth seemed to accompany his stooped, slow movements. The boy wondered how many seasons the man had been coming to matches as the old-timer gave a brown teeth stained smile and ruffled the boy's blond hair. The old man shrugged his shoulders up and down in an attempt to achieve a brief respite from the icy cold around him as the young lad shoved his hands further into the pockets of his coat, wishing he had remembered his woollen gloves.

He turned around in the hope that he might see some of his school friends. Several of his classmates had confirmed in no uncertain excitement that they had obtained tickets. However, such was the crowd's size, he doubted if he would see any of them until the morning: then would begin the dissection of what could and should have happened. What they would have done had they been given the same shot on goal that David Hawes had had in the closing minutes of the first half. What could have been when Colin Walsh's long range shot beat the keeper but rebounded back off the post? What might have happened if the opponents had been awarded the penalty in the first few minutes?

His father glanced down, his moustached face breaking into a compassionate warm smile. He bent down and lifted the lad onto his shoulders, much to the annoyance of the shorter supporters behind him, the six plus feet of his father already causing an observational hindrance. Immediately, the full vista of grandeur was available in all its glory. From his lower position, his small frame gave sight to just enough to take in the battle in front of him, but he relied on the noise and faces of the crowd to relay to him what was happening when he was not completely able to keep up with the play.

Now he could really see!

The glare from the floodlights had turned the dark, starless, cloudy winter night into day. Across on the opposite side of the pitch, behind the wall, he was able to take in the hoards of red and white scarves of the home supporters. They sang, in unison, driving their team onto greater effort.

He pondered the possibility that the players were actually from another world as the ball was thumped upfield from defence; the heavy breathing of the defender closing down an opposing forward; the disappointed growls of those around him after the referee's whistle for a free-kick decision to the visiting team: the surreptitious knee in his opponent's thigh not discreet enough.

His eyes widened as he could now clearly watch the nearest players to him. The opposing team, all in blue, were attacking down the near side. The number eleven jinked and turned, his long, free-flowing, dark hair moving in time with his bodily swerves. He finally accelerated past the fruitless, attempted tackle of a red and white defender. The expectant noise this time came from the visiting supporters as the winger powerfully crossed the ball to the far post. The blue number nine timed his jump to perfection. As he leapt he twisted his head back and then forward as he connected with the ball. To the relief of the home supporters, and the goalkeeper who was left stranded some yards from his line, the ball clipped the crossbar and went over into the massed, swaying hoard of blue and white clad fans behind the goal. As they rolled their way forward, the striker, both his hands on his head, cursed as he looked up to the heavens in disappointment.

The boys stomach turned.

That was close!

His father shook his head in angst. "I can't help but think it's a matter of time before they score, do you?" the boy's father commented, glancing up at his wide-eyed son. "We've got ten minutes left to hang on for extra-time."

Those last two words caused mixed emotions within the young lad. The thought of another half an hour's play was an exciting prospect, but so was walking into the security of the hall of his home, just a few miles away. A cup of hot chocolate, toast dripping with butter followed by the comforts of his bed was an unwelcome but nevertheless comforting distraction.

He settled for a wrapped sweet passed up to him by his father. It was not only the thirty minutes extra football that could delay the eventuality of their arrival home: there was also the several minutes it took to get out of the ground and trudge through the ice and snow back to the car. But this was Woodmouth Albion and such thoughts of comforts to come were dismissed as his senses returned to the spectacle in front of him.

No one was leaving the ground before the end of this game. The lad smiled as he remembered his father recounting how much that hasty people had missed a few weeks before. Woodmouth had trailed 2-0 against Newport County. The crowd began to filter away, heavy hearted, having been confronted by seventy-four minutes of what the papers the next day had described as 'pure torture'. Those who stayed, his father further explained, were rewarded with one of the greatest come backs ever witnessed at Wiltshire Park. His father, annotating to workmates, could only chronicle the phenomenon by crediting 'the other eleven players who played the last quarter of an hour.' Woodmouth ran home winners 4-2, a turnaround which prompted the home team's manager to run on the pitch when Alan Hamilton had scored his second and the club's fourth goal with thirty seconds of play remaining. That was the club's last win.

Another home supporter passed his father, raised his hand and grunted a greeting with a mouth full of hot-dog. The boy's mouth drooled, as he smelt the warm, savoury food and greasy, sloppy onions. His attention returned to the events on the pitch. A loud cry filled the stadium as a home player was fouled in the penalty area to the boy's left. Twenty thousand spectators jumped up and down as if their team had scored in response to the referee blowing his whistle and pointing to the penalty spot. Four blue players ran to the referee in animated protest. In the fracas that followed, the blue number three, the club's captain, was shown a yellow card. As the player turned away, he thumped his temples with both fists and shook his head in frustration.

The boy glanced to the spectators to his immediate right and from his newly elevated view saw a husband and wife gleefully hugging each other along with the other members of the crowd in support of the home side. After a few minutes the crowd gradually quietened as the home number six placed the ball on the spot, looked up to the sky as if praying for some divine assistance, stared at the ball as he took four carefully paced steps backwards. He momentarily looked towards the goal and the spread-eagled figure that stood between him and a possible unexpected match-winning goal.

"Come on Johnny!" the boy's father mumbled under his wintery breath. The old man next to them produced a small transistor radio from his coat pocket to check on other results, and found coverage of their match. Jordan could just about hear the faint, crackly voice of presenter Mike Benton.

"Thanks, Paul, there at Highbury. It seems Arsenal are safely through to round four, but we are going over to Wiltshire Park where in the closing minutes, it seems there could be a dramatic upset. We go over to our man at the game, Jim Norman."

"Yes, Mike, it certainly is drama here. Woodmouth have been awarded a penalty with just three minutes of the regular ninety left. Garry Phillips went down in the area, adjudged to have been fouled by Chelsea left-back Kevin Peterson. The task of a potential match winner for the minnows from the third division has been given to midfielder Johnny Macnamara......," Jim Norman excitedly enthused.

Macnamara turned, promptly charged at the ball and thumped a left foot shot into the top right-hand corner of the net, the keeper already having committed to the opposite direction. The twenty thousand supporters renewed their celebrations whilst Macnamara raised his arms, his triumphant cry inaudible from where the boy and his father stood. Macnamara was immediately jumped on by three teammates.

"Gooooaaaal!" Jim Norman hysterically announced, "As you can hear from the delight of the home crowd here, Macnamara has scored! He put all his effort into the power of the spot kick, sent the keeper the wrong way and Woodmouth are in front! It's Woodmouth 1 Chelsea 0 and we are in the closing minutes now. Back to you, Mike."

"Thanks, Jim. Well, maybe another upset tonight at Woodmouth, we'll return with any further developments in the closing stages and also at the final whistle. We cross now to Old Trafford where Manchester United have comprehensively beaten Mansfield Town by four goals to nil....," the tinny sound trailed away as the old man clicked the device off as the voice over the tannoy brought more delight to the already gleeful crowd.

"Woodmouth's first goal in the eighty-seventh minute was scored by Johnny Macnamara!"

Meanwhile back on the pitch, the captain in blue, head and shoulders above the official in question, ambled past the referee, angrily voicing his protest. He firmly tapped the man in black on the shoulder who promptly reached into the pocket of his shirt and animatedly raised a red card. The home supporters' cheers started up again. The player turned, scoffed in anger and began his long, slow, dejected traipse to the tunnel.

"We've done it, Jordan! We've actually done it!" the boy's father exclaimed, with a fleeting glimpse at his elevated son.

The lad returned a broad smile.

The remaining three minutes were played in a similar vein to that of a mediaeval castle siege. Woodmouth kept eleven men behind the ball and their goalkeeper had to make several close range saves. Twice, the ball was cleared off the goal line, seemingly by invisible angels, stretching the tired legs of the home defenders. In the final seconds, the opponents even had the ball in the net, but the goal was disallowed for a foul on the home goalkeeper. In the ensuing chaos, several players again surrounded the referee who booked two visiting midfielders and also sent off their centre-forward. Ten seconds later, the referee blew for the culmination of the match bringing with it cheers of jubilated relief for the home supporters, dispirited gloom for the travelling fans.

Scores of Woodmouth fans, despite loudspeaker appeals, and also a strong police presence, streamed onto the pitch to join in the celebrations with their idols. The boy was gently helped down to his feet from his father's shoulders. They shuffled their way to the open gates and joined the thriving mass of anonymous figures, energetically singing as they weaved their way across Herald Park Road's cavalcade of traffic to their own vehicle parked some half a mile away. The boy finally spoke his first words for over an hour.

"One day Dad, I'm going to play for Woodmouth and guess what? I'm going to be their manager as well." His father paused to look down at him with a gentle smile.

"Well now, young man", he said cheerfully, "that would be quite an achievement. If you play anything like your Dad, you'll be lucky to be a sub at the park!"

"No Dad," he continued, "I mean it. I can do it, you'll see."

His father, knowing how hard the cold evening had been for his son, simply ruffled the lad's hair. "Sure you will, son. Sure you will."

Jordan Westward's mind briefly skipped a couple of years ahead to a distant, unlikely, imaginary future.

****

2 ½ years later: November.

Westward was, for once, playing on form and everyone, to his elation had recognised it. On this rare occasion, he was actually the hero. For once, when he did manage to kick the ball, it went where he intended it to. For once, when he tackled someone, he didn't foul them. To add to the moment, the goal he had scored a few minutes earlier, to complete his hat-trick, was still firmly in his mind as one of the best scored by a player for his young team - ever. The excitement was still bounding around inside as he returned to his position at centre-back for the re-start. Bending over to pull his socks up over his tatty shin-pads, he heard one of the other boy's fathers call to encourage him. He responded with a beaming smile.

His first goal, after just ten minutes was a simple tap in from about three yards, but he somehow managed to keep his head as he toe-poked the ball home. His second goal, even though it took a deflection off a yellow and black-striped defender soared its way into the top right-hand corner. He was jumped on by several delighted team-mates. Now, his third goal, making the score 7-1 with five minutes left was his piece de resistance. The ball had been crossed from a corner on the right, a defender had mis-kicked a clearance which, from waist height, Westward had somehow hooked a shot that bounced powerfully off the turf and back up past the keeper and two defenders who were poorly guarding the goal.

As the final whistle blew a few minutes later, he left the pitch, beaming from ear to ear. It was an amazing feeling, he thought to himself, to hear people's approval. "Well done Jordan!"

"Great job, son!"

"Wow, I never thought you had it in you!"

I just wish mum and dad had been here.

Later, he was dropped off at his home. He waved at the departing estate car as he jogged up the driveway, so excited to tell his family of his achievements. His exuberance lasted but a short while as he could tell that his mother, once again, would show no interest. An hour later, his father returned from work and the tense atmosphere between his parents began its usual descent. As much as he needed some kind of praise from his father, he wasn't sure whether he would show any attentiveness either. It had been a long time since he had seen him even smile.

****

Later that evening, Jordan's father was washing the dishes and his older sister Susan was doing her homework in front of a music related programme on the TV. His two younger sisters, Amy and Annie were already in bed. His mother was taking a bath. The radio in the kitchen poured out the crowd dominated sounds of commentary from the midweek European Cup match from Anfield. Jordan poked his head around the door and watched his father at the sink as the smell of fish filtered its malodorous way into the hall and lounge.

Dip. Brush. Rinse. Dip. Brush. Rinse.

He could tell that his father was more than just preoccupied. Recently, he become accustomed to his father's distance, but tonight he seemed more quiet and short-tempered than usual.

"Dad," he called sheepishly.

His father, without turning his head, mumbled unintelligibly in acknowledgement of Jordan's voice.

"Will you help me with my reading before I go to bed?"

"I'm listening to the football."

"Will you be long?" Jordan pleaded.

"I said I'm listening to the football."

Dip. Brush. Rinse.

He placed another plate on the draining board. He still did not turn around.

He resigned once again to the rejection. "Oh. OK."

Jordan sadly returned to the lounge and tried to be interested in the TV. Not really understanding the programme, he picked up his reading book and for the fifth time still did not fully understand its purpose and was easily distracted by his football magazine. In the background he was aware of the familiar 'slurp' of the sink emptying as his father replaced the empty washing up bowl.

Moments later, he expected his father to appear in the lounge, but he never came. Jordan carefully placed his magazine on a shelf with other newspapers under the smeared, glass top of a coffee table. He jumped up and darted to the doorway, half expecting to run into his father but did not so continued towards the kitchen. The hallway was dark as the light bulb had blown. Doubtless his mother had moaned again at his father for not replacing it, Jordan thought to himself.

In the small kitchen, a bare bulb hung. A small gate-leg, mahogany table which had seen better days was closed up against the wall to his right. A chair sat at each end, one occupied by his father. The radio had been turned off, and his father sat staring at the wall opposite. Jordan wondered what had gained his father's attention.

"You alright, Dad?" Jordan meekly asked as he stood in the doorway leaning against the folded, plastic, concertina type door.

"Jordan, leave me alone. I am trying to think!" His father barked as he turned with a harsh stare. Jordan was taken aback by this side of his father, a temperament which had become accentuated the longer the evening went on. He had noticed that his parents seemed to be different. They were arguing more and rarely spoke to each other apart from to complain or criticise one another.

"Dad.....I just...."

"Jordan, just give me a break. I have had a long day, I am tired and I just want to be on my own!"

In the awkward silence that followed, Jordan's stomach turned in fear. His thoughts briefly drifted with sadness to one boy at his school who had announced that his parents were divorcing. Jordan had never heard of the word. Now, over the recent weeks, he propositioned to himself about the reality of a similar situation for his own family. He became aware of the fists which both his hands had curled into as a roller-coaster of emotions turned up and down within him.

Jordan pushed his hands into his pockets. "Is there anything wrong between you and Mum?"

His father sighed and nodded his head as if to summon his son towards him. "I'm sorry, son. It's not your fault. I am sorry I shouted at you. Things are, well, hard at the moment. I don't expect you to understand. I only hope that when you are older, it will be better for you."

Dad, Jordan pleaded inside, *open your arms like Jesus did in my book at school.*

His father rubbed his moustache and shook his head. "Jordan, your Mum's struggling at the moment and...," he sighed as he got up to put away some crockery, "I can't explain why very easily for you to understand. We are finding it hard to sort a lot of things out."

Dad, Jordan begged inside, *just for once, tell me that you still love me - just say it!*

"You need to get to bed." He clipped as he trudged heavily past his bewildered son and pulled his coat from the bannisters at the bottom of the stairs. "I'm just going for a walk. I'll be back soon."

With a few business like movements, he placed his jacket on and left, closing the door like an escaping thief. A few moments later, his mother appeared at the top of the stairs in a warm, pink dressing gown, hair wet and curling.

She placed her hands on her hips. "Where's your Father?"

"Dad just went out," he replied sensing an increase in the intimidating atmosphere, "He said he needed to think and wanted to go for a walk".

"Typical. Disappear when things need sorting out. Always the way with him."

"Mum, what's going on?" Jordan began to feel afraid again. First his Dad, now his Mum.

Why are you both acting so weird? I'm frightened!

She brushed past him to the lounge. "Jordan, you ask too many questions. Go to bed."

Now fear joined loneliness. He returned to the lounge to say goodnight to his sister. He walked past the TV set to pick up his magazine. He really didn't feel like tackling his reading book now.

"Jordan, get out the way!" Susan yelled with flaying arms, "I'm trying to watch this!"

"Why is everyone doing this?" He asked, slapping his hands on his thighs and flopping heavily onto the old, worn-out couch, covered in the yellow blanket which hid old spillage stains.

"Be quiet! This is my favourite song!"

"Jordan!" his mother roared, taking a cigarette from a packet on the coffee table, "go to bed. Now!"

Does anyone really love me anymore? Does anyone even like me?

He shuffled his way out of the room, just as his mother exhaled a billow of smoke towards him. He stomped upstairs to his room, flicked on the light and sat on the edge of his bed.

He stared at his hands and noticed a nail that had begun to grow. He nibbled at it until it was no longer there and then began to chew the skin at the side. Huffing as he watched the small arc of blood appear, he undressed and crept under his blankets. He hated the musty smell of the room, partly from the bedding that had not been washed for months and also the chill from the unheated house on a November evening.

The first year in the new house, particularly the winter, had been hard without any proper means of heating – a comfort that Jordan enjoyed when visiting school friends. He relished the pleasure of the alleviation from the discomfort of the chill when the 'dryer' was in his room – the strange device that his father had been given to put wet clothes in. That particular evening the antagonism of his family was not helping matters.

The old house had happy memories. His youngest sister had been born there. He had left for school as usual, one autumn morning, almost three years ago and upon returning that afternoon, had found his mother sitting up in bed with a new baby girl in her arms. He remembered how gentle and kind his mother had been that day, how she had smiled when he had dashed upstairs and paused in the doorway to her bedroom. She had patted the bed for him to come closer to see his sister. He remembered the tied-up, laced bonnet on her head and her tiny body, mostly hidden under a newly crotched blanket from his grandmother. She had her eyes closed and he had beamed at his joyful, but exhausted mother. She had returned the smile and had held the baby out for him to cuddle. He sat, gazing in awe at the newborn infant and his mother had placed her hand momentarily on his shoulder in an act of kindness. It was a happy memory, one of many from that house.

This new house had not been happy. He had no friends nearby, it was busy outside the front door, and it was always so cold, even in the summer. His father had decided to buy the house in its present condition at a lower price as he had intended to do the improvements himself, but the constant overtime at work severely restricting his father's free time.

He lay huddled under his bed covers, straining to hear his mother talking in low tones to his older sister.

Her music programme must have finished, he thought to himself.

He strained to hear, but every now and then he heard his mother raise her voice in anger. He pulled the cord above his bed to turn his light off and tried to sleep. The constant noise from the traffic outside and the yellow light from the street-lamp directly in front of the house didn't help.

He yanked the blankets over his head.

Some curtains would help, he groaned to himself.

He was on the verge of sleep when he was disturbed by the distant sound of a key in the front door lock.

It must be Dad, he ventured to himself, shifting on to his back so he could hear more clearly and was immediately aware of his mother coming to the hall.

"Where have you been?"

"Just for a walk," he grumbled, wiping his boots on the near threadbare mat at the front door.

"Could have told me, I've been sitting here like an idiot wondering where you were."

"I only went for a walk. Can't I do that?"

"You can drop that sarcastic attitude now!"

"Look, all I did was go for a walk. I've got a lot on my mind as you are well aware."

"Oh yeah, work, work and work. When are you going to do something on this house, Graham?"

Jordan quietly got out of his bed, his teeth chattering as he considered taking a blanket. He sat at the top of the stairs, just around the bend where he could not be seen. He heard his father nervously clear his throat and throw his coat over the unpainted bannister at the bottom of the stairs, his heavy boots clunking on the bare floor boards.

"When are you going to give me a break?" his father spluttered as he coughed.

"Give you a break? That's choice! I am stuck here all day on my own. I cook, take kids backwards and forwards to school and still have to suffer this hole. When am I going to get a new kitchen, hmm?"

"Gwen, I know this is hard for both of us, but I am trying," his father pleaded.

His wife stomped on the bare boards. "How about some

carpet in this hallway? What about the vegetable patch? Flowers on the garden, hmm? All you offer is loads of promises and no action. I've had enough."

"You've had enough! Oh, come on now! You've been nothing but a misery for a whole year. Could you at least try and be a bit more sympathetic? I work long hours, pay all the bills, see that everyone is taken care of and all you've done for a year is moan and moan. I've had it!"

"So, what are you going to do?" The sarcasm was back now. Another exhaling of smoke. His father stood silent for a few seconds.

"Well? And please stop that awful habit of jangling that change in your pocket!" his mother continued in an intimidating manner.

"To be honest, Gwen, I can't stand this any more. Something has to change."

"You're going then, are you? Walking out like a coward? Always thought you had no backbone. Just like your father: selfish, cowardly and lazy."

"What! What are you talking about?"

"Exactly what I said: you're a waster."

"You bitch!"

"That's it, start on me!"

Susan ran into the hallway and placed her hands over here ears. "Mum,! Dad! Please stop arguing!" she pleaded as their mother stared, red-faced, eyes bulging. "Susan, please stay out of this!"

"Mum, I am fed up of hearing you fight. When is it going to stop?"

"When he gets out of my life, I think."

"When you get out of mine, more like it!"

"Then bloody well go!" she roared, lunging at her unprepared husband and kicking his shins, "sod off!"

"You ungrateful cow! What do you want?" he screamed, on the verge of tears.

Jordan's mother was now crying. "Just get out of here! Leave us all alone, we're better off without you!" she grabbed his coat, threw it at him, and covered her face with her hands as tears flooded out. "Get out! Just get out!" she screeched.

He turned to the door dramatically and slammed it shut as

he left. Somehow, the lead-light opaque glass which ran down the centre of the door rattled but stayed in place. By now Jordan's older sister was crying and his younger sisters, disturbed by the commotion, appeared next to him in their grubby nightdresses, sucking their thumbs.

"Mummy," one sleepily called, "why are you shouting?" The two girls and Jordan trampled down the carpet-less stairs and hugged their distraught mother as she embraced the three of them, Susan sobbing on her mother's shoulder. The ignition of the car could be heard and through the glass of the front door Jordan made out the headlights of the family estate reversing off the driveway. It roared away down the road and was soon gone into the night as Jordan was surrounded by four wailing females. He stared at the floor and wondered what would happen now.

Will Dad come back?

Will I have to walk to school if the car has gone?

He hated having to do that. His shoes hurt his feet because they were too small. He also wondered if there would be fish cakes for dinner at school as tomorrow was Friday.

I hate fish cakes.

****

A few weeks later.

Jordan was bored and frustrated as he lay on his side on the threadbare carpet of the living room, his head resting on his arm. He turned another page of a comic, leafing through it for the third time. In the background, the sound of commentary of a horse race filtered from the TV set in the corner, but Jordan was almost oblivious to it.

He flipped the comic closed and rolled over onto his front, propped his face on his hands and stared at the TV screen. He sighed heavily. No one would hear him. His mother had left to do some grocery shopping with his two younger sisters. He glanced at the clock above the fireplace. It was already two-thirty. Once again, his now permanently absent father had not turned up like he had promised. Since he had departed, he had returned at two o'clock on Saturday afternoons to take him and his sisters to a park and on to his Grandmothers' for tea. He had missed his Dad. He liked it when he kicked a ball so high that it seemed to go out of sight but then eventually plummeted and bounced high in front of him. He had missed seeing him standing at the sink washing dishes. He had missed being woken with a cup of tea at six o'clock – even if he did hardly ever drink it, sleep calling louder than thirst.

Perhaps he will ring, Jordan thought hopefully.

He got up, switched off the TV set and made his way to the kitchen. He filled a glass with water. It was full of muck and sand. He sighed once again and poured the water down the sink and opened the door to the back garden. How he wished he had friends nearby that would come round. How he wished that he could visit them, but his Mother's behaviour had become even more erratic still since his father had left. She would not allow anyone round and apart from school, he was not to leave the house without her.

Funny how it's OK to leave me alone at home though.

He trudged through the overgrown lawn, his trainers soon drenched as he searched for a football. All that was on offer was a deflated plastic ball depicting a character from the big hit children's movie of earlier in the year.

Dad took us to that film, he remembered.

In frustration he slammed it right-footed into the 'Wendy House', the family's shed-cum-play-house. The thin glass rattled as a gust of wind whirled around the scrappy ropes attached to a home-made swing on the adjacent apple tree, long since relieved of its fruit for the year.

The clouds parted and the sun shone a few late rays on a damp, autumnal sky. A few gardens away he could hear the chugging of a petrol lawn mower, reminding him of how he had stood in front of his father, holding on to the handles as he pushed it up and down the length of the garden. He loved watching the grass shoot from the rotating blades as it settled in the container. The mower had now been taken and the grass continued to grow. His mother had spent some of her hard earned cash from her part-time supermarket job on a non-motorised machine, but his tender years were sadly not enough to have the strength to propel it around the extent of the overgrown lawn.

He found a tennis racket, buckled from being left out to the elements of the wet weather. He picked up a mouldy apple, tossed it in the air, his first two swings missed, but the third made full contact. The apple disintegrated into countless wet, decaying pieces that showered him and the side of the 'Wendy House'. He heard a quiet 'splat' as the major part of the apple had hit its back panel. He wiped his mouth and face and tossed the racket aside in boredom. He trudged towards the end of the long, narrow garden. This was where his father had intended to dig a big patch over and plant various vegetables, a task that young Jordan had been looking forward to.

Not anymore, he grumbled to himself, *and Dad's not coming today.*

Just then, he looked up as through the open fanlight window of the kitchen, he faintly heard the phone ringing. His face lit up, as he sprinted back to the house.

It must be Dad! he thought, *it must be! He is just a bit late, but he is coming!* With renewed hope, he picked up the phone.

Composing his breath, he picked up the receiver. "Hello, Jordan Westward here." He eagerly anticipated his father's voice, but his joy was soon stolen.

"Hello Jordan, it's Granddad here. Is Mummy there?"

"Oh, hi Granddad. No she's gone shopping. She said that she would be back about four o'clock. I'm just waiting for Daddy. He said that he would take me to the park today, but he's still not here."

"And you're there all on your own? Didn't your mum tell you?"

"Tell me what, Granddad?"

"Your Dad won't be coming today."

Jordan didn't hear the remaining part of the sentence regarding his father going on holiday. He had already retreated into his private world, where no one could hurt him, where nothing could touch him.

His grandfather continued talking, but Jordan did not take in anything. "I'll tell mummy you called," he replied, shedding a tear as he returned the tangled phone to its yellow cradle before plodding dejectedly upstairs to his cold box-sized room. He lay on his bed and stared at the ceiling as his "mind people" began to attack him once again.

He never really loved you, did he?

Anyway, you forced him to leave.

It was your fault. You were an accident.

If you hadn't been born, your Mum and Dad would still be together.

He put his hands over his ears and closed his eyes as tight as they could go.

"Stop it! Just stop it!" he managed in a weak, childlike voice. "It's not my fault!" He moved to his side and rolled back and forth, trying to gain sanity. The voices continued.

You were never wanted.

Let's face it, your family don't like you.

You have no friends and now your father has deserted you.

No one loves you. You are a misfit.

It's not like you do that well at school. You're no where as good as anyone else.

Jordan began to cry as he curled up into a tight ball and sobbed.

Maybe they're right, he reasoned to himself. *Maybe no one does really love me. Maybe I would be better off dead.*

I wish I'd never been born.

****

"I remember young Westward as quite a likeable lad, maybe lacking in confidence but academically quite sound. He didn't seem to fit in with his peers very well but wanted everybody to like him. I had him in my classes for languages and he seemed to have a great aptitude for them. Yes – I would say he was a likeable chap."

Edward Torrence,
Headmaster,
Woodmouth High Grammar School.

Chapter 2

May 23rd - four years later.

"WESTWARD! MAN ON!" a voice from behind him screamed as an opponent bore down on him. He side-stepped a tackle, looked up momentarily and launched a high ball down the centre of the field, causing him to lose his balance for a few seconds and end up sitting on the turf. The ball was jumped for by the centre-forward on Jordan's team, along with the right-back for his opponents. The striker was a good couple of inches taller and made the connection to divert the ball into the path of the oncoming right-winger. He weaved his way around two defenders before unleashing a shot aimed at the top left-hand corner of the goal. The ball was just a few inches out of the reach of the desperate dive of the goalkeeper. It clipped the top of the left hand post and rippled down the back of the net before nestling neatly on the turf.

There were few people on the sidelines of the pitch brave enough to give up their time on this cold, rainy, spring, Sunday morning. Nevertheless, they shouted their approval as the goalscorer ran back to his delighted team-mates with his arms aloft and a jubilant smile. The yellow-shirted youngsters huddled together, hugged each other and jogged back to their positions for the resumption of the match.

"Three minutes," shouted the referee, holding three fingers up for all to see. The score was 3-3. Extra time was not an option at this level, so that would mean penalties to ensure a conclusion of the match on the day.

Straight from the kick-off, the red-shirted opponents launched an attack, but again good defending re-gained possession for Jordan's side. Their central-midfielder however lost possession when his pass was too short for the team-mate just ahead of him. The opposing midfielder threaded the ball to his right-back who had made a rare foray to support on the over-lap. His first time cross was headed down by a striker, but Jordan's sliced clearance landed at the feet of an attacking player who at first could not believe the opportunity for an attempt on goal that this had created. The 'keeper responded but his frantic dive in front of the player was just a second too late and he could only look back as he watched the ball cross the line past a desperate defender. Jordan knew that his mistake could have cost his team the game.

From hero to villain in seconds.

Charlie Brown. The blockhead. The goat.

He tried to hide the rising hurt inside as he bit his lip.

Several of his team-mates expressed their disapproval by calling him names. His captain simply looked him in the face, said 'never mind' and screamed for his players to get back for the kick-off. By now there would be less than two minutes left. Jordan looked down, pulled his socks up and returned to his position. His team kicked off but despite several thwarted attempts were unable to break down the defence. All his team pushed forward for one last attempt to equalize, but, right on the edge of the opposing goal area, they lost possession again.

Once more, quick passing and shear gritted determination saw the team with a one on one situation between Jordan and the opposing striker. His goalkeeper shouted for him not to commit to a tackle at the first chance. Jordan however wanted to make amends for his earlier error and slid in. In a brief moment, his whole world changed. He made contact with the player's ankle and not the ball, which trickled harmlessly back to the safe arms of the goalkeeper. The opponent fell forward, arms out in front of him to cushion the fall. Both players yelled out in pain as the player landed on Jordan's bent left leg.

The referee blew sharply to indicate his awarding a penalty, just to add insult to injury, but neither player were getting up too quickly. Jordan rolled over in obvious agony whilst his opponent sat and gently nursed nothing more than what was found to be a bruised left leg. The referee signalled for the first aider for Jordan's team to come on as he stood over him, a consoling hand on his shoulder. The trainer immediately ran on, bag in hand but took one glance at Jordan's obvious pain before shouting for a stretcher. Each player looked on, hands on hips, enjoying the moments to regain breath, none offering any solace. As Jordan left the pitch on the stretcher, he was carried down a gauntlet of team-mates, all verbalising their own brand of abuse.

"Thanks, Westward. Last time you play for us!"

"Yeah, idiot!"

"Definitely lost us the game now - thanks a bunch!"

"Stupid thing to do!"

He tried not to look anyone in the eye as the demons once again added to his already strong thoughts of self-annihilation. He held back from crying and took deep, raking breaths to put on a brave face.

"Jordan, there's only a couple of minutes left. We'll need to get to hospital. Do you want to wait to see what happens? They'll put Danny Griffiths on in your place." The kind voice of midfielder Josh Harris's father Ian, an amiable, slim man in his early forties kindly spoke as he held one end of the stretcher. Jordan simply nodded, staring at his knee. The delayed penalty kick was then confidently dispatched as Jordan sat on the park bench which had been swiftly bought over to the touch line for him. For the final two minutes he was breaking inside as he watched his side concede another late goal to finally lose 6-3. He got up to try to walk but soon gave up when he needed support from a couple of nearby, sympathetic parents. Several of his team mates muttered more insults under their breath as they past him.

He remained quiet the whole journey to the town's General Hospital and most of the two hour wait in the A&E before he was finally seen by a nurse who took x-rays, gave him some strong pain killers and then shortly afterwards by a thickly bearded, friendly Asian doctor in a blue turban.

"Hello young man," he began with a smile, "I am Doctor Singh. My goodness, you really have done yourself a mischief, haven't you?"

Jordan nodded nervously as the doctor sighed.

"Now then, your knee," he began as he gently attempted to straighten Jordan's leg, "is the largest and most complex of joints. Obviously, it is the most used and therefore the most stressed joint in the body. There are a number of issues which could cause the injury that you have. It could be a break, it could be what we call ligament damage or it could be meniscus. If you are really unlucky, it could be a combination."

He stepped back, folded his arms and looked on thoughtfully for a moment before continuing.

"Can you try and explain what happened and what you felt when you fell, Jordan?"

Jordan stared at his already swollen knee feeling very scared. "Well, I went into a tackle, probably a bit hard, and as I bent my leg back I twisted it. I kind of felt this snap - but not like a broken bone. I know what that's like as I did break my arm once. This was, I don't know, really deep inside."

The doctor nodded sympathetically as he toyed with his pen before continuing. "The knee joint is very delicate and lots of knee injuries occur in sports, especially football and rugby. A ligament injury can occur in many ways, mostly by landing from a jump onto a bent knee then twisting," he paused as he performed a kind of fifties 'twist' dance, "or landing on a knee that is over-extended." Jordan nodded and stared at his knee. The doctor cleared his throat before continuing. "Because of the amount of force that is required to damage the cruciate it is possible for other areas within your knee such as the meniscus to also be damaged."

Just then, his mother, out of breath, burst into the room.

"Hello Doctor, I'm Jordan's mum. Oh, Jordan, I got the

bus here as soon as I could. Mr. Harris called me. What have you done?"

What have I done? Whatever happened to how are you? She covered a hand over her mouth in shock at the sight of the swelling.

"Please, Mrs. Westward, take a seat," the doctor waved a hand at the vacant chair next to the bed. She sat, adjusting her wide-bottomed trousers around her boots.

The Doctor introduced himself, told his mother not to be worried and gave a brief synopsis of what Jordan had explained and what may have happened. Jordan listened intently to the doctor's enthusiasm but all he wanted to know was when he could he play football again.

"Why is it some people can carry on playing with this injury?" Jordan ventured, recounting a recent game on TV where a player had been brave enough to attempt to play on with a knee injury during an important match. The player was eventually stretchered off fifteen minutes later.

The doctor nodded in agreement. "An interesting situation, really. You may feel that you can carry on, but as soon as your knee is put under strain, it will become unstable. The reason why you can't carry on in the end is that the kind of 'holding back' mechanism of your ligament has gone. So, as soon as you overuse your shin in relation to your thigh, your whole knee joint will become unstable. Looking at the swelling, I think it is likely that you have torn a ligament. The swelling is what is known as haemarthrosis."

At this, Jordan interrupted. "Haema – I guess that must have something to do with blood, does it?"

The doctor smiled kindly and nodded. "Yes, it does, well done young lad! It is actually bleeding within the joint. This swelling is your knee's way of saying 'don't use me any more', if you see what I mean."

Just then, another nurse entered the room, passed on an envelope to the doctor whilst whispering something in his ear. The doctor nodded his thanks before drawing the x-ray pictures from the envelope and placed them both on a magnetized white board which illuminated as he flicked a switch.

He tilted his head and paused thoughtfully, his chin in his hand.

"OK, the good news is, I don't think that there are any fractures. The femur here," he pointed to the large bone in the thigh area above the knee, "seems intact and I can't see any damage either to your fibula or your tibia. Hmm."

Jordan nodded, still confused.

"Having said that, Hmm," the doctor began his thinking again, tapping with his fingers, "I think the sooner we get you into theatre, the better. What do you think, Mrs. Westward?"

"I, well," his mother stammered, clutching her handbag nervously to her chest, "is it that serious?"

He turned the off the light and stood staring at Jordan for a few moments. Jordan was relieved to hear of the fact that there were no broken bones, but he had little understanding of the long-term implications of ligament injuries.

"I think what we need to do is some internal examination. We will need to put a tiny camera inside your knee to explore a bit deeper. This is quite new technology but it gives us a very good picture of the extent of the damage." He pulled a diary out of his pocket. "Now, I am breaking a few rules here. I want you to go home for now, keep an ice pack on it to control the swelling and rest, rest, rest until I get you booked in, which will hopefully be next week. For now, I think we'll just get you bandaged up so the knee won't get used too much and we'll get you some crutches."

Jordan's mind was in a spin.

Next week is ages away!

Mr. Harris entered the room after a courteous knock and looked at his watch.

"Gwen, I-"

Jordan's mother stood, brushing down her trousers. "Oh, of course, yes, Mr. Harris," she began, "I know, you've been very good to wait for us. I guess we need to go."

"OK. Mrs. Westward, give your son's details to the receptionist and you should get a letter very soon. Don't worry, I'm sure things will work out fine," the doctor re-assured Jordan with a final smile before shaking hands and leaving the room.

Jordan was carefully aided into a wheel chair and manoeuvred to the reception. He was gingerly bandaged up and wheeled to the Harris's car by his mother where Mr. Harris gingerly helped Jordan into the back seat. He and Josh hardly spoke on the journey back as the pain killers began to wear off. Jordan stared out of the window at the rows of bleak terraced houses passed by and wiped a lonely tear from his eye as he took a deep breath to stop his bottom lip from quivering. This was not part of his 12th birthday plans.

****

Jordan was grateful for the fact that he could not get to school. At least it would be a while before he saw anyone who would remind him of his crazy penalty incident. His mother, as always, was out at work all day so he busied himself with watching old football re-runs and, checked out a number of old manuals for various school subjects. On the Wednesday, the letter for his knee procedure arrived, clarifying that his appointment had been set for the following Monday.

****

His mother, in a rare moment of compassion, took the day off work to take him to the hospital for the operation. They arrived, as scheduled at eight o'clock, having had to allow twenty minutes awaiting a taxi. He was taken to the pre-op room and given a brief but thorough run-down of exactly what was going to be done. A large iodine orange arrow was painted on his left thigh, ensuring that the correct leg was worked on. He was then wheeled to an area just outside the theatre and the gowned staff gave an explanation of the anaesthesia. They were going to put a transparent mask over his mouth and he was to breath normally and count to ten.
He began: *One, two, three, four.....*and he was gone.

****

A little over two hours later, he awoke and noticed his mother next to him. He was groggy and wanted to go back to sleep – it was such a wonderful place to be. No one disturbed him, no one abused him, no one could get to him. It was a netherworld of peace. He neither dreamed nor had nightmares – it was perfect.

His mother noticed his brief movement and closed her magazine. "How do you feel?" she asked abruptly.

"How did it go?" he quizzed, shifting to sit up, aware that his knee was now in a stiff cast.

"The doctor should be here in a few minutes – he said he would come back when you came round."

"What have they said?"

She sighed. "I think it is not good, but I'll let them explain. All I know is you will be off your feet for several weeks. No more football until next season at least," she paused, "maybe longer."

Jordan's impatience showed as he slumped back on the slightly inclined bed. He pulled back the flimsy sheet and was shocked to see a cast from the top of his thigh to his ankle.

Strange, he thought. *Even kids with broken legs don't get this much plaster.*

A nurse appeared and took an order for lunch. The night before, Jordan had thought about how hungry he would be having not eaten for sixteen hours. He was surprisingly not that bothered – he rationalised that it was his nervousness about the operation. Shortly after, the doctor who had seen him the week previous arrived with his superior and gave his best attempt to look positive.

"Hello Jordan. Hello Mrs Westward. Pleased to meet you. I'm Doctor Turner, the chief knee specialist. You have quite a competitive athlete here, I understand. Well, I can tell you the procedure went well, we got a very good look at your knee and you took one heck of a clump, didn't you?" he began, gently smiling with the best re-assurance that he could give.

Jordan was interested in one thing. "OK, but when can I play football again?" His question was followed by a very un-comfortable silence. Doctor Turner sighed and curved the corner of his mouth up as he tried to compose kind words in a tough situation. Jordan stared, expectantly, anticipating some shock news.

"Jordan, I might as well be honest with you. But," he paused, "first I need you be honest with me. Have you had any pain in your knee leading up to your incident last week?"

Jordan shrugged his shoulders, "Yeah, most of the time. I just play through it and put up with it. I'm pretty slow running but being a defender, I don't cover much ground during a game. Why?"

"Well, from what we could see, you've had an injury there for a long time. I don't know how you've put up with it, to be honest."

OK, Jordan thought, *get to the point.*

"Jordan, I-," he surprised himself at his hesitancy to bring the news. "I think there is a very strong possibility that you won't ever play football again. Your knee was in quite a mess. Do you remember I mentioned the ligaments that can get damaged in your knee? Well, there are four. I didn't bother mentioning the other two as they rarely get affected. Jordan, all four of your ligaments have been ripped, as well as a tear in your meniscus. We cleaned your knee out and there was quite a lot of loose tissue. You'll not be playing any sport for several months."

Several months! Jordan thought, *several months!*

"You mean, I'll be out for the rest of this season?" he asked aghast.

"And...... probably next season as well."

Jordan's mother remained silent as her son and the doctor made verbal negotiations as to the severity of the problem.

"Jordan, as you get older, there is a very good chance that you will develop arthritis as well. Any sports injury leaves an area in a drastically weakened state. You have youth on your side so healing will be quicker and easier than if it had happened to the likes of me or your mother here.

His mother interjected in astonishment. "Arthritis? What do you mean? He's only twelve!"

"Yes, I know that this is extremely rare. The severity of the exploration today will only exasperate the arthritis as well. It puts quite a strain on the joints. In all honesty, Jordan, I -," he paused and placed his hand on Jordan's shoulder, "Well, I hate to say this but, I would not advise you to play competitive sport again."

His mother glared at the doctor as she shot to her feet.

"What?"

"I know that this will be a disappointment, but you could still be able to kick a ball around in your garden in a few years, but serious full matches," he shook his head, "not an option."

"Doctor, he's not even a teenager yet, you can't be serious; football is his life!"

As the conversation continued, Jordan just sat and stared into space. The pain in his soul began to hurt as much as his knee. Already, he knew that he had to face the ridicule of his friends at school soon but not playing football again was a pain that he could never have been able to prepare for. The doctor explained some exercises for Jordan to do, but his mind was not concentrating. Trying to come to terms with losing the love of his life was a distraction he had not expected that day.

The remaining hours, few though they were, dragged for Jordan. His mother, unusually for her, tried to console him, but he knew that they were just words. To say goodbye to football was more than he could take.

As the taxi carried them home, he silently imagined children kicking a ball around in their garden. How different the day may have been had he cleared the ball successfully and not plunged in for the tackle that caused the injury that he now nursed both physically and mentally. He began to drift. He was aware of his mother's voice in the background but he couldn't listen. He closed his eyes and let his head fall back on the seat as the voices inside began again.

Let's face it, Jordan, they told him, *life isn't worth living now is it?*

The demons inside rejoiced. They held a party as they dug into his consciousness. Constantly, they tormented and re-minded him of the devastation and the helplessness that he was in, that he no longer had any value. After all, he was to blame for the defeat.

Unforgivable.
No way back.
No friends.
No hope.
May as well give up now.
No one really likes you.
You're finished.
End it all now.

****

Five years later - August

Jordan trudged up the driveway and stepped through the overgrown grass at the centre of the path. His mind constantly went over the crazy back pass by the Woodmouth defender, handing their opponents an injury time 1-0 win in the opening game of the season. He was not in a good mood, his frustrations taken out on his key as it was forced into the lock of the yellow entrance door, the paint flaking off in several places.

He jiggled the key the usual three or four times before the door was able to be pushed with force. The moment he entered the dark hall he remembered another light bulb had gone and despite his mother reminding him to buy one on the way home from school, he once again had forgotten. He cursed under his breath.

He screwed his face up at the pungent odour of pilchards as he accidentally kicked a carelessly removed pair of shoes on the bare boarded hallway. He sluggishly removed his coat and red and white scarf and threw them over the bannister. He stopped by the half closed lounge door, rested his hand on the wallpaper-stripped wall and noticed a voice that he did not recognise along with that of his mother. A television programme was on, low in the background.

"Anyone home?" he called nervously.

He stood a while trying to place the voice before going to the kitchen and pouring a glass of water. He noted again that no one had washed up the dishes.

That stink of fish is awful.

He wiped his mouth on the back of his hand and looked around the kitchen at the mess. The sink piled high seemed to complete the scene.

Oh well. Up to me again, I suppose.

His mind showed him a vision of the last time that he saw his father in this house, standing washing dishes. He had tried to start a conversation, but his father had not engaged.

I tried to talk to him but he just wasn't there. I really miss Dad.

Jordan shook his head to return his thoughts to the present, placed his hands on his hips and sighed. Just then his mother, uncharacteristically dressed smarter than usual came into the kitchen.

"Oh, Jordan, I didn't hear you come in," she quietly said almost nervously as she brushed past him to fill the kettle. She plugged the lead into the appliance, leaned against the grubby worktop and folded her arms.

"Got in five minutes ago. Woodmouth lost," He mumbled without making eye contact with his mother, nervously pushing his hands deeper into his jeans pockets. She fumbled around in her trouser pockets for her cigarettes. Her hands shook as she took three attempts to strike a match, took a deep drag of the cigarette and exhaled the smoke towards the ceiling, where it hung and swirled in a grey storm-like cloud.

She scoffed and flicked some ash into the sink. "Don't know why you waste your money on rubbish football all the time." She precariously placed the burning cigarette on the edge of the worktop as she made two cups of coffee. Jordan opened his mouth to plead his case but thought better of it.

I wonder if there is someone else here? I am sure I heard another voice.

He thought kind remarks might have staved off the hostility. It was only then that he heard the front door close very quietly. He turned at the sound but saw no one.

"Who was that?" he quizzed, his suspicions confirmed.

His mother nervously replied. "Probably Amy on her way out. Don't you have homework to do?"

Jordan felt the unease about the moment but attempted to dissolve the atmosphere.

"You look really smart. Are you off somewhere?"

She swung round, her anger overflowing. "Why are you so nosey? Can I not do anything without you having to know details? You are just like your father – so nosey. He wouldn't let me have a life of my own either. For God's sake, leave me alone!" She pushed past him to pick up her cigarette, chewing her lip as the ash of the cigarette lengthened. Finally, she swore as she knocked the ash onto the floor. It immediately made a burn mark on the linoleum which she trod down with her shoe.

"Mum", Jordan began, "when will we start to sort the house out and do it up a bit? I mean, just keeping on top of the washing up would help...."

"What's wrong with you doing it?" she interrupted abruptly, exhaling more smoke towards the ceiling.

He didn't respond.

"Just like your father. Bone idle. You'll never amount to anything."

He imagined where he would really like to take this conversation: him bellowing out his frustrations with his mother overwhelmed and unprepared to respond. Instead, he said nothing as if his lips were unable to part.

"Why do you never have anything to say for yourself? You truly are useless, Jordan. Lazy, good for nothing and useless."

She turned to look out to the darkness through the greasy window before shaking her head, tutting and storming out of the room. A car horn hooted in the distance from the driveway. "I'll see you later," she muttered, grabbing a coat from the bannister without turning to look at him. She opened the front door and was gone. He raced to the front room window and peered out, hidden behind the thin, tobacco-browned net curtain. He watched as a short, smartly dressed man, with tight curly hair opened the front passenger door of a Ford Cortina to let his mother in. He obviously cracked a joke as she paused, laughed, kissed him on the cheek and smiled. The man, also smiling, bounced his way around the front of the car and jumped into the driver's seat. It was a newish car, Jordan considered, and almost marvelled at the engine which started first time.

Jordan watched the car disappear down the street until it eventually left sight at the tight bend a few hundred yards down. He trudged upstairs, aware of the rock music coming from his younger sister's bedroom.

Jordan could not help the rising bitterness. Was it surprise? Anger?

No, this was betrayal. Simple, outright betrayal.

Jordan's thoughts were interrupted as his sister and her boyfriend bounded out of the room, giggling.

"Oh, hi Jordan, we're just off out. Be back later. Annie is staying overnight at her friends. Did you know?"

Jordan, embarrassed for a moment, shook his head and shrugged his shoulders.

"Hey man, you're always so full of such enlightening conversation!" the long-haired, skinny boy joked in a slur as the two stomped their way down the stairs past him.

The giggling continued as they collected their coats and once more Jordan was aware of the emptiness of the house as the front door shut. It was now quarter to ten and he was nowhere near ready for sleep. He slumped onto his bed and stared at the threadbare carpet on the floor. He sighed deeply and laid back with his hands behind his pillow.

Then, the idea came into his head.

He made his way into his sister's bedroom, suddenly aware of a very unusual dank, musky smell. In the ashtray on the window sill next to a paperweight containing a picture of David Bowie from the cover of Aladdin Sane was a half smoked cigarette. Or what he thought was a cigarette. He picked it up to examine it closer. It was still hot and he was aware of the tiny embers still alight inside. He gently blew on them several times and before long it was smoking again.

He had tried cigarettes before, once, but coughed so violently he had never gone back to them. Yet tonight, this was different.

This is exciting!

This was hidden, no one would know, no one could see him. He was all alone. He took a long puff from it and let the smoke go deep into his lungs, held it, and then slowly exhaled. He amazed himself that he did not cough, and was mildly surprised at its different taste.

Why does this taste so different? Must be because it's a 'roll-up'.

He took another drag and within minutes began to feel so relaxed, so care free. He took the 'cigarette', still unaware of its contents, downstairs. He sat in the lounge, pitch black apart from the minor light from the street lamplight edging through between the curtains which did not quite meet at the centre of the bay window.

He turned the TV on just in time to hear a short report of Woodmouth's game that he had attended earlier that evening. He lay on the sofa, smoking and watching television. What a strange situation he thought to himself as he felt his body get more and more heavy, but at the same time, so unstrained.

Until the car outside bought him back to reality.

He quickly threw the item into the fireplace, still alight. It felt like his heart was nearly in his mouth as he heard the key turn in the lock and he heard his mother's voice.

Oh hell, he paniced, *what do I do now?*

As she shook her shoes off, he heard her say quietly, "what on earth is that smell?" She traced it easily to the lounge where Jordan stood completely unsure of what to do or say. His mother stood in the doorway as she flicked the light switch on which caused Jordan to squint briefly. She stood aghast, seeing the smoke in the fireplace, taking in the smell.

She took three strides towards him and began repeatedly slapping her son around the face. The man with her attempted to pull her back which only spurred her on, her anger having full force now.

"JORDAN! OH, OH, HOW DARE YOU! HOW DARE YOU!" she screamed, continuing the onslaught as Jordan put both his hands up to block the blows. It was only a matter of time, he knew before the emotional blackmailing tears would start. "YOU SNEAKY, SNAKE-LIKE, GOOD FOR NOTHING IDIOT! OH!"

"Mum, you don't understand...." Jordan ventured.

"DON'T UNDERSTAND? DON'T GIVE ME THAT! THIS TIME YOU'VE GONE TO FAR!" she roared.

"Go easy, Gwen," the man gently intervened. She eventually backed off and stood shaking, held by the arms of the man with her.

"I just found it in Amy's room. I was just curious, I..."

"Don't you lie to me!" she spat viscously, "You, you.....agh!"

Jordan shook as her verbal onslaught continued.

"What do I tell the neighbours? What do I tell anyone who comes round – I have a drug taking son! Oh, how could you? I can't believe it – my son smokes dope!"

"Mum, it was in Amy's room!"

"You coward! You won't even admit your guilt even when you are caught red-handed. Lazy, good for nothing, useless, lying .... Oh, don't try to implicate your sister. This is all you, Jordan! I should have known it would be you."

"Mum, go up to her room, you'll see an ashtray, you'll smell it there! I'm telling the truth!"

"Stop lying! Now, you, just get out, GET OUT! GET OUT!" she barked, her anger increasing.

"No, Mum, I won't!" he said meekly, vainly attempting to stand up to his mother.

"I beg your pardon?" she said almost in shock that Jordan had had the audacity to argue.

"I won't!" he again spoke with little conviction, cowering with his hands behind his back.

"YOU LEAVE NOW!" she bellowed and pointed towards the front door. A moment later, for good measure, she simply added, "NOW!"

Do I go quietly or do I make a scene? Jordan thought to himself through the fog of drug induced confusion. He knew he was simply still too afraid to face up to his mother so strode past her without looking at her face, shoved the man out the way and grabbed his coat and scarf. Now, fighting the tears back, he simply slammed the door, momentarily aware of his mother's tearful whimpering in the arms of the still unknown man.

He wondered where he would go as he slipped his coat on and knotted the scarf around his neck. He checked his watch. Ten-fifteen. He checked the contents of his pockets and a strange, eery feeling crept over his soul. He remembered the sign outside the off-licence on the way back from the football ground earlier that evening. There was a special offer on a popular extra-strong lager. He figured that he had just enough to buy one can of beer if he could make it there in fifteen minutes.

Then, amongst the overgrown grass of the central reservation slicing the dual carriageway in half, he noticed from a distance what looked like a piece of paper. As he approached it, it flapped about, trapped between blades of grass. His heart skipped a beat as he realised what it was. It was a ten pound note. He picked it up to closely to examine it, but realised straight away the precious seconds which were slipping away. He stuffed it into the back pocket of his jeans as he jogged a few painful paces before returning to a brisk walk.

But now, he thought to himself, *this puts a whole new slant on the situation.*

He now had enough money for several cans of beer, a chocolate bar and who knew what else with the change. At ten twenty-seven, the grey-haired man behind the counter, not unfamiliar with Jordan, bade him a good evening as Jordan shyly picked up not just one can, but what joy, a whole pack of four. Plus a chocolate bar. He pushed the note towards the man behind the counter. The man examined it closely, held it up to the light to check its authenticity, pulled a face at Jordan and counted out the change.

"Didn't know you were over eighteen?" the man behind the counter quizzed with a frown.

Jordan stumbled a moment. "Erm, yeah, couple of weeks ago."

Liar. Well done!

Jordan pocketed the change, turned and left swiftly, the thick glass door offering the usual chiming as it opened and closed. He stood outside, examined one of the cans that he pulled from the plastic and read the details of its contents.

Man, he thought, *eight per cent alcohol!*

He watched a bus crawl past as he pulled at the ring of the can and threw it to the pavement. Behind him, the lights of the off licence were turned off as he took a long draw from the thick tasting, almost treacly, effervescent liquid. He finished half the can in one gulp before wiping his mouth on his hand and belched loudly. He took another look at the lettering on the can before finishing the rest of the contents and dropped the empty can into the waste bin next to the entrance.

I didn't think it would be that easy, he thought to himself, as he carefully unwrapped the chocolate bar, finished it in three bites, before pulling open another can and walking towards the town centre. For a few brief moments, he had not a care in his world. In his mind, the demons celebrated. They didn't think it was going to be this easy, either. With Jordan Westward, they had thought that they might have had a fighter on their hands.

No, this was so easy.

Who cares? Jordan thought as he emptied the second can and pulled on another.

****

Nineteen months later – December.

The evening had begun in a joyful way for Jordan Westward, having seen Woodmouth win 2-0 at home but had disintegrated once again in direct proportion to the amount of alcohol that he had consumed. The music was weaving its tentacles around his mind and body as it drifted from the speakers and spoke its message to his soul. He closed his eyes, took another drag on a cigarette. He slowly exhaled the smoke and then opened his eyes to watch it hang in a cloud in the demon infested atmosphere of the sleazy bedroom. A young girl giggled as she sat on the lap of a teenage boy in a tatty armchair in the opposite corner. A small crowd of youths laughed in the kitchen next door as they attempted to make hot drinks in the greasy unwashed cups which had sat on the draining board for days.

Westward's head was spinning from the effects of drinking too much alcohol on an empty stomach and also from being intoxicated by other substances. He took another swig from the large vodka bottle as if it were water. Despite the liquid, his mouth was dry.

His knee also ached due to the cold weather. Even so, as he stubbed out his cigarette and opened yet another can of beer. He watched imaginary birds emerge from the arms of the chair in which he had slumped. He allowed his head to fall back as once again he closed his eyes in the vain hope of steadying himself. His head began to spin so he once again looked ahead trying to focus. Through the rips in the net curtains which tried to cover the windows he watched the snow tumble endlessly as a rare vehicle slushed its way through the wet roads. He coughed heavily as he got out of the chair and tried not to show his difficulty in walking.

He bumped into the broken coffee table in the middle of the room covered in overflowing ash trays, crumpled cigarette packets, beer cans, glasses and sections of the day's newspaper. He glanced at his watch. 2:35. He needed to get home. He had no money and he knew it was a four mile walk back. And his knee was really aching.

He left the lounge and immediately was shocked by the temperature drop in the hallway. He pulled himself up the stairs by the rail, the top of which was dangerously loose. The tall, leggy blonde was still here. She was talking to someone he did not know at the top of the stairs. She seemed disinterested in the acne-ridden boy in a t-shirt showing two caricatures of two well known musicians of the time and Westward wondered why she was even there. He caught her attention and embarrassingly smiled as he made his way to the bathroom. He locked the door and took in the surroundings and wondered why he had even bothered coming. The sink and bath were simply disgusting. The smell of urine was overpowering. The crusty flannel left on the dirt-ridden pink bath-rug finished the scene. Through the frosted window, Westward's angst built as he watched the accumulating snow on the sill.

He flushed the toilet, and tried his best to walk in a straight line as he came out. He fell back against the wall behind the blonde girl who was clearly getting tired of the other boy's company. Westward closed his eyes.

"Hey, do you mind?" the boy sarcastically said, staring forcefully at Westward, who stood several inches taller.

"No, I'm OK where I am, thanks," Westward replied returning the sarcasm.

"No, you don't seem to understand," the boy continued, pushing past the girl, tilting his head as if with authority, "I don't want you up here."

Westward opened his eyes. "I couldn't care less what you want, pal," Westward slurred, "I am happy where I am." Westward folded his arms. The other boy mumbled something under his breath as he turned back to the girl.

Click.

There it was. The demon hit the 'respond now' button in Westward's fragile mind.

Westward assumed it to be an insult to him and the demon pushed, demanding an immediate response. "What did you say?" he questioned, pushing the youth in the back. "What did you say? Come on you filthy piece of...." Westward never saw the fist coming even though it bairly made contact with his chin. His head turned from the impact. As he wavered, he shook his head to gain straight vision again and with all his anger began pummelling punch after punch into the youth's face. The girl began screaming for the fight to stop.

Then the adrenaline rush hit him as he smashed one final, angry fist into the youth's face, satisfaction at the sound of splintering bones from his onslaught.

"Don't ever," he paused for good measure, catching his breath, "don't ever do that to me, ever again, do you hear?"

The youth looked at him through fear-filled eyes, nodding his head with a painful, hazy look. Westward smiled evilly, spitting at him as he casually turned and stumbled down the stairs. Several people appeared from the lounge in wonderment at the commotion.

"What the heck.....! Jimmy, you OK? What on earth happened?" A skinny, long haired boy in his early twenties glanced first upstairs and then at Westward as he stood triumphantly in the cold hallway.

The blond girl behind the youth on the landing, through sobs, stared down the stairwell. Westward sniffed as more blood continued to flow from his broken nose.

One lad stood between Westward and the front door. "Where do you think you're going? You just hurt my friend here, mate!"

Click. Again, the demon urged him on.

Westward smiled sarcastically, momentarily looked back and then, before the other youth could even have a chance of moving, forced his forehead onto his nose. Again, blood spilled, some spraying onto Westward's greasy hair. The lad immediately held his head in his hands as two other boys stood speechless at the spectacle. For a moment, the scene froze as no one knew what to do. Westward's last victim wept uncontrollably.

Wow, I've never done that before. What came over me?

He stumbled his way back to his chair, retrieved his vodka bottle and returned to the hallway. He scanned the stunned faces around him.

"I...er, I think I'll be off," He said quietly and slipped out into the cold of the night and gently closed the door after him. He briefly slumped outside and placed the bottle on the wall before pushing his hands deep into his jeans pockets. He sniffed, aware of the pain from his broken nose and then took a deep breath. He coughed up blood before spitting it away.

The demons danced.

A few moments later, despite the fact that the snowfall had increased, he stopped to light up another cigarette, grabbed the bottle and started to walk home. He stumbled over an empty milk bottle that spun its way, still intact, towards the flaky brown paint of the metal gate hanging delicately by its solitary, top hinge. He looked back to the house from where he had left and took a long, satisfying swig of vodka and wiped his mouth.

He passed the pub on the corner and kicked a stone which bounced erratically towards the other side of the street before bouncing and settling by the rear tyre of a parked panel van. He made his way towards the football ground which guarded the way between him and home.

Home, he thought to himself. *I don't really live there, I just pass through.*

The relationship with his mother had been semi-restored but continued its fractious, strained status. He swore under his breath as the cold, accentuating the pain in his knuckles, caused him to drop his cigarette. He rubbed them under the armpit of his thin jacket and as the journey progressed his heart grew heavier.

His anger began to give way to remorse, then to sadness, and finally, loneliness, the brokenness overwhelming him. He stood and stared up at the metal floodlights of the ground as he fell rather than sat on a low brick wall. The full weight of his emptiness hit as the tears came with full force. His body shook as he hid his face in his hands and wept as the snow continued to fall without mercy. He had never been a great fan of Unholy Alliance, but the demons began to feed his soul with the lyrics of *'Funeral for a Broken Life'* that had been played earlier that night at the party..

> *All desert you, you are nothing,*
> *Hopelessness your only friend.*
> *Count the days, the months, the years.*
> *Always borrow, never lend.*
>
> *God may hold the keys for you now,*
> *But will He ever let them go?*

Take a chance, there's nothing here, so
Surely hell's a better show.

And now, you're all alone,
And nothings ever gonna change,
And now, forever and a day.
What's the use in telling lies?
No one ever hears your cries,
Please don't tell me that you want to stay, yeah,
Please don't tell me that you want to stay.

In between tears, Westward took long swigs from the vodka bottle, oblivious to the burning, tasteless liquid as the flakes showed no sign of abating their tumbling from the unnatural brightness of a snow-filled sky. Eventually, the bottle emptied, his insides at least warmed for a while. Westward considered simply throwing it with all his might at the high brick wall outside of the football ground, yet a tiny atom of conscience stopped him. The demons were taken aback momentarily, a brief respite of peace before they continued their mental onslaught.

Westward got to his feet but was halted by a searing pain in his knee which settled into a gnawing ache. He rubbed it briefly, but soon realised the futile activity before staggering on. He was soon aware of a presence with him although he looked around several times and saw nothing. It was now 3am and even the taxi drivers carrying late night revellers leaving the night clubs had long since ceased their slushy journeys down the road from the town.

A voice spoke in his heart.

"Jordan."

Again, he looked about him. At first, he just put it down to the combination of drugs and alcohol. There was no one there.

Then, a few moments later, there it was again.

"Don't give up, Jordan."

This time, he could do nothing but halt in his steps.

Westward turned anxiously and saw no one. But, the voice persisted.

"Jordan, I can help you?"

"Who are you? Where are you? Show yourself! I know

you're there!" he screamed, turning about himself.

"Let me in, Jordan! Let me in! I can turn your life around. A new life. And I will never let you go."

Never let you go. Never let you go. Never let you go.

The words rang around in Westward's head. In the Spirit realm, the man in white stood by the throne. The demons knew that He had to be invited to sit. They re-grouped, just in case Westward refused.

Westward stood still, his mouth open, without a sound.

"Jordan, you can trust me."

Westward put both hands to his ears in a futile attempt to stop the voices.

"No! I can't trust anyone! No one is my friend! No one! No one will ever be!" he roared at the top of his voice.

Before he had finished the scream, he stumbled as he attempted to run, at least as best he could in his alcoholic stupour. Within a few hundred yards he had to stop, breathless as he held on to the wire mesh of the surroundings of the park, desperately trying to ignore the pain in his knee. He was still a long way from home.

"I am here when you need me, Jordan. Always here."

✱✱✱✱✱✱✱✱✱✱✱✱✱✱✱✱

Eventually, Westward shuffled and limped his way back home. It was 4:30am. The snow had piled eight inches on the driveway and the roofs of nearby cars. He eventually laid in his bed, exhausted, his head spinning profusely. He sat up in an effort to shake off the movement. The warning his stomach gave him was just long enough for him to reach the bathroom as he vomited its contents. His head throbbed, but the gastric onslaught was brief. He returned to his bed in the chill of an unheated house. After many more minutes of contemplating the evening's misgivings, he eventually fell into a fitful, fear-filled sleep.

The final thoughts in his mind were the voice.

"I am here when you need me, Jordan. Always here."

✱✱✱✱✱✱✱✱✱✱✱✱✱✱✱✱

It was just after 2pm before he even awoke. The closing of the front door jerking him out of his repose. The house was now empty. He remembered that his mother had planned to visit his grandparents that afternoon and he realised that she must have just left.

He sat up slowly, the hangover in full force. He lay back down again and closed his eyes but there seemed no respite from the pain. Eventually, he slowly, very slowly, pulled on some clothes and made his way downstairs past the piles of dirty laundry on the landing. As he stumbled his way, he was aware of an incredible sensation. His eyes felt like they had enlarged to several times their normal size, his mouth felt like he had eaten the contents of a full ashtray and anything louder than his own breathing was torture. Yet what he wanted more than anything at that moment in time was another drink.

Something, anything.

He suddenly had a brainwave. His parents had always kept a healthy supply of beer and spirits in the cupboard under the stairs, left over from Christmas visitors. They were not aware that he had watched them as they had hidden it away. A strange joy came over him when he found six cans of strong lager, a fresh bottle of vodka and a half-finished bottle of basic, but nevertheless, very welcome scotch whisky. He kissed the vodka and took it, along with the lager from the cupboard, ignored that his stomach was empty and made his way to the lounge. It looked like his sister had had company round the night before as the smell of stale tobacco filled the room, adding to his nausea. Ashtrays dotted around the room overflowed onto furniture and the floor as he clicked the television on just as the afternoon football highlights started.

The main match was the seven goal thriller between Tottenham and Newcastle the day before. Here he was, watching football, alone and happy with his own company accompanied by enough alcohol to keep his escape from the real world firmly secure.

"I'm still here for you, Jordan," the voice reminded him.

Yeah, but so are we, and there's more of us! some other voices countered.

Jordan smiled and nodded his appreciation as the first goal for Tottenham went in after just two minutes. He pulled the ring on a can, guzzled several long mouthfuls and slumped back. The stormy war over his soul continued as a few moments later, Tottenham scored again. He felt that he was ignoring the vocal competition – but little did he realise by the emptying of the second lager can and the second long swig of vodka, the group of voices, like Tottenham, was on its way to a victory. Even though his knee ached more than ever, he didn't care a bit.

He felt free, liberated.

No, he thought to himself, *hopelessness is not my only friend. I have a way out of this hell.*

Before the end of the football programme, the cans and the vodka bottle were empty.

****

"Jordan was a funny kid. Always trying to impress but failing miserably. We didn't like him, really. One parent family kid, you know. But who would have ever imagined that he would have got to where he is? Remarkable really."

Richard Yates,
Former school colleague

Chapter 3

Four months later – End of April.

THE CROWD WERE GROWING more and more impatient. Westward anxiously glanced at his watch and willed Woodmouth in his mind. All his team needed was a point to avoid relegation. A draw against the club two places above them - Woodmouth were at home. Surely they could manage that? The visitors had scored in the sixtieth minute, totally against the run of play. In the meantime, Woodmouth had missed a penalty and hit the post twice. Their opponents, in an effort to hold on to their lead, took off a striker and put on a fifth defender. Woodmouth meanwhile, took the unprecedented move of doing the opposite.

Four-thirty. Ten minutes left.

"I'm going. It's all over." Gary Lockhart tapped Westward on the shoulder as he nodded towards the exit.

"Oh come on, are you going as well?" Westward sighed as Chris Taylor and Simon Ronald shrugged in a depressed mood, and said their farewells and followed Lockhart towards the high, blue gates which had been wheeled open fully.

Westward raised a hand in lamentation from the wall on which he rested his arms. He never liked the view low behind the goal and after a few moments trudged up the steps of the terrace in an effort to be able to see more of the action.

Their opponents took up a staunch rear-guard action as wave after wave of Woodmouth attacks came to nothing.

Two minutes left.

The Woodmouth goalkeeper took a long goal kick which was headed on by a midfielder on the half-way line. The ball reached the Woodmouth centre-forward, on the edge of the opponents box with his back to goal. Sloppily, but just well enough, he managed to bring the ball under control as he was shadowed by two defenders. His fellow striker screamed for the ball as he ran into space to his left. The ball holder casually laid a pass straight into his path. He let go a thumping, rising shot which left the diving goalkeeper stranded, but players and supporters alike grimaced in agony as the ball cannoned back off the crossbar and was immediately cleared. It was controlled quickly by the opponent's right-winger who sped into the chasm of open space left by the Woodmouth full-back as he had been caught up field.

The winger, however, aware of an approaching defender, stopped the ball under his foot as his adversary slipped, before crossing the ball through an unprepared defence. The opposing striker chested the ball, evaded the sliding tackle of a Woodmouth centre-back before turning and shooting casually past the home side's goalkeeper to the delight of the small group of travelling supporters. Woodmouth players stood distraught. They knew there was no way back now and what should have been an afternoon of joy had turned into a disaster.

Westward now, with many other disgruntled supporters, made his way towards the gate. Many showed their vocal displeasure, calling for the resignation of the Woodmouth manager. Once again, he felt betrayed. He could no longer play football and now the town had a team that was not worth following.

And why is everybody staring at me?

They surely don't know what I do, do they?

Is there anyone or anything left in this world really worth living for?

One thing for sure that Westward knew at that moment: more than anything, he needed alcohol.

****

Westward, in a noticeably melancholy mood, caught up with his friends later that evening. They sank a few beers in their habitually attended pub before heading for the main high street where the cruising cars snaked from one roundabout to the other. They made their way towards the row of arcades, full of video games and slot machines.

"Anyone going to matches next season?" Chris Taylor, the short, overweight companion to Westward's right ventured, lighting another cigarette.

"You gotta be kidding!" Gary Lockhart voiced above the rock music blaring out from an arcade, "It was bad enough paying that money to see a Third Division team. You going, Jordan?"

Westward was quiet. He drank deep from the open beer can in one hand and used his red and white scarf to wipe the dregs from his mouth. Taylor tried to grab a can from the three in his other hand. Westward spilled some and cursed his companion.

"Quit messing around, you sh...."

"Oh come on, Westward, lighten up! What's the matter with you?"

Again, Westward swore as he tossed the empty can into a bin as he passed.

"So, what we doing tonight? I'm bored with this. Any parties on anywhere?"

"Do you think we're welcome after what he did a few months ago? No, tell you what, we'll go and leave him behind."

Westward pulled the tab on another can.

"I told you," Westward tried to justify, "I'm better now. I'm off the vodka."

"Yeah, look at you now, though. Knocking back beers like they're going out of fashion."

Westward wanted to throw the open can at his sarcastic friend but screwed his hand up in conscious temperance.

"Man, I'm bored."

Just then, a glossy, white car pulled up alongside them. The passenger window wound down as a pretty, blonde girl sat back allowing the driver of the Ford Capri to lean towards them to get their attention.

"Hey, what's happening?" Michael Shore, the young driver and old school friend of the small group asked.

"Dunno, really. Just hanging out I suppose."

"Well," Shore paused to drag on a cigarette and press the hazard light button, "word has it that there's a do at Heather Hunter's place."

"What, that ta.."

"Hey, I don't care," Westward interrupted, "I'll go."

Taylor, Ronald and Lockhart looked at one another.

"Sorry, only three seats, one of you will have to make your own way there. But bear in mind that he," Shore pointed at Westward, "probably won't be welcome."

He arranged to meet them in the car park a few hundred yards further on as a policeman on foot ushered Shore to move on.

Westward was already beginning to realise that his company for the evening was separating and he hung back a few paces. He finished the beer and opened another. The demons as always enjoyed the inebriation process. Then he heard his name in a sentence from in front of him.

It must have been a sarcastic comment about me, he thought to himself, mumbling a profanity as he drank more beer.

Lockhart didn't even turn to address Westward as he voiced an opinion on behalf of the small crowd. "Jordan, I think we're going to have to leave you here. You can get a bus easy to the party."

Click.

The demon was going to enjoy this outburst.

Westward waited a few seconds during which his insides boiled over as his anger reached a crescendo. He then threw the beer can at the three youths, its liquid spraying an arch about them, before launching a two footed kick to Lockhart's back, sending them both sprawling.

Lockhart tried to stand, gasping for air and shocked by Westward's sudden actions.

"What's got into you?" he screamed, brushing his clothes down and pointing to the patches of beer on his suede jacket.

"Westward, for God's sake, what's the matter?" Taylor joined in.

Remember, no one really cares. You are a useless waster, and nobody likes you, the demons reminded him.

Westward got to his feet and took a deep breath. "I thought you were my friends!" he roared as passers-by glanced in the direction of the fracas.

Oh God, now they've seen me blow out as well. The whole town will know soon.

Westward, demonic anger all over his face, grabbed Taylor and Ronald by the hair, shook them loose before turning and walking in the direction from which they had come.

"Man, shall we get a copper?" Ronald ventured.

"No", Lockhart said quietly, before screaming, "idiots like that are not worth knowing!"

Westward turned, gave an obscene hand gesture with and continued walking.

Why did I do that?

What had he done? He had not intended any of it. It was like something other than him was in control, like at the party, months before. He wanted to go back and apologise, but the demons persuaded him otherwise.

Let's face it, Jordan, you are a drunken, drug-taking waster. They won't listen anyway.

As he meandered to the emptier places of the town, he came to a conclusion.

I hate Woodmouth Albion Football Club.

He hated everything to do with it. He hated, with a vengeance the club, the ground, the players and the supporters. Then he took the thought a step further.

I hate football, full stop.

He could not care less whether England were in with a shot of winning the ever-nearing World Cup finals. He could not care less whether Woodmouth dropped out of the football league. He couldn't care less if he ever saw those so called friends again. The walls around his world were now complete.

He began the walk home, again, a solo walk, stopping briefly at a pub overlooking the river where he sank two double vodkas. As soon the local news on the TV screen showed the goals and near misses from the match he had earlier attended, Westward made his way to the Off Licence. He found he had just enough money for a small bottle of his ever-faithful companion. It never let him down. It comforted and kept reality surreal. Just him and his only friend. He took the bottle and continued his way along the riverside towards the farm fields further away, enjoying the last moments of the spring sun setting.

Then came the voice again.

"Always here for you, Jordan."

In his alcoholic insensibility, he span in a circle and screamed.

"I don't care who you are, leave me alone! I just couldn't care less, do you hear? You're just another liar like the rest of them!" he paused as he kicked a fast food drink carton away in exasperation, "get away from me! Get away from me!"

"I'll still always be here for you, Jordan."

Westward carelessly tossed the now empty bottle amongst the early poppies that fringed the weed-filled perimeter of a ripening rape seed field. He clasped his hands over his ears in a vain attempt to shut the voice out. Then it spoke again.

"Let me in, Jordan, I want to be your friend."

Again, he screamed, aghast at the idea that there was really anyone who could be a friend. Above his laboured breathing, Westward roared.

"NO!"

"Always here for you, Jordan."

A few yards further on, Westward shrank to his knees, disorientated and perplexed and wept hard, wracking tears. He put his head into his hands and sobbed as once again the voice returned.

"Always here for you, Jordan."

His tears eventually subsided as he fell into a drunken sleep against the hedge bordering the now silent road.

****

Some hours later, Westward became aware of some blue flashing lights to his side and two men in black speaking to each other as they tried to rouse him. One shone a torch into his face making him squirm as he slowly raised a hand to shade his eyes.

"What the...?" he mumbled, his head ripping apart in pain.

"OK, sergeant. No problem, he's OK. Saturday night reveller that's all. Come on, son, up you come."

Westward sat up and breathed deep whilst keeping his eyes firmly closed. "Not a chance, mate. Leave me alone. I'm OK, thanks."

The man in black became slightly more persuasive. "Time to move on, sunshine. You must have a bed at home, come on."

Once again, the policeman tried to get Westward to stand up as he shrugged the arms off and swore at him.

"OK, I'll make it a bit easier for you. Either we help you up and you start walking or you can have a lift to the station with us. You choose. I'd say it is not a difficult choice, but it's a choice all the same."

Westward now had a new person on his hate list. And this one figured quite high up at that moment. Again, he swore under his breath.

"Last chance to get up, son."

Westward drunkenly, but immediately, shot back with a sarcastic look.

"Last chance to lick my boots."

The other man in black then made what Westward considered a mistake. He gently nudged Westward with the tip of his boots.

"What these?"

Click.

At that, Westward with all his remaining strength got to his feet. The officer, thinking that he had got the drunken youth to see sense was not ready as Westward sneered and forcefully spat at him. Before Westward could even consider his next move, he was aware of metal shackles being tightened around his wrists as his arms were swung behind his back. He was then roughly pushed into the back of the waiting car, one of the officers enjoying a shove to Westward's shoulder.

The policeman, now firmly Westward's number one

enemy, read out his rights. "Blah! Blah! Blah" Westward mumbled, interrupting the man by swearing as he let his head fall back onto the head restraint. The man continued but Westward did his best to ignore the words, but deep inside he began to take stock of the situation. It was 3 am, he was drunk and handcuffed, travelling in the back of a police car, probably now being charged with assaulting a police officer. If he was prosecuted, he would probably lose his job.

If he lost his job, he would probably be kicked out of home. If he was kicked out of home, he would top his own hate list. The bitterness of his life was almost complete and the demons danced at the closing stages of the destruction of yet another existence.

And how easy it was.

And Westward marvelled at it all and came to a glorious conclusion: he didn't care.

Not one iota.

****

At five-thirty that morning, Westward's uncle arrived at the Woodmouth Central Police station. His shocked face said it all. He shook his head, sighed and looked slowly down in absolute disgust at Westward's condition as he was led to the front office from the cell in which he had been taken to cool off. He retrieved his belt, loose change and wallet and scribbled an illegible signature as his hangover began to kick in. His Uncle assured the Police Officers that he would do all he could to ensure that this kind of activity would not happen again and persuaded the officers to let him off with a caution.

What do I care? Westward pondered. *What do I care?*

Secretly, inside, his breaking, lonely heart, he convinced himself that he really didn't.

Not about himself.

Not about life.

Not even about football.

He no longer lived, he simply existed in this world that had been created specifically to hate and destroy him.

****

Just over a week later.

"JORDAN! FOR GOODNESS SAKE! IT'S HALF PAST EIGHT!"
Westward forced his eyes open with a start as his mother's voice finally got through at the third attempt in forty minutes. He scrambled for his watch and panicked. It wasn't Sunday after all; it was Thursday morning and he was now going to be hopelessly late for work – again. He jumped up, stormed into his clothes, spent thirty seconds on cleaning his teeth and ran in a panic out of the house. He checked his watch again.
8.39.
Even if he jogged, he knew that he would be hopelessly out of breath and in agony from knee pain within a hundred desperate yards, but he may just get the 9.00 bus. That would get him to work at 9.40. *Surely they would understand, wouldn't they?*
Buses run late... not my fault... trying my best.
But he remembered what the manager had said. The next time would be the third strike - and he would be out. He hobbled along as quickly as his tortured knee would allow, the extra pounds he had gained from drinking did not help.
He got to the bus stop just too late as he saw the double-decker pulling away.
Those people in the back were staring at me. They know as well.
He sighed despondently and blurted out a string of expletives, as he popped headphones over his ears and pushed the adapter into the radio. The news was concluding and the sport took over. Another reminder that Woodmouth were relegated didn't lighten his day at all, so he turned the radio off and stuffed it back into his pocket and scrunched the headphones in with it.
"Jordan! What are you doing here?"
Westward span round to a young, smart suited, smiling lad of about his age. Despite the fact that the lad recognised him, Westward could not place him.
"It's me," was all the person said.
"Sorry, do I know you from somewhere?" was all he could muster up, patting his jacket for cigarettes.

"Yes, we've met before – and I am sure this will not be the last time, either. Are you getting this bus?"

Westward looked next to him and had not even noticed the bus which seemed to have appeared from nowhere.

"You going to Millford? I didn't see what number you were," he asked the driver as the doors swished open.

"Yep. Hop in," the driver nodded jovially, "this is the fast one, be there in fifteen minutes." He shrugged and realised that he would be at work by twenty past.

Better than not at all, he thought to himself, then considered the likelihood of his dismissal. *Not that I care.*

He frowned as none of this was making sense. There had never been a fast bus to his place of work. He scratched his head, paid for his ticket, worked his way to the back of the bus and casually swung by way of a pole onto a seat. The person who had greeted him sat directly opposite him and continued to look so happy.

But that smile is fake. He knows as well. Everybody is after me. And the guy behind me. Oh man – and that woman just looked up from her book. She knows too!

"You still don't know who I am, do you?" the young lad asked, bringing Westward back to reality.

"Should I?" Westward shook his head and tried his hardest to ignore him. He patted his jacket again, stared out of the smeary window and wished that he had a cigarette.

The young man leaned forward to get Westward's attention further.

"Do you remember a football match from many years ago when you injured your knee? You tackled someone and got sent off?"

Westward's video memory was immediately rewound to the occasion. He could still recount every second, every partial moment of a second, as since he had not played a competitive match.

"Yeah. Sure. Why?" he asked casually, shrugging his shoulders.

The lad still smiled. "You still don't know, do you? I'm the guy that you tackled when you gave the penalty away!" he triumphantly announced.

Westward frowned. "You're kidding me, right? That was

seven years ago, nearly."

"Jon McDermott," the boy announced, "I work in Millford as well – at the Building Society. Well, actually, today's my last day – I hope to be working with my Dad soon. He's a football scout. We are moving back to Liverpool next week."

Westward's heart sank a little further. He hated everything to do with football and also anyone who had a connection with the game. "So?" was the best that he could muster up as he watched the shops and terraced houses slip by.

Then the paranoia began.

That woman with the book is watching me again.

McDermott's smile remained, and he was clearly not ruffled by Westward's continued brush offs. "Do you still play football – erm – it is Jordan isn't it? Oh, would you like some chewing gum?" he asked, offering his new packet.

Westward, conscious of his potential bad breath, showed no lack of gladness as he took a piece. Within a few minutes, Westward had warmed to McDermott and had overcome his initial antagonism towards him until he asked what Westward now did at weekends. He explained that he usually went to watch Woodmouth, went to pubs with his mates, searched out a party or went to the cinema, but he was now finished with football. He couldn't play any more and it wasn't worth paying to watch a Fourth Division club.

For the first time ever, Westward found a person whom he could talk to who genuinely seemed to care. They arranged to meet for lunch later that day. It seemed 'the gods', as his grandfather had referred to when things went well for someone, were watching over him when he arrived for work both his manager and sub-manager were not in and so his tardiness would not be noted.

After an uneventful morning, Westward and McDermott met later and flew a few stories back and forth about school days. The restaurant began to crowd as the pizza makers frantically attempted to keep up with the demand. Westward took a beer, finished it in a few gulps and ordered another.

Now the pizza guy just saw me. I can't stay here.

"Can we go somewhere else?" Westward asked, standing up.

McDermott gave a look of concern mixed with confusion but decided to ignore Westward's request and simply motioned for him to sit down.

"So, what do you do?" McDermott quizzed, pushing lettuce and tomato on to his fork, "for work, I mean."

Westward nodded towards the bank opposite them. "Took the first job I was offered. Didn't need to be a genius to start there. Interviewer seemed happy with me and they took me on ahead of exam results.

"Oh, wow! That must be exciting!"

Westward scanned the room, several enemy troops in the paranoia war firing darts of attack. He scoffed, shaking his head. "Not in the slightest. Manager really doesn't like me, the rest of the staff are so boring. Barely pays enough beer tokens for a weekend. I suppose there's prospects if you want to tow the line but I'm so bored there."

McDermott watched Westward sink another bottle. "I'm gonna get some more pizza. Coming?"

"Erm, actually I think I have enough. You go ahead."

McDermott prayed as he eyed Westward glaring at almost everybody, checking them out. He eventually gave in and joined the crowded pizza bar and returned with another four slices and called a waitress for another bottle.

"Jordan? I sense that you are troubled."

"Troubled? What makes you say that?" he retorted sharply as he shuffled in his seat, swigging from his bottle. He nervously studied everyone present, scouring and evaluating.

"I....do you remember a conversation we had many years ago about God? You came to the church I was attending back then, one day during the summer holidays."

Westward tore into a slice of pizza as he stared out of the large window beside them, carefully observing each shopper that passed by.

The guy with the briefcase. The woman with the pushchair, no - the tall guy with the leather jacket!

"Erm, yeah, kind of. Didn't you say Jesus was God or something like that? To be honest what's God done for me? My dad left home, my mum hates my guts, I have no relationship with my sisters any more and I am barely hanging on to this job," he laid out with concise, tragic disdain.

Mcdermott paused briefly before quizzing, "Why do you blame God for that?"

"Who else is there to blame?" he shrugged, "I thought God was all powerful and he was in charge of everything. If that's the case, why should I give him the time of day? He's done nothing for me."

McDermott nodded in understanding as he chewed on a pizza crust. As he swallowed, he continued. "I understand, but if you look at all those unfortunate things, they prove the very reason we need God, not why we should reject him."

"Huh," he mocked, "It's no problem to reject someone who shows no interest in my life?"

"Well, it proves what a sin filled world we have," McDermott continued, slicing an illusive cherry tomato.

"Oh, please, don't talk about sin – you'll be having a go at me for drinking next – what are you? a Mormon or JW or something?"

McDermott smiled kindly to show his understanding about his potential association with those groups.

"No, Jordan, I am nothing like that. I am just a Christian."

"What, Church of England or something like that?"

"No, we now go to a Pentecostal Church in town."

Westward was puzzled. He was aware of a few denominations, Baptist and Methodist, but not Pentecostal.

"So what's so different about your church then?" he asked draining his bottle of beer and pushing the sparse pile of salad around his plate.

"Nothing really. We just love God, worship His Son Jesus, and believe that through a relationship with Him we can have eternal life and forgiveness of sins."

Jesus. Wow. Yes – I remember that name. That school book. All those years ago. Dad washing up. Open your arms, Dad. Like Jesus did. Forgiveness of sins.

The last few words struck a resounding, tuneful chord within Westward's heart and mind.

A tiny hook, a tiny piece of bait, was lowered, gently into Westward's heart. Until that moment, he had never considered himself a sinner, just a victim of circumstances.

Who wouldn't have become the person he was with the same set of problems in life? Wouldn't everyone be the same? Wouldn't everyone have a justified hatred for life, the things that they used to love – even a hatred for themselves?

"How does that work? How can that happen?"

Westward sat spellbound for the next few minutes. Words spun in his head.

Sin. The cross. Christ. Repentance. Salvation.

McDermott finished with a quiet smile.

"You know, Jordan, God has a plan for your life."

Just as Westward was about to ask another question, McDermott glanced quickly at his watch. He stood up immediately, pushed his chair out and grabbed his jacket from the back of his chair. "Oh man! it's ten to two, I have to go."

Westward patted his own pockets and realised to his embarrassment that he had left his wallet back in his office. To his relief, McDermott pulled out his. "I've got this, Jordan, don't worry. By the way, this is my new number if you want to keep in touch," he said, scribbling on a notepad and ripping it off.

"Thanks - and thanks for the chat. Shame we met just as you are leaving town."

McDermott paid the bill and they left to be greeted by the usual gridlock of traffic on the one way system. It gave them a chance to cross the road, reaching the building society where McDermott worked first.

"Well, nice to meet you again, Jordan," McDermott smiled, offering a hand.

"Yeah, thanks, Jon. I'll try to keep in touch."

"I understand if you don't, it's OK. Just remember what I shared with you. God loves you, wants to have a relationship with you. And, like I said, He has a unique plan for your life."

They shook hands, parted company and Westward pushed his way through the swing doors of the old bank building. As he tried to work that afternoon, all he could think on was those words, over and over again.

A plan for your life... A plan for your life... A plan for your life.

That plan seemed a million miles away when he took a call from his distraught mother that afternoon with the news that his grandfather had been admitted to hospital, likely for the last time. He watched every minute pass during the last couple of hours until the end of the work day and made his way to the nearest pub.

By the time an important European football match was switched on the television behind the bar, his resentment for the game now boiling inside, he was already drunk enough to barely stagger to the bus stop. He couldn't play, so what was the point of watching? Yet inside, despite his ongoing self-destruction, he yearned for the love that McDermott had described.

Two days later, his grandfather died, Westward's despair for life now complete. He now had no relationship as such with his father, no grandfather for stability and his previously beloved football had been taken away too. All that was left was alcohol, his only lasting friend, one he now took solace in during every possible waking moment.

As he dragged his body into bed that night, he cried out from his heart.

I hate myself, like everybody else does.

God, please help me.

****

Another week later.

Jordan Westward was vaguely aware of a distant voice, growing louder, calling his name in a very gentle but per-suasive manner. His head pulsed in pain from the excess drinking from the night before. His eyes opened gradually, eventually having to shade them from the bright light that seemed to emanate through the whole room as he became aware of another person with him. The room had changed and at first Westward was scared and taken aback. He sat bolt upright and pushed down with both hands and stared, wide-eyed.

He looked first right, then left and noticed that the whole room apart from his bed had gone, to be replaced by the pure white light which seemed to exude powerfully from the person who stood at the end of his bed. The man was dressed in white, the purest white that he had ever seen, his arms, strong looking arms, hanging relaxed at his sides. He somehow seemed so familiar and yet Westward knew that he could not have met him before.

"Hello Jordan," the man gently said with a gentle, kind smile, "I've waited a long time for you to call on me."

"Who…who are you?" Jordan stuttered, narrowing his eyes to focus in the brightness. "Where am I?"

His senses slowly tried to come to terms with the improbable reality that surrounded him.

The man sat down on the edge of the bed and smiled once again.

"Have we met before?" Jordan asked, shaking his banging head. He felt so sure that they had met many times before, but he knew they could not have done. But this man was so, so familiar. Then, he noticed the holes in the man's hands and took a sharp intake of breath as the realisation hit him as to who the man was.

"I think you already know who I am," he answered, the kindest smile accompanying a voice of such gentleness and comfort. "Do you remember that snowy night several months ago?"

"Oh, God. Oh, Jesus. It was you! Oh, no. I'm not ready to go. Not yet. I'm too young. I……"

"Jordan," the man replied to comfort him as he moved closer to Westward. He lay an understanding hand gently on a terrified shoulder, "I haven't come to take you with me. You're going to take me with you. Do you remember all those dreams you have had? All those ambitions? All those disappointments? Well, I died for you many years ago and have waited for you to see that you needed forgiving. I took all that pain for you. I died so that you could be healed. I died so that you could have life. Life like you could never have imagined. In short," he paused, pointing to Jordan's very heart before continuing, "My Father has given you another chance. Do you know that all your past will be pushed away and you will, according to my Father, be a new creation?"

New creation.

He recalled those words from Jon McDermott.

Westward sat startled, his head slowly shaking in disbelief. He felt inside a mounting up of emotions ready to explode and felt an initial tear fall down his face. The solitary tear, he knew, was just one drop breaching a very high, seemingly impregnable dam.

But these were not tears of hopelessness.

These were tears of release.

But I am not going to let go. I don't trust anybody.

"You, Jordan Westward, are a very special person," the man stated compassionately, smiling and laying a playful punch on Westward's chest.

Westward sat in silence.

Special. No one has ever called me that before.

"Well, to my Father, everyone is. But for this moment, you are the special one and for this moment, no one else matters. Just you. I have followed you every step of your life and have seen everything, good and bad that you have done. I have protected you," the man continued, again gently resting a hand on Jordan's shoulder. Jordan felt a wave go pulsing through his stunned body. The tears began to flow more rapidly.

The man in white smiled again warmly. Somehow Westward knew that his fragile mind was being read. Not suspiciously though, but out of love that wanted to heal. The man nodded as if in appreciation of Westward's pain. He knew that there was nothing he could possibly hide. In fact, there was nothing that he even needed to hide. It was as if the worst crimes that Westward had ever committed did not even phase him and the kindest, most generous deeds that Westward had ever done, few though they were anyway, would never be able to impress him.

Westward pondered. *If I had to describe a best friend, then this man would be one.*

The man in white continued to smile and nod his acceptance as to what was happening. He understood. He moved closer and put both his arms around Westward at which point he fell apart and cried like he had never cried before. His whole body flopped against this person and shook. Every pain, every hurt, every sin, every crushed moment in his life came flooding out like a torrent of an unstoppable tsunami.

Every time he had been made fun of.

The times that he had shut his heart off.

When his father left.

When his mother screamed at him.

When people let him down.

When he let others down.

All of it. Right down, right the way down to his very depths. With every sob, he was cleansed. With every tear he was purified.

At first, it did not seem appropriate, but now he could no longer hold back. His arms slowly went around this strange person and after some time, maybe minutes, maybe hours, he could not tell, he moved away and looked into his face. His eyes spoke of just one thing – absolute, pure, unconditional love. An acceptance that Westward had never experienced before.

But it was the love that drew him. This person had a smile that could never be forgotten. This love was beyond that of a mere man because it did not come from a human heart. It came from the heart of the God who created him. It dispelled all his hatred, all his loneliness and all his hopelessness.

Westward was suddenly very tired, but just before he drifted off, he heard the man speak. "I will never leave you or forsake you, Jordan. My Father has great plans for your life. Let me stay in your heart. I will comfort you, protect you, and guide you - if you will let me. You need never be afraid again." Then Westward felt his eyes roll as they slowly closed to take him asleep with a peace that was alien.

Even the hangover had gone.

****

Another week later.

The last seven days had changed him. He knew that the difference was not merely temporary - unlike his flirt with eastern mysticism from a few weeks back had been. It felt real and that it was to stay. For the first time in many, many months, he felt no one staring at him.

He had kept the encounter to himself, but even he knew that he was different. His drinking was not totally gone, but was drastically reduced. He had distanced himself even further from the usual crowd that he hung out with and was, for the first time, not just used to being alone but actually enjoying it. Instead of reaching for football magazines, he was drawn more each day to the Bible.

He had also had the news that he had been offered the job

he had applied for at the credit card operations centre that had just opened on the outer ring road that circumvented the town. Five hundred jobs had been made overnight – and he was to be on shift work as an operator. A huge pay-rise – plus a week off every three weeks.

With no one else home, instead of turning the television on, as was regular habit in such circumstances, he began fishing around in the cupboard where he had found alcohol before. His gaze was caught by a half bottle of whisky, not his favourite drink, but alcohol all the same. But something inside drew him away. Today, he picked the bottle up, read the label and, not even disappointed, he replaced it and closed the cupboard door.

"Come unto me," the voice inside spoke again.

He returned to the lounge, yet as he sat down and picked up the Bible, he felt a warmth and comfort that he was becoming more and more accustomed to. He checked his reading plan, the New Testament passage for the day being Matthew 11. As he read the words, the familiar peace began to envelope his soul. Then he reached the end of the chapter. Those words again.

"Come unto me, all ye that labour and are heavy laden, and I will give you rest. Take my yoke upon you, and learn of me; for I am meek and lowly in heart: and ye shall find rest unto your souls. For my yoke is easy, and my burden is light."

"Lord," he quietly spoke out loud, "I am so much happier than a few days ago. But still I worry. Still I feel angry. Still I am lonely. I give you my life once again. Take my pains away. Set me free. I want friends – people who really do care, not drinking friends. Lord, I want a girlfriend, someone to marry, someone I can love, someone who loves me for who I am – like you do. Lord, thank you for understanding. And oh – would you heal my knee? Lord, I want to play football. I so much want to play football again. And, Lord, I don't want to drink. I know something inside me is changed, but I am still not free. Lord, I ask that you would set me totally free...."

His prayer was interrupted by the voice again.

Wings as eagles.

He quickly opened his eyes and turned to the concordance in the back of his Bible. He turned the pages, excited. He found W and dragged his finger down to the word.

Wings. There it was. A reference in Isaiah 40. He excitedly turned back to the Old Testament prophet. He found verse 28 and read it out loud to himself.

"Hast thou not known? Hast thou not heard, that the everlasting God, the Lord, the Creator of the ends of the earth, fainteth not, neither is weary? there is no searching of his understanding. He giveth power to the faint; and to them that have no might he increaseth strength."

Westward's lips began to quiver as he surrendered to the power behind the words. He went on as hope rose in his soul. It was certainly true, he was weary, he was still burdened. He sometimes felt powerless and had no might. He needed strength – specifically in his knee. He continued reading.

"Even the youths shall faint and be weary, and the young men shall utterly fall: But they that wait upon the Lord shall renew their strength; they shall mount up with wings as eagles; they shall run, and not be weary; and they shall walk, and not faint."

Could it truly be possible that God Almighty, Jesus Christ, his personal Saviour and creator of the world, penned those words...for him? Did God know him that intimately that these words were written for his situation right at that moment in time? He was overwhelmed as he realised, once again a step deeper than before, that his strength was in Christ and nowhere else and that even in his weakness, God could be his strength. When he felt weary, he could be elevated. It certainly seemed sometimes that when he walked, it was a great effort. Not just physically in his knee, but in his very soul. But right at that moment, he felt some warmth, almost liquid once again, running through his body from head to toe.

"Oh, God", he cried, "I don't care anymore, I just want you. I know you care. I know you really, really care about me. I don't care about football, I don't care about a wife, I don't care about anything else – just you. Just you! Oh, God!"

He felt the need to kneel in front of the chair in which he sat and once again his heart overflowed with joy. Not just happiness, but real joy.

****

He had not been aware how long he had wept – it did not seem that long, but when he looked at his watch he was shocked – it had been three hours. He had been in the presence of God for three hours. He stood up some time later expecting the usual pain to shoot through his knee.

When it didn't, he frowned.

He stood on his right foot and bent his left leg back and forth. There was not a trace of pain. For a brief moment, he was sad at the thought that no one was there to share in his joy. But then he realised someone was there – his Saviour Jesus.

He ran to the back garden and scouted for a football. The one he found was a little under-inflated, but it would do. He jogged to the patio and threw it in the air. He began to try to keep it in the air. At first, he swore at himself as he had to come to terms with his rustiness. Then, gradually, the rhythm returned. Right knee, left knee, right foot, left foot, head, left knee, head, chest, right foot......

He was flying.

He laughed to himself.

Wings.

Thank you, Lord.

****

Westward's first few days at his new job passed with little incident. The night work enabled him to avoid his mother and sisters – he was out the house the moment he awoke and so hardly saw them. On breaks, he kept himself to himself and spent the time studying. As he left the sterile white corridors of the new building, he paused to check the new notices on the board. One particular handwritten piece of paper caught his attention:

Football players wanted.
Under Twenties vs Fathers.
Kick-off 2PM.
Withersdale Park.
Ring for details.

Westward scribbled the number on the back of his hand with a pen. He was excited. A chance to play football. Then the excitement turned to fear. How would his knee hold out? What if anyone he knew was playing? Would they trust him to play? He paused to wonder at the wisdom of attempting to be involved and then pondered on the fact that he had nothing left to lose. He had no friends – something that he realised he was very content with.

His usual pessimism was gradually dissolving and he purposed to ring up. *Chances are,* he reasoned, *they already have enough players.*

I'll ring anyway.

****

His call was returned a few hours later and to his utter surprise, Westward would not only be in the squad, he would be in the team. Not many, it seemed, were interested in playing at centre of defence, so he was a starter. He then had an idea. Maybe his father would come? He punched in some numbers as he pictured his father with his new wife and the children from her first marriage.

"Hello." Westward's contact with his father had been sparse for several years and his father sounded as grumpy as always.

"Hi Dad, It's Jordan."

An uncomfortable pause.

"Oh yeah. You alright, Jordan?"

Surely he's going to be impressed – a new job and I'm playing football soon, he thought to himself.

"I'm OK Dad. I'm sorry I haven't been in touch much. I know you have a new family and stuff but actually things are really good. I got a new job. I just started last week."

Another uncomfortable pause.

"Do what? What on earth possessed you to leave the other one – you had a good job there!"

"To be honest, I hated it, Dad, I-,"

His father's sullen attitude continued. "Not many of us actually like our jobs."

"Well, this one's doing alright, actually. I just finished a night shift."

"You're doing shift work?" His father huffed. "That won't be any good for when you get married. Shift work's awful for married blokes, I can assure you."

"Well, I did get a massive pay rise – I'm going to start getting driving lessons now I can afford them."

"Yeah, Darren's started driving now. He's doing really well."

And I bet he'll have a Ferrari as a first car, no doubt. If a manned mission to Mars was scheduled, guess who would be on it? Yes, Darren would either become Prime Minister or write a best-selling novel, no doubt.

"Dad, I was ringing to let you know that my knee is better and I'm playing football this weekend. I know I haven't seen you for ages and I thought I'd let you know in case you wanted to come."

"You – play football?" his father scoffed.

"Yeah, what's wrong with that?"

"Doctors said you'd be foolish to play again – anyway Darren's got tennis and golf this weekend," he clipped.

Click.

The demon gave the prompt right on queue.

"Dad," Westward's voice was gradually raising, "I've never said this before, but to be honest I don't care about Darren. I'm your son, not him – and you've done nothing to support me in anything I've tried to do. This is my first game of football for years!"

"Jordan, look, I have a new family now and..."

"And let's face it," now it was Westward's turn to interrupt, "you did nothing when you were at home anyway, did you?"

"Jordan! How dare you speak like that!"

"It's true, Dad! You never cared for me at all!"

"Jordan!"

"Dad! Just one game, that's all I called to ask for – one lousy game, and you can't even manage that. You don't change do you? Well thanks a bunch!"

Westward slammed the receiver down and thumped the wall several times.

Will I ever know what a father is really like?

His heart pounded in gripping anger.

Just then, the comforter spoke to his heart.
"I am the Father."

****

"Working with Jordan Westward was truly unique. We all came in for a laugh, to be honest. Got the bare minimum done, took the money and that was that. But to Jordan: everything was taken so seriously. We would be playing cards on our breaks on a night shift but not Jordan – he would always have his head in some book to get on in I.T. I suppose that's why we never progressed far and he is where he is."

Peter Foster,
Former work colleague,
Major credit card company.

Chapter 4

A few days later.

F OR WESTWARD, IT SEEMED that life was complete once again. He was full of joy as he pulled on his red and white striped shirt and laced up his boots. He ran his hands over the outsides, the leathery smell as familiar as his last game several years before.

This feels so good! he thought to himself, *I never imagined that this could happen again.*

He sprang up and as he stretched his hamstrings, he examined the team sheet pinned on the notice board of the very basic changing room. Unpainted benches backed by glossy, but pitted and dimmed, whitewashed walls ran around the small bare-boarded floor.

There it was. Number five, centre-back, Jordan Westward. He smiled to himself and felt the pangs of nervous excitement building inside. Not knowing too many of the team, and those who did recognise him seemed to be keeping a wide berth, he ran out on his own. He didn't care one bit. He had discovered the love of His Saviour, was now not drinking at all, felt fitter than he had for a long time and was running out on to a football pitch.

He picked up a ball from the sidelines, trotted on to the pitch and simply ran from one end of the goal-line to the other, keeping the ball close to his feet. He stretched various muscles and as some of the other players joined him, he took a place as a defender as they took turns passing and making shooting op-portunities for each other. After a while, they practiced a few corners, every single one he managed to either head clear or, if he was encouraged, pelt a header goal-ward. He even had the pleasure of watching a low, left-footed drive rebound off of a post and into the net.

A couple of the other boys were nodding towards him and pointing at him, talking under their breath. They seemed to be taking things very casually – yet to Westward, this was foot-ball! How could they be so reluctant to revel in such an opportunity?

As the dads joined them on the pitch, how Westward wished his father was on the same pitch as him or even just standing, watching him. He quickly re-focused on the game and smiled as he watched some of the dads. Most in their late forties and obviously had had a few too many beers and roast dinners. One of them he could even see stubbing out a cigarette under his boots. But they were here and playing against him.

After a few minutes, the referee called the team captains and each player lined up on the centre line to be introduced to each other. Just then, Westward scanned the ever-building crowd around the pitch – even the mayor was here, complete with his gold regalia.

Wow, he thought, *there must be a couple of hundred people here!*

And he was playing again.

From the kick-off, the dads team, immediately began taking advantage of the gusting, spring breeze by pumping long balls up the centre of the pitch to the strikers. Westward had no problem gaining control of and feeding the ball to his wingers and mid-fielders. One particular ball he chested down with relative ease, avoiding a tackle from a slow striker on the dads team and sortied into the opponents' half. He played a one-two with a short, quick winger to his right and was only just off target with a shot from thirty yards. As time continued, he grew more and more in confidence.

The score was goal-less after half an hour when the younger team won a corner. The younger team's goalkeeper, recognising Westward's height advantage over many on the pitch waved frantically for him to go up to add his stature to the attack. He stood, un-marked in the 'D' of the goal area and as the corner was lofted over, timed his run to perfection and his excitement reached new heights as his unchallenged bullet-like header found its way into the net just off the right hand post.

He trotted back to his half, right arm aloft, beaming. Several of his team-mates took the time to shake his hand, albeit in a subdued manner. For the rest of the half he took authority at the back, barking orders and advice when needed.

Five minutes before half-time, the dads won a corner. He gave instructions to several of his team-mates to man-for-man mark opponents as he stood at the back post. A short corner was played to one of the slower dads. Westward yelled at the right back to run and press him before he could get a cross in. He did so but moments before his tackle, the ball came over. Westward followed the path of the ball attentively, headed the ball, albeit fortunately into the path of his left-back who, having skilfully controlled the ball with the outside of his right boot, sprinted into the huge space in front of him.

He pointed forwards. "Now!" he hollered as he sprinted up the middle of the field.

Stay onside, he told himself.

The defender chipped a perfect ball into his path which he swung at with a left-footed half-volley from about twenty yards out. The goalkeeper stood rooted to his spot as the ball flew past him for Westward's and his team's second goal. A penalty by one of the lad's strikers was missed just before the half-time whistle to leave them with a 2-0 lead.

Wings.

Westward wasn't just flying. He was gliding, above the highest clouds, not another soul around.

This cannot be happening, he grinned to himself.

It was as if he had never stopped playing.

No, it was more than that.

He was a totally new player.

****

As Westward marched confidently off the pitch, his team receiving a passionate ovation, one of the dads jogged over to him.

"Hello, Jordan, long time no see."

Westward slowed to a walk as the man caught his breath.

"Hi, erm -?" Westward questioned.

The kind faced man extended a hand and introduced himself. "Kyle McDermott. You may not remember me, I'm Jon McDermott's dad."

Westward's face lit up as he remembered the person who now seemed most responsible for his salvation.

"Jon! Wow, how's he doing? Oh gosh, I said I was going to ring and I never did."

Kyle McDermott, still remarkably fit for his age, put his arm around him. "That's OK, though this is pretty awesome to see you running around after your injuries!" he beamed.

"Mr. McDermott - "

"Oh, please, Kyle is fine. Go ahead, sorry to interrupt."

"Kyle - can you let Jon know that something amazing happened a couple weeks ago. I was woken up in the middle of the night and I was visited by Jesus Himself - in my room. I got saved!"

McDermott's face creased into a gentle, loving smile. "You know, I thought when I saw you running on to the pitch before the game, I knew there was something different about you! Praise God!"

Westward continued. "But that's not all. Just a week ago, I got a total miracle healing. I haven't played football for years. To be honest, I'm pretty beat after that first half although I won't say anything – this is the most amazing thing – I don't want to stop now. And tell Jon this as well – the drinking's

absolutely, completely gone!"
Westward began a brief account of his changed life.

As they approached the changing rooms, McDermott gently patted Westward's shoulders, even though he was a good two inches taller than himself.

"Well, you have a great second half. I'm coming off now – I want to give one of the other guys a run out. Well played Jordan, and so pleased about what's happened. I'll tell Jon I saw you. He's playing back home today." McDermott waved and smiled as he disappeared into the room opposite Westward who, despite his efforts, received a cool reception in his room. He didn't care. Nothing was going to stop him enjoying the rest of the afternoon.

****

As they returned to the pitch for the restart, the sun had dipped behind an ever growing group of low, white, silver bordered clouds and the wind had increased. The dads started an attack which resulted in an overweight, unfit, short man with balding hair hammering the ball way over the bar from twenty yards, not before it skimmed off Westward's head.

From the resulting corner, the same man had a close range effort cleared off the line by Westward. The ball found its way to the dads' right-back who lobbed the ball high and over the advancing boys' defence as Westward joined in the wide-eyed yelling for offside. The referee signalled to play on. Westward sprinted to get alongside the dads' centre-forward, slid in a perfectly timed tackle and with great relief watched the ball trickle off for another corner. The dad in question shook his head, ruffled Westward's hair and simply said with great enthusiasm, "well done, son!"

****

Howard Peterson pointed out Westward and had noticed that McDermott was constantly encouraging him and had spoken to him at half-time.

"Who's the big lad – the number five?"

McDermott smiled. "Yes, he is big isn't he? He's six foot-four, would you believe? Jordan Westward is his name."

Peterson, an amiable, well-dressed man in his fifties, nodded as he unwrapped another piece of gum.

"Bit of a gut on him for a young lad though, do you reckon? Does he play regular anywhere?"

McDermott shook his head and swigged from a sports bottle as he tossed one to Peterson. "This is his first game for years – he did his knee in as a youngster and packed up playing. He's done well, hasn't he?"

Peterson looked at McDermott with a 'that's an understatement' look on his face. "So what's the deal with his knee – doesn't seem anything wrong with him today?"

"He's just become a brother in arms, if you know what I mean. Says he had a miracle healing a little while back. I got one of the guys to offer him a game – at the time I didn't even know how long he would play for though."

Peterson glanced at his watch. "He's played an hour and he's looking strong. When did you say he last played?"

"Oh, about six years ago."

"What? Look at him, don't be silly!"

"I'm serious Howard, did his knee when he was about twelve and hasn't played competitively since."

"So what you're saying is he is unfit and he can still play like this? How well does he know the lads he's playing with?"

"Well, that's the other interesting thing – he doesn't know many and the ones he does, well, he just doesn't seem to fit with them off the pitch. He's a clever lad as well. Why, something on your mind?" McDermott turned to Peterson with the question just as Westward out-jumped the tall, well-built figure of Michael Southgate, father of nine year old Jamie Southgate who watched eagerly from the far touchline.

The ball was cleared by his defensive partner but was promptly heavily thumped back high in the air. Westward ran towards the ball and chested it skilfully down, tapped it up with his right foot and, as he was about to be pressured by an oncoming midfielder for the opponents, side-footed it neatly to his right-back. A few minutes later, the ball went out of play for a goal kick.

Peterson listened intently as Westward animated some instructions to his players. "Hey, Graham – push up! Mark

and Steve, three man defence with me. Find a bloke to mark –
and stick to him like glue. Trust me. I've watched the tactics –
this will work."

Peterson once again looked at McDermott in amazement
at the authority with which Westward barked orders around.

McDermott had one word for him. He nodded and simply
said, "watch."

Peterson laughed heartily. "Tactics – at this level? Who
does he think he is?"

"Just watch!"

Westward's defensive trio shrugged their shoulders and
reluctantly obeyed.

"What's he thinking - three man defence?" Peterson muttered to himself.

McDermott had prayed and had seen Westward's plan.

"Simple. Look at the older guys. One man down the
middle, two wide men. Why do you need four in defence
against that? The fourth lad wouldn't know what to do with
himself."

"So.....where's he gone?"

"Well, I'm assuming he will sit just in front of the back
three – a second playmaker if you like."

Peterson frowned at the irregularity. "Doesn't sound
sensible football to me. Who was he telling to push up? "

"Watch the number two. He's going to push up further to
add an extra midfielder."

For fifteen minutes, the fathers found no way around the
plan. Then, with a lot of space in front him, despite his
draining energy, Westward shifted a gear. He evaded two
tackles before swiftly glancing up and seeing the number two
racing towards the far corner flag. Westward chipped a perfect
ball to his feet seconds before he was upended by a harsh
tackle by one of the dads' midfielders. The referee waved play
on and Westward hobbled back to his defensive position as he
watched the cross evade everyone apart from an unmarked
midfielder for the boys who casually and calmly stroked the
ball home.

McDermott once again applauded the move and showed a
fist of delight to Westward who quietly nodded back.

Peterson did not miss the moment. "How did he do that?

How did he see that? He had a split second – this kid's vision is amazing!"

Moments after the re-start, the lads forced a corner.

Again, Westward stood with his back against the rear post as the ball came over from the corner, this time only three yards from the goal. One of the dads' central defenders had gone up for the corner. He and Westward both went for the ball but Westward's height advantage allowed him to head the ball clear into the path of one of his midfielders.

Westward scanned the pitch. "Down the centre, now!"

The tall, unshaven, dark-haired lad glanced back, then ahead, saw what Westward had noticed and duly dispatched the ball for one of the boys' strikers to chase. Between him and the goalkeeper was one defender.

Westward motioned for others to support the lone striker. It seemed that the cocky, over-confident lad considered assistance unnecessary and ploughed on towards the goal, relentless. He swept past the defender but just as he swung his leg back to put an effort in on goal, the dads' goalkeeper threw himself at his legs at which point the lad acrobatically tumbled over and watched the ball harmlessly bobble away. The referee immediately pointed to the penalty spot.

The boys' captain nodded for Westward to come forward to take the kick. Westward, shocked, shyly pointed to his chest, but having received the nod, jogged forward. With his back to goal he placed the ball on the freshly painted penalty spot and walked several paces back. The referee blew his whistle at which point Westward ran forward, closed his eyes and hit the ball as hard as he could to his left hand-side. The goal keeper had gone right and the ball rippled its way down the back of the net, a foot off the turf. Westward opened his eyes as the cheers from his fellow players and supporters confirmed he had made his hat-trick.

Wings.

He closed his eyes again as the sun broke through a cloud and warmed his tiring body. He felt like he was back where he belonged. Yet the feint pangs of emptiness still saddened him that no one from his family or from his friends were there to see it.

But Jesus saw it.

And looking on excitedly, again, so did Kyle McDermott and Howard Peterson.

****

Peterson smiled and shook his head as the young, lanky number five trapped the ball, feinted one way and then the next and triumphantly slipped the ball through the legs of the player in front of him right to the feet of his captain.

"Jordan Westward, that was absolutely awesome!" McDermott called through cupped hands, hoping Westward would hear him above the excited din of the crowd.

McDermott and Peterson exchanged glances.

"I think we need to talk to your boy afterwards......"

****

The boys managed two more goals, Westward marshalled his defence majestically and the boys walked off the pitch at the end 6-0 winners. It had been so long since that terrible day when he had injured his knee and yet he felt like he had never stopped playing. It seemed his alcohol abuse had not touched him and he would have played on for another two hours if he could have done.

"Well done, Jordan Westward!" applauded Kyle McDermott from a distance. Westward nodded and waved humbly in acknowledgement as he dashed to take a swift shower. As he left the changing room, the fact that few of the boys congratulated him on his performance hung slightly heavy on his heart. They were happy to joke and laugh amongst themselves, but he still felt like an outsider.

Kyle McDermott and another one of the Dads had waited for him.

"Hey, Jordan, before you go, let me introduce you to someone. This is Howard Peterson, he manages Calverley Wanderers – I am sure you know who they are."

Westward dutifully shook hands, not sure why this introduction was necessary, and totally unaware of what was about to happen. He had expected to get some kind of abusive backlash for one of the few mistakes that he made in the game such was his lack of confidence still.

"Yeah, sure, Northern Premier League – amateur level, is that right?"

Peterson, smiled at Westward's clumsy description. "Well, actually, we have a number of lads who are now semi-professional. I'm not sure if you were aware but Jimmy Newton was signed last week on full pro-terms by Doncaster Rovers. Next season he's a League One Player."

Westward, wide-eyed, had read a few months before of this potential move but had lost touch with the outcome.

"Jordan, Mr. Peterson was watching you with great enthusiasm today. He was very impressed with your game and wanted to know what your status was with regards to playing." McDermott's words seem to come so fast that Westward at first did not fully comprehend.

Peterson graciously grinned. "Jordan, I'll make this quick. I'll get to the point. We are short of defenders and wondered if you'd like to give us a try? I watched you today and you are a natural at centre-back. You're tall, quick, tackle well and I think you'd fit in perfectly. What do you say?"

Westward, in his brief memory of local results knew the quality of Calverley. Promotion two years out of the last three, runners up in the Northern Cup the previous year.

"Sure, why not?" he casually replied, still not completely aware of what was taking place.

Peterson continued, puzzled. Most kids at least would smile at the prospect. "OK, erm, how about a phone number, maybe?"

Westward shook his head embarrassed. "I'm sorry. Yeah, sure." He peeled off his home number, shook hands with both men and made his apologies before sprinting towards the park exit to catch the bus home.

Both men watched him intently. McDermott broke the silence. "Poor lad. He's hurting inside. He's had a hard time. To be honest, I think he just needs a father figure, dare I say?"

"Hmm. That's what I wondered. Heck of a footballer though. I haven't seen such tenacity in a young kid for a long while. And today was a friendly, but did you see him charging around? Let's hope he keeps that up."

McDermott smiled as he offered a hand to shake.

"Yep. Let's give him whatever encouragement we can. Anyway, Fancy a pint?"

Peterson grinned as he shook hands and patted McDermott's shoulder.

"I thought you'd never ask!"

****

Peterson, against all regular football practices, called Westward and invited him along to train with his squad. The two bus rides necessary hardly phased him and Westward made every practice that his shift patterns allowed. Westward increased quickly in fitness and the other players welcomed him despite his initial sense of being overwhelmed by the talented squad.

He made two cameo appearances for the final five minutes in games that Calverley were in control of. Then, the following Thursday after the evening training session, Howard Peterson announced that Westward would be making his first appearance in the starting line-up. The season had ended, Calverley just outside the top honours in their division.

"Jordan, I want to say how much I have noticed and appreciate your patience – that is a rare thing in a lad of your age. Other guys, all they want is the glory and the prestige. But, you son, are so very different. As you probably have been made aware, we have a friendly organised against Woodmouth."

Westward's eyes widened with passion and excitement.

"This Friday? May 23rd?"

What a birthday present, Westward thought to himself, *Woodmouth!*

Peterson nodded and continued. "As a reward, you'll be starting."

Westward's surprise and delight was now hard to hide.

"Thanks, Mr. Peterson – I don't know what to say!"

"And what's more, we have decided to take you on full terms as of next season. We want you as a semi-professional footballer at this club."

Westward looked astonished.

Peterson smiled and nodded. "Yes Jordan, you'll be playing football and getting paid. It won't be much to start with, but who knows what's ahead?"

Westward stood speechless, his fist covering his mouth in shock.

"We are thinking of a two year contract to start with. We can't pay much to start with - fifty quid a week, an extra twenty when you play plus twenty for a win and ten for a draw. How does that sound?"

All Westward could do was extend a hand to shake. After saying farewells, he trotted to the entrance of the tunnel leading to the changing rooms. He turned to scan the tiny stadium, recalled the four hundred or so fans that had braved the rain and howling wind from the previous weekend. He glanced behind and up from where he stood and scanned the initials C W F C strategically patterned on white seats amongst the blue of the main stand.

Surely this can't be real?

In just a little over twelve months he had gone from being a potential suicide with problems from drug and alcohol abuse to a semi-professional footballer.

I can't wait for Friday, he thought with a smile.

He found himself smiling a lot more these days.

****

Two days later.

Westward pondered whether deja-vu actually did exist. Was this familiar feeling a reality, the motion of being carried, stretchered? He stared up at the enormity of the night sky above his head, floodlights guarding the four corners and bordered by the low, partially roofed stadium.

Surely God must be huge, he considered.

He closed his eyes, partly to hold back a tear, but mostly because his knee was in agony. He raised his head to look down, shocked at the expanse of swelling, now bigger than a grapefruit. The colour, the bruisey purple partly camouflaged with the green of the grass stains, he found quite sickening. In fact as he was passing players heading for the tunnel, the look on their faces spoke the volumes that their voices did not. Moments before entering the tunnel, to a standing ovation, those close to the clear perspex covering grimaced at the sight.

They know, he thought to himself, they know. *I'm never going to play again – again. Maybe God is not that huge. Why has this happened?*

Then another thought engulfed him and gave him brief hope: perhaps this really was just a dream, a nightmare and any moment the sweet bliss of sleep will be almost gratefully disturbed by the morning's waking. But then one of his carriers almost tripped and the jolt sent a shock of pain up his left leg - through his left knee. He gritted his teeth, the absoluteness of the truth of his true presence in the real world bringing the old familiar sinking feeling in the pit of his bowels.

Just ten minutes earlier, things had been very different.

****

"It's just a friendly, boys. Let's just have some fun. I know the crowd are going to want to see us beat these guys. Give 'em a show! And Jordan," Howard Peterson paused as he broke Westward's daydream, "I don't want you to think there is anything to prove. You've already done that. You don't have to give every tackle everything you have tonight. Loosen up, lighten up – at the same time, don't be overawed by these guys – they're just footballers like you, eh?"

Westward shyly smiled, pulling socks over his shin guards. Still not completely certain of his acceptance as part of the team, he had consciously not joined in much of the changing room banter. But tonight felt so different. This was not just football – this was against his home town. He wondered if even playing Barcelona or AC Milan would have seemed any more exciting.

At that moment, the referee knocked at the door.

"Let's go, guys."

The room was filed with the frenzied turmoil that only pumped up, expectant sportsmen could evoke. As both teams walked out in two lines onto the pitch to the all too inadequate ovation of a capacity stadium of 3,500 fans who had braved the torrential rain.

The formalities over, the match soon settled into pressure by Woodmouth and dogged defence by Calverley and Westward was soon subject to much praise by his team-mates clearing a thunderous shot off the line and out-jumping a Woodmouth striker to clear the ball from a corner. His sliding tackle on the slippery surface stopped the pacey Woodmouth right-winger a few moments later, the resulting throw-in also cleared strongly by Westward's ever-strengthening left foot.

After a scoreless first twenty minutes, Woodmouth pulled off the pressure and allowed Calverley an opportunity to come at them. James Pendleton, Calverley's midfield playmaker, threaded a short pass through to striker Jack Devlin who had the ball taken from him just as he was about to shoot. The Woodmouth defender immediately attempted to thump the ball into the crowd for a throw in but his kick was carelessly sliced and ended up going out for a corner much to the delight of the Calverley contingent of the crowd. Peterson motioned for Westward to get into the box to add height to the attack.

Chris Langley, Calverley's left-winger ran over to take an inswinging corner on the Woodmouth right. He raised his hand to ensure the crowded box was ready. Westward, as was his habit, standing just inside the 'D', unmarked. As the corner swung over, he carefully timed his run, leapt fearlessly into the throng and, although eventually crashing heads with a Woodmouth defender, the cheer from the crowd confirmed the reward for his effort. His stomach flipped. He had just scored for Calverley Wanderers, against Woodmouth Albion.

At first, the denial inside. Then the embraces of congratulations. Then the acceptance. The raising of the arms in triumph.

Jack Devlin was first at his side to lift him off the floor. He shook his head and smiled. Patting Westward's back, the happy-go-lucky Irishman simply said, "Well done, Son! Where'd you learn to do that?"

Westward simply grinned, shrugged his shoulders and trotted back to his defensive position as the announcer confirmed his strike. "Ladies and Gentleman, Calverley's first goal was scored by Jordan Westward!"

Westward simply raised a hand in acknowledgement of the crowd's applause. It seemed every tackle he attempted, every pass he completed, every call he made, every run he coursed, Jordan Westward was nigh on invincible. His confidence was soaring and despite the greasy surface, he kept his footing and began spraying passes around like any seasoned player on the pitch. He was used to Match of the Day, hearing teams being cheered for every pass they made. Tonight, it was his stage. It was him the crowd cheered for. It was Woodmouth's striker, Matt Henderson, who they booed when he, out of sheer frustration stuck both elbows in Westward's back when he once again beat him to a header. Westward regained his breath as Henderson was booked, the stocky striker standing hands on hips, wiping the sweat from his face with the back of his hand as the rain streaked down his forehead from his drenched hair.

Westward launched a firm free-kick into the Woodmouth box, Devlin seeing his strike partner Steve Mason, arm raised, unmarked a few yards to his left. Devlin's cheeky back heel was perfectly placed for Mason to take in his stride and slot a sublime finish cooly under the advancing Woodmouth goalkeeper.

Howard Peterson was on his feet. Westward's evening was already way beyond his expectations.

A few moments later, the half-time whistle was blown, Calverley still leading 2-0.

"Well done, Jordan, come back next season!"

"Westward for England!"

"Jordan Westward walks on water!"

He briefly scanned the crowd around the tunnel and applauded his supporters as he made his way to a very jubilant changing room.

****

"What on earth are you doing, son? What on earth are you doing?" Peterson exploded as he rubbed his hand through Westward's hair, "I thought you were Franz Beckenbauer out there!" he continued, referring to the German international sweeper.

Westward shyly smiled. "Thanks, boss, we're doing well, aren't we?"

Peterson threw his head back and roared with laughter. "Doing well – listen to this kid! Ha! Jordan, one day my son, you are going to amaze people if you carry on playing like that."

"Thanks, boss!"

"How am I supposed to keep you at this club when you play like this? Sheesh!"

The changing room was a buzz.

For now.

****

In the Woodmouth changing room, things were different. It was silent apart from the clattering of studs on the concrete floor and the raging voice of a manager under pressure – despite the fact that it was just a friendly match.

"Mr. Henderson! What do you think you are doing? Are you going to continue to play like a girl all night or are you actually going to do something constructive? I will give you fifteen minutes. You either start putting that ball in the net or you can start playing for the reserves, son!"

Henderson remained silent as he glanced up from his tea and, aware that he had now gone nine games without scoring.

"This kid - Westward - is in his late teens and he's running rings around you. Grow up!"

Henderson jumped up, threw the remains of his drink against the wall and shouted at the top of his voice.

"You're such an expert motivator, aren't you? You really make your players want to put themselves out. I'm sick of this!" The door slammed behind him as he stormed out.

"Take it easy, boss!"

"Give him a break, boss!"

"Man, go easy, we all need to get going, not just him."

"Boss, leave him be. He is not to blame for everything. It must be frustrating. We are all going through tough times."

Outside, Matt Henderson, through clenched lips, was fuming. He decided there and then what he would do.

****

As the teams took to the field for the second half, Westward was aware of a change in atmosphere on the pitch. He glanced around at the opponents and caught a glimpse of Matt Henderson. The man looked like a bull looking down a red sheet. A few minutes later, Westward was laid a casual side pass. Henderson charged in, sliding with both feet towards Westward.

"JORDAN! WATCH OUT!" Westward's defensive partner Ricky Maxwell shrieked. Westward had a split second to drag the ball back as Henderson slid past and thumped the turf in frustration. Westward wasted no time as he pushed forward into the centre circle. Chris Langley raised a hand on the left flank as Westward duly chipped a ball into his path and continued his run forward. Langley stepped over the ball to trick the Woodmouth full-back and then accelerated past him. His cross was carelessly pushed away by the Woodmouth keeper, but out of the reach of the Calverley strikers.

The crowd's anticipation was heightened as the goalkeeper was unable to pick himself up in time. The ball bounced as Westward found himself with the opportunity to unleash a half-volley from twelve yards which went between two defenders and into the centre of the goal. The crowd erupted as Westward this time sprinted away, arms aloft in triumph, chased by several Calverley players. He closed his eyes and smiled at the heavens.

Several yards away, Matt Henderson shook his head and emptied the build up of saliva from his mouth.

Next time, he thought to himself, *I'll get you.*

****

Howard Peterson was on his feet shaking his fists and applauding Westward. He turned to Fred Turner, the physiotherapist.

"Have you ever seen anything like this lad in years?" he asked gleefully.

Turner shook his head slowly. "No. But don't expect to hang on to him for too long. He's a wee bit special, this lad."

"That he may be. Have you ever seen a defender so quick, so energetic, so calm – I tell you, he reads the game like a veteran. His anticipation is incredible. How many defenders would have the gall to get that far forward?"

"Your main problem," Turner continued, scratching his nose pensively, "is where to play him. Is he a central defender, a central midfielder, and if so, defensive or attacking? Or dare I say – is he a striker?"

Peterson threw his head back in mirth. "If that's my biggest problem – there must be a God! Come on Jordan!"

****

The crowd urged Calverley forward even at 3-0 up. Westward, although congratulated on his second goal, was reprimanded by Ricky Maxwell for deserting his post, Westward duly acknowledging. Meanwhile, Henderson's game had not improved. He glanced over at the sidelines and saw a board with the number nine being retrieved. They had played just under an hour when Westward received the ball. He moved to the side to get a better view of who was open to pass to.

The pass never took place.

Maxwell looked on in horror as he screamed "NO!"

Henderson's sliding tackle this time had all the effect that he had intended previously. He missed the ball and caught both of Westward's ankles from behind. Westward's cry of excruciating pain seemed to echo around the stadium as he fell, not forwards, not backwards, but just down into a crumpled heap, arms above him. One leg did not fall in its usual way and the crowd's shocked silence only accentuated Westward's awareness of the pop in his left knee. The all too familiar agonising, searing paroxysm followed as he ended up on the wet turf. The referee's whistle was explicitly clear as a great silence followed a universal sharp intake of breath amongst players and spectators alike. Henderson simply got up and, in anticipation of the red card that was inevitable, casually trotted towards the changing rooms amidst an uproar of boos and whistles from a disgusted crowd.

Westward was immediately surrounded by several players as he attempted to move his knee, the tell-tale swelling growing before him. Fred Turner raced on to the pitch and fell at Westward's side. Westward screeched in agony as Turner barely touched his knee. The short, grey-haired man screwed his face up as if he knew the pain himself. He shook his head as he pursed his lips.

"Let's get a stretcher here please guys, now!" Turner barked.

"Holy.....," Devlin whispered under his breath.

Several other players joined the throng.

"Hell, Jordan, I..."

"Oh, man..."

One of the younger midfielders had to turn away to stop the rising sickness from his stomach.

"Alright, people," Turner bellowed, resting a calming hand on Westward's shoulder, "give the kid some air, would you please?"

Westward closed his eyes at the increasing pain as the stretcher arrived.

****

By the time Westward's ambulance arrived at Woodmouth General Hospital, his leg was completely numb. The doctor's assessment was simple: anterior and posterior cruciate ligament tears, medial and lateral meniscus tears and a displaced patella. His recommendation: to never even attempt to set foot on a football pitch again.

That's it, he finalised with a renewed resolution to himself, *no more football.... again.*

As Peterson bade him a heavy hearted farewell late that night, Westward's mind was drawn back to the cupboard back home. Once again, he had been betrayed, once again he would find solace in copious amounts of alcohol and once again he would simply withdraw to the place where no one could touch his body or his mind. Fortunately, by the time he was released from hospital several days later, the loving voice of the Holy Spirit spoke quietly and compassionately to his soul:

"I will never leave you nor forsake you."

****

Six weeks later.

Westward limped awkwardly along beside the gently flowing stream, and enjoyed watching its journey meandering beneath the rough stone bridges connecting the small terrace of cottages to the village road. The calming warmth of the sun kissed his back as he flicked his sunglasses further up onto his nose. He walked until he reached a small brick bridge and stood momentarily to enjoy the view of the small cluster of stone cottages opposite.

This is a really nice place, he thought to himself, *but Lord, what am I doing here?*

He swung his jacket over his shoulder and continued walking, albeit hobbling, towards the pub and tea room a hundred yards or so further on. He shoved his hand deep into his pocket and pulled out an assortment of coins. It amounted to a little over three pounds. He looked up, tutted as if deep in thought and sighed. Would it be a pub lunch or a sandwich and coffee in the tea room? He pushed the coins back into his grubby jeans pocket and ran a hand through his now shoulder length hair and continued walking.

Where are they? he thought to himself.

His friends should have been there by now. It had been two long hours since they had parted, agreeing to meet in the village. He stopped to stare through the gift-filled windows of the shop next to the tea room.

Are they in there? He pushed his face against the window, his breath on the glass momentarily obscuring his vision. All he could see were two holiday makers choosing postcards, oblivious to their small son who mischievously drew out a plastic sword from a bucket.

Westward walked on and for no apparent reason continued to the edge of the village. A few yards further on, the road continued into the rural wilds of the Cotswolds, a national speed limit sign confirming that there would be little else further on to tempt an already hungry stroller. The last establishment was a purveyor of equine products. Two large, wooden gates were open revealing the expanse of a neat concreted forecourt area. A pair of healthy looking horses were being tackled up by a tall blonde girl, perhaps his age, as their potential riders tried on a variety of hats to size. A year old, deep green Range Rover took a dignified place in a parking space next to the sizeable, light wooden framed window filled with saddles, reins and bridles. Partially obscured by the large vehicle was a walkway where the stables were located.

He could not help but watch the girl, so confident in her activities. He rested his arms on the concrete pillar at the bottom of the drive.

Wow, she's nice, he thought to himself, her jodhpurs clinging tightly to her shapely legs, the collar of a rugby shirt sitting on the top of a loose navy blue sweatshirt bearing 'Sinclair's Livery', the logo for the business.

At that moment a short, casually dressed man in his late forties bounced his way happily out of the shop, spoke something inaudible to the girl, patted her shoulder on passing and pointed his keys towards the Range Rover. The headlights flashed twice before he pulled open the heavy door, jumped in and turned the keys. The huge 4.6 litre engine growled into life and he negotiated slowly around the horses down towards where Westward stood.

He slowed further as he approached the gates and pushed the button to wind down the window.

"Can I help you at all?" he asked in a concise, well spoken way.

Westward shuffled, uncomfortable. "Erm, no... Err, sorry, erm, I'm just waiting for some friends of mine. I thought they may be around here."

The man in the Range Rover briefly looked down to his side as he clicked his belt in and before accelerating away simply said, "No one left in the shop, old chap. Must be somewhere else! Keep looking, must be around somewhere, eh?"

Before Westward could reply any further, the Range Rover rumbled its way effortlessly towards the village centre and beyond.

The man must be doing all right for himself, Westward contemplated, *what a number plate – HSL46. All Range Rovers seem to have personalised number plates!*

He glanced back to the yard and watched, fascinated as one of a pair of riders shoved a foot into a stirrup and swung a leg over the saddle. A confident grabbing of the reins and the horse was soon making its way towards the gate. The clatter of horses hooves on the forecourt area followed as they approached the entrance side by side. Westward took a few steps back so that he was out of sight as the horses turned right and meandered their way contentedly into the relative quietness away from the village. The girl assistant brushed her hands together, placed her hand over her eyes to shield them from the sun as it glistened through the shuffling branches of the oak trees at the entrance, and once satisfied that the riders were away, returned to the shop.

For a brief moment, there was silence apart from the ethereal breeze blowing through the bushes next to him. Then, for no apparent reason apart from the fact that he wanted to see the girl again, he walked towards the shop. As he entered, he saw her straighten up having bent over to place some things under the counter. She walked back to the centre of the shop and re-arranged some items on a rotating display. She smiled briefly as she noticed him. He nervously returned the smile.

He walked around trying to make it seem that he belonged where he was. The truth was, of course, he did not have the first clue about anything to do with horses. He fiddled with a very expensive wax jacket, peaked at the price, his eyes widening in shock and backed clumsily away into a rack of riding boots. He bounced back, embarrassed, his knee causing a brief pang of pain as the girl turned, hands on hips to address him.

"Hello," she said in an eloquent tone, "Is there something particular that you are looking for?"

Westward awkwardly rubbed his stomach as it rumbled.

"No, erm, I, er..."

The girl tilted her head to one side and frowned in a friendly way. She folded her arms and examined him quickly from head to toe.

In the end, he smiled, looked down and shuffled his feet nervously. "Actually," he began, "I've lost some of my friends and I just wondered if they were possibly around here, but...clearly.... erm, they're not, so I, erm, guess I'll be on my way."

The girl unfolded her arms revealing her tall, slim figure. Westward gazed with youthful attraction at her, his stare unfortunately obvious. The girl tapped her fingers on her thighs several times, and simply said, "Well, they certainly are not here, I am afraid."

"No, erm, they aren't," Westward stalled.

Then, like a bolt out of the blue, he spoke, shocked by his own boldness. "Would you, erm...I mean, do you have a lunch break...could I buy you something to eat, perhaps?" he clumsily asked rubbing the back of his head.

The girl, hid her shock well and took a good look at Westward. He was, she considered, underneath his shyness and obvious scruffiness, quite a good looking lad. *Tall, for sure for his age and quite broad,* she thought to herself. *Give him ten out of ten for bravery,* she quietly smirked to herself.

She glanced back to the clock above the counter and smiled. "My father will be back in ten minutes if you can wait."

Westward beamed.

This will be one heck of a story to tell the crew. This girl is top of the league. And then he remembered that he only had three pounds in change! He had walked the length and breadth of the village several times and there was no sign of a bank or a cash machine. This could be potentially embarrassing.

"Abigail Sinclair," she confidently confirmed, offering a youthful, elegant hand.

"Jordan...Jordan Westward," he returned, clumsily lunging forward to shake her hand. "So, I take it that was your Dad in the Range Rover?"

"Hmm. His pride and joy. He's always wanted one, got it just last week. My mother wasn't happy as it's quite costly to run. Daddy convinced her it was OK."

Westward stood, mouth open, trying to think what to say next. "So, do you live here, in the Cotswolds?"

"Good heavens, no. Mummy would love to, She's always saying it's an area that has class. No, we live in a place called Woodmouth. Do you know it?"

Westward was dumbstruck. *Do I know it?*

"That's amazing. Yes I do know it. Actually, I live there too."

"No way!" she exclaimed momentarily stopping the tidying up of a basket of soft toys, "what a coincidence!"

"Woodmouth's a big town, which part are you from?"

"We're just outside actually, in Chesterford, you know, the village just east of the town. I always say Woodmouth, but I suppose it isn't Woodmouth at all, really."

Westward had cycled through Chesterford many times and admired the large, individually built properties, all set back on tree lined boulevards, the spire of its fourteenth century church completing the picturesque setting.

A bit different to where I live, he pondered.

"How about yourself?"

Man, this will be embarrassing....

"Erm, we're just round the corner from the hospital."

"Ok, that's where our cleaner comes from."

The two awkwardly looked away at the realisation of the social chasm between them both. *Your cleaner. That's almost funny.*

"So, how come you're here? Woodmouth's a fair way away," he ventured.

"Well, I could ask the same of you, couldn't I?"

Westward was stumped. "Yeah, I suppose you could. You first."

"This is a great time for business, you know, the horse show etc; Daddy's shop is so busy during this time. We own twelve horses and they're all out. Do you ride?"

"Actually, yes I do – but only pedal bikes," he grinned. Abigail sniggered as she returned to the counter.

"So what do you do when you are not horseying?" Westward ventured.

"Horseying!" she chuckled, "that's a funny phrase! When I'm not horseying, I'm at Uni - Med. School actually, at Woodmouth. Quite handy not having to move away to go really. I think that's partly the reason why Mummy and Daddy always saw me as a physiotherapist or something like that. Easier to keep tabs on me, I suppose. But," she sighed, "I'm not sure. Maybe midwifery. We'll see. What about you?"

Midwifery? Maybe she's the maternal type, he hoped.

Westward wondered how to best describe his job. To him, it always sounded fancier than it was. He was after all a simple computer operator. "Oh, I'm in IT."

Abigail's response surprised him. "Oh how interesting! I'm actually useless when it comes to computers. Daddy's quite a whizz, though. Exactly what do you do?"

Now he was cornered and would have to either bluff or be honest.

"Well, you know the guys who stay up half the night putting tape disks up to ensure that your credit card records are kept up to date? Well, that's me."

"You do shift work? Nights must be horrid."

"You get used to it. The shift allowance is handy. I get a week off every three weeks too. Dangerous I suppose to give an extra third on top of your salary to a decadent teenager."

Abigail smiled. She didn't really see this young man as a decadent teenager and her thoughts were broken by the phone.

"Sinclair's Livery," she spoke with clarity, confidence and helpfulness, "yes...erm, yes...certainly...no sorry, he's already out. We have Dragonfly if you'd like him. For two hours? No problem. Mister...Pemberton-Jones. OK, see you about nine-thirty in the morning. Oh – and if I remember, you like the western saddle, is that right? Yes, of course, sir. OK, bye for now," she scribbled some notes whilst slipping a loose strand of hair behind her ear.

At that moment, the sound of the Range Rover growled its way across the courtyard and a few moments later, Harvey Sinclair sprang through the door rattling his keys and whistling happily. "Hello Sweetheart. Everything OK? Sorry I was a bit longer than expected. You know how things are, can't be done in a flash, eh?"

Abigail looked up and smirked quietly to herself as she finished her notes. "No, Daddy, they can't, can they?"

"Oh, hello again," he continued, recognising Westward from their brief meeting a while back, "did you find your friends, old chap?"

"Erm, not yet, actually, I..."

"Hmm," Sinclair grumbled as he eyed Westward suspiciously.

Abigail swiftly jumped in to break up the potentially embarrassing moment. "Actually, I'm off to lunch, if that's all right. This nice lad has invited me out."

Harvey Sinclair's suspicion vanished as he raised his eyebrows in surprise. "Oh, really! Super," he nudged Westward's chest, "Consider yourself very fortunate, young man. Not everyone gets a yes when my Abigail is asked out, you know. Very choosy. Have to be these days!" Harvey Sinclair laughed heartily as he scratched his hand, revealing an expensive looking Swiss gold watch, "OK then, darling. Mummy will be back shortly, you two disappear, see you when you get back. Rose and Crown's a good place, you know. Jolly good baguettes. Great value. Nice pint too, if you like that sort of thing, real ale and all that stuff."

Abigail glanced at Westward as she took a beige jacket from the back of a chair. "See you shortly then, Daddy." she kissed his cheek, sliding her jacket on. The two walked towards the door, Westward still wanting to pinch himself to see if he was truly dreaming. This girl was gorgeous, and here he was, on a date with her.

They strolled along slowly and crossed the narrow street to the Rose and Crown, a bustling, ivy covered, old fashioned village pub. A number of tables with umbrellas strategically positioned outside were in full exposure to the sun as it competed for sky space with the scattered clouds gently buffeted along by a cooling breeze. The question of money resurrected itself in Westward's mind as the two shuffled their way through the crowd to the bar. At that moment, his financial challenge was solved as a finger tapped him on the shoulder. He turned to see one of the colleagues that he had travelled down with.

"Hell, where have you been?" Adam Fuller demanded.

"I could ask the same. I've been walking up and down for two hours killing time! Listen, can you lend me a tenner?"

"A tenner! Flipping heck, you're in a generous mood. I'll have a lager shandy while you're at it then," he said peeling off a brown note from a small wad in his back pocket. Westward nodded to Abigail standing patiently behind him. Fuller frowned, confused. Then he understood, eyes widening. "You are kidding me!" he whispered, pulling Westward towards him. "You've pulled her? Man, how'd you do that? We've been all over and there's no women under forty around here."

Abigail cleared her throat to get attention.

"Sorry, Abigail, this is my pal Adam Fuller. You can call him Rat, that's his nickname. Abigail Sinclair."

"Hello....Rat, if that's what you are known as!" she held out the same elegant hand that Westward had held earlier.

"Anyway, Abigail, what do you drink?"

"Pineapple juice is fine please, with ice, thanks," she replied picking a menu from the bar. Westward ordered the drinks and having paid, suggested they go out to the beer garden at the rear.

"Where's the rest of the crew?" Westward enquired scanning the garden for a free table and then remembered that he had not ordered any food. Now he was left with the unenviable position of leaving Abigail in Adam Fuller's company whilst he returned to the bar.

"What can I get you to eat, Abigail?"

"I'd love the tuna and cucumber baguette, please. Oh, and could I have wholemeal if possible," she advised, "white flour is pretty horrid."

Fuller stared at Westward from behind Abigail's back and pulled a face to insult her. Westward looked away in the hope that it would hide his ill-timed smirk. When he had composed himself, he turned and said, "I'll order some nosh and I'll be right back." Westward rushed knowing full well that Adam Fuller was not known for his kind treatment of girls. Upon his return, Westward looked on in horror seeing Abigail at the mercy of not only Fuller, but all of Westward's other companions. He swallowed nervously as he approached.

"Hi boys, I guess you've been introduced to Abigail."

"Yeah, she's just been filling us in on your equine knowledge, Jordan. Saddle up, kid!"

Abigail hid her blush by taking a sip from her glass, swirling the dissolving ice around as it chinked against the sides. Westward smiled defeatedly, his expressions not un-noticed by Abigail. Westward tried his hardest to hint his strong desire that his friends move on and eventually, only after having embarrassed him enough did they make their excuses and said they would meet up to leave for home within an hour. Moments after their departure, their food arrived. He looked on in awe as she delicately opened a napkin and took gentle bites of the enormous sandwich.

Now I've got to try and eat this without looking like an animal, he thought to himself, sincerely regretting ordering the greasy sausage and onion roll. Abigail's disapproval of his choice was well hidden, but a strange sensation of needing to look after this boy came over her.

"So," she broke the silence, "what brings a bunch of rowdy teenagers to the Cotswolds?"

"Hmm. Well, some of the guys wanted to go to the Motor Museum and all of them wanted to do the brewery while they were here. To be honest, neither interest me at all."

"Oh. I see. OK, so, tell me about your family. Mother and father? Brothers or sisters? What do they do?"

Now here's where I lose her for sure, he thought to himself.

"I live in a bed-sit now. Mum and Dad divorced when I was young. Haven't seen my Dad for ages – he remarried and moved down South – I think. Mum still lives in Woodmouth, but again, not that much contact. I have three sisters, two younger than me, one older. Haven't got a clue where they are to be honest, we live different lives." He paused as he contemplated out loud. "I would have loved a brother." He stared at a stain caused by a recent spillage of beer on the table as he spoke and Abigail became more and more aware of wounded areas in Westward's heart as they spoke on.

After a brief silence, Westward nodded as if to say, 'how about you' as he took another bite from his food and wiped ketchup from his lips with his napkin. She swallowed and placed the remains of her food on her plate. "One sister, Stephanie, my best friend. She's wonderful. We really are pals. She's five years younger than me, however."

"Is she down with you?"

"Yes, out with Mummy at the show today. Isn't it a glorious day for it?"

"So, how come you aren't there today?"

She smiled as she emptied her glass. "My turn tomorrow, it being the Bank Holiday. Mummy has the shop today. Daddy kind of floats between the two places."

"Do you enjoy riding horses?"

She smirked. "That's a bit like asking someone like, er.. oh, bother, what's his name?" she clicked her fingers trying to recall a particular player's name. "That's it! Glen Hoddle. It's like asking him if he enjoys playing football."

Westward frowned.

"I'm sorry," she continued, "that's sarcastic, I didn't mean it to be. Yes, I love riding. What do you like?"

"To be perfectly honest, I remember being out on a horse when I was about ten, but I was petrified. Never been near one since. I heard you mention a 'western saddle' when you were on the phone. What's that?"

Her face lit in anticipation of talking about the subject. "Well, not many people use them over here. It is exactly what it says it is – western, cowboy type saddle. Made for people who would spend a long time on the horse. It is a little more comfortable for that type of use."

"Any other differences?"

"Well, the main difference is you have what is known as – and don't laugh – a horn on the front of the swell." She blushed and looked away, embarrassed.

Westward did his best to comfort her. "It's OK," he giggled, "I'm sure it's a bit awkward when people come up with phrases like that, but I get the picture. It's the bit the guy hangs on to while the bronco bucks, yeah?"

Abigail chuckled. "Well, I guess that's one way to put it! I better not mention then that the guy sits on a part called a skirt!"

"Ha! No kidding! er...Another drink?"

Abigail simply nodded. Westward soon returned, eager to hear more.

He placed her glass in front of her her. "You were saying?"

She gently rubbed her lip recollecting where she was in the conversation.

"Saddles?" Westward ventured.

"Ah, yes! Actually, there are a whole range of saddles; simple riding, competing, show saddles, trail riding saddles – and work saddles. Then there are those for racing, learning and also ceremonial ones – kind of like what the Queen would use for say 'Trooping of the Colour'."

Westward smiled as she continued, enjoying her passion for equestrianism. "What about stirrups?" he ventured, "are there lots of those too?"

"Yes," she quickly replied, sipping her pineapple juice, "the most common are what are known as 'Prussian Side Open' – they are the typical English ones. But then you get fillis stirrups which give you more balance in the saddle, leather covered cowboy type ones and also you can get these sort of rubber treads to give you extra grip."

Westward nodded as she continued to detail the differences between pelham bits and snaffle bits.

"You still haven't told me what you enjoy."

He knew how few girls actually liked football so he left it out. "Music. I love music. Classical."

In the back of her mind, a counter clicked again. *Classical music. This boy really was different.*

"Any particular composers? Mummy adores the stuff."

He smiled briefly. "I quite like Rachmaninov. Heavy piano stuff. Schubert, Chopin, some opera. I love the Marriage of Figaro. And, dare I say it, I really like Edith Piaff – I know she's not exactly classical, though. I know that may be a bit weird for a bloke of my age, but, well....anyway, did you know.." Westward spent several minutes developing the story line of the previously mentioned Mozart opera as Abigail listened intently, her head resting on delicate, feminine hands. She seemed lost somewhere wrapped up in his voice and nearly didn't hear him ask what she liked.

"Oh, me, er...well, I was bought up on Jazz, vocal stuff. Forties and fifties. Sinatra, Ella Fitzgerald, Billie Holliday, you know..."

Westward then spent a few minutes giving his opinion on the little Jazz that he knew. She could however hear in his voice a sincere interest in what she liked.

An hour past far more quickly than either of them wanted before they walked back to the stables.

"So," he said, still clumsy and awkward, "thanks for a really nice time. I-I'm so glad you came out."

"Well, thank you, Jordan. It truly was a special surprise. Oh, I guess you'll have to find your friends now. I do hope they are sober somewhere for you."

"Er...can I see you again? Can I take your number?" Westward ventured bravely.

She strangely found herself glad that he had asked. "Do you have a pen?"

"Er..no. I don't, but that's OK. I'll remember it."

Her heart sank. *No one remembers phone numbers,* she thought dejectedly. This was perhaps the 'nice to have met you, but see you around' moment.

"01991 338748."

Westward repeated it several times as he closed his eyes briefly and looked skyward as he nodded his head. "OK, its the same code as me, so I've only got six numbers to remember!" he laughed as they shook hands, "I will call – I promise."

For the first time in her life she had met someone who she really hoped would call. There was a strange feeling inside that remained with her. If anyone asked her to describe what it was, this emotion instilled from a shy, seemingly lonely boy who did not fit with those he classed as friends, she would not have been able to do so. But it was there all the same, as she watched him hobbling back to the village. She wondered how he had ended up like that.

She would ask next time they met.

If there was ever to be a next time.

****

Seven long days later, to Abigail's surprise and delight, Westward did call. Weeks turned into months as they walked or sat in parks, bouncing life experiences back and forth. She, from a wealthy, successful family, he from a what seemed to be another victim from the ever-growing statistic of broken families. Yet, the chasm of circumstances in which they were bought up seemed to dissolve as they got used to each other's company. To his wonderment, he soon discovered that Abigail shared in his faith which not only bridged their social differences but had generated a solid approval from her parents.

"You know, I so much want to be a dad one day - a good dad. Abigail, it seems like I've known you all my life," Westward began as they walked hand in hand along the quayside, "I-I, don't want to get too familiar or sound weird or anything, but, none of my so called friends have offered what I have with you. It seems like you actually care."

The sun retreated behind a cloud as she took off her large tortoise shell sunglasses. He stopped walking, she turning to him. "Abigail, I-I, oh man, I don't know how to say this." He took her face in his hands and gently kissed her on the lips, aware of the mixture of responses that could happen. To his amazement, she placed her hands on his shoulders and responded whole-heartedly.

At that moment, a barge passed by and hooted loudly, the man at the tiller shouting his approval. Embarrassed, they pulled apart and both smiled and briefly waved at the man. They looked back at each other, blushing but still smiling.

His stomach continued to do somersaults as he looked for the right words. "Abigail," he asked, "I have something to ask you. You don't have to reply straight away."

She looked at him quizzically and dipped her head to one side. He stood speechless, for several moments. He looked away at another passing boat as two seagulls circled above them and landing on the war memorial.

Eventually, he mumbled his way through what he desperately wanted to get across, whilst looking down at his feet in embarrassment. "Would you like to, I mean, how do you feel about, erm- oh, what the heck," he looked her in the eye before continuing, "will you marry me?"

She stepped away at first and covered her face with both hands in shock.

Now on the defensive, Westward continued. "Abigail, I love you. I am totally and utterly in love with you and want to spend the rest of my life with you. I cannot offer you much, but..."

She walked on ahead, clearly dazed and sat at the next available bench. Westward joined her, unsure of what to say next.

Now I've blown it, he speculated, overcome by disappointment. They sat in silence watching the fountain in the centre of a grassy area spring into action. Several young children ran to its base and swished their hands in its cool pool of water. Westward sighed, but moments later, she turned to him, beamed and simply replied, "Yes."

****

Later that day, the couple made the short car drive to the Sinclair residence – a place that Westward had grown very fond of. As Abigail pulled her Mazda onto the meticulously kept driveway, two frisky squirrels scooted up one of the poplar trees that lined each side. As they passed the high hedges which obscured the property from passers-by, Abigail turned to the right and brought the car to a halt in front of the detached triple garage, Westward enjoying the wealthy sound of the crunch of the loose gravel beneath the car tyres. He cast his mind back to the first time that he had visited – overwhelmed by the social division between the two of them, yet also, how he had been lovingly accepted by her parents and her sister.

****

Months before

"Hello! Yes, I remember you! Lost your pals in Broadford-on-Stour if I recall, eh?" Harvey Sinclair's memory was as sharp as ever as he briskly shook Westward's hand having opened the heavy oak front door.

Westward was immediately taken in by the meticulously clean and neat appearance of everything. He inhaled the scent of the fresh flowers which graced the hallway, perfectly complimenting the fragrance of the air freshener which hung delicately in the air. As Harvey bounced his way happily to the lounge, Westward in tow, Abigail grabbed the moment.

"Apple and Elderflower room spray. Mum loves M&S!" she whispered, smirking.

Westward nodded as he paused a moment. As he took in the chandelier of many individual glisteningly clean glass pieces, he considered that had he known what elderflower smelled like he could have known whether to be impressed or not. As it was, he enjoyed it anyway.

The hall, simply emulsioned over a quality anaglypta, set off the plethora of paintings and wall ornaments. His feet, having removed his heavy boots, enjoyed the depth of the multi-coloured axminster carpet. The staircase to his left was a gallery of heavy framed replica paintings from a bygone age, atmospherically lit by strategically placed wall lighting.

I bet all the bulbs work here, Westward considered to himself as Harvey leaned around the door to invite Westward into the lounge.

Westward hid his sharp intake of breath at the grandeur. It amounted to a full thirty feet long, by his estimate and at least twenty feet wide into a huge bay window to the far side adjacent to the largest set of sliding patio doors he had ever seen. Heavy, deep green velvet curtains accompanied by matching pelmet and contrasting tie backs offered a magnificent frame through which to enjoy the vastness of the neatly manicured lawns and shrubs thoughtfully placed in the rear gardens.

And no mole hills, Westward thought.

"Hello, I'm Fionna – with two 'N's!" a slim, attractive woman in her forties announced, smiling politely from a high-backed arm-chair next to an Adam style fireplace as she placed her china tea cup and saucer on the mahogany coffee table in front of her, "You must be Jordan, yes?"

Westward, in a speechless state could simply muster, "Yes – pleased to meet you, Mrs. Sinclair."

"Oh, please – Fionna is fine!"

He gazed around the room. *All that's missing are the bronze stands with thick, red ropes attached and a sign telling visitors which areas were not open to the public.*

Harvey looked aghast as he suddenly recognised Westward.

"Good heavens – I know you! You're Jordan Westward! I thought I recognised you but couldn't quite place you!"

Westward nervously pulled his lips in. "Yes, that's right, sir."

"Oh come now, none of this "sir" nonsense, young man, Harvey is fine!"

"How do you know me?"

"Well, I was at Calverley a few weeks ago watching this young lad having the game of his life before that big old brute Henderson ended it. Don't go to football hardly at all but some pals forced me to go. Noticed you limping. How's you knee now?"

"Good and bad days," Westward shrugged.

"Too bad. Anyway, fancy a drink, young man? Tea, coffee? Scotch?" Harvey asked rubbing his hands.

"Erm – just water, please."

Harvey looked awkward as Abigail stepped in. "Jordan doesn't actually drink tea or coffee. He doesn't smoke or drink either," she emphasised proudly, pulling a 'beat that' kind of face at her mother.

Abigail was not sure whether her father's frown that followed was of disappointment or simply adding the snippets of information that he was collating about Westward to make a picture of him. In the end, he shrugged and went off to the kitchen, Abigail following.

Westward, feeling that sitting without invitation was inappropriate, walked over to the patio doors. A series of water sprinklers attended to their duty of keeping the green of the grass as a brace of pheasants wandered contentedly at the back of the lawns just in front of a curtain of well established and carefully kept leyland Cypress conifers.

It all seems so grand, Westward thought, shaking his head.

"Please, Jordan, have a seat, please feel at home. I have looked forward to this day – Abigail has never bought a young man home before." Westward's brief moment of discomfort was relieved as Harvey and Abigail returned.

"So, Jordan, I understand that you like classical music? I'm a bit of a jazz buff you know, but Fionna here's partial to a bit of the old stuff though," Harvey announced dropping his slightly paunchy figure ungracefully into his accompanying chair to Fionna's. Abigail considered cuddling up to Westward but decided against such an outward show of familiarity too soon and remained a few inches away.

Fionna added to the conversation. "Just this morning as I was cleaning some ornaments, I thought I'd let Harvey choose. What was it today, darling?"

"Oh, that – the Radetsky March, Strauss. Cracking piece of music. Do you know it, Jordan?"

Abigail smiled at Westward, immediately aware of the moment he had looked forward to – impressing her parents with his knowledge.

"Yes, I like that one. Did you know that Joseph Radetsky von Radetz, the guy who it was named after was actually responsible for bringing Wiener Schnitzel from Italy to Austria?"

"What?" Harvey looked shocked, his cup stopping just before it reached his lips. "You mean it's not actually Austrian?"

Westward cleared his throat after sipping his water. "No, it originates from Italy."

"Well I never," Harvey exclaimed, "and all this time, I thought my favourite meal was Austrian."

Abigail joined in now. "Dad loves Tyrolean cuisine, don't you Daddy?"

"Oh, You bet! Went skiing in Innsbruck, again, earlier this year. Smashing place. Stayed at the Grand Europa, we did. Amazing place. Took our time choosing it though. You know how things are, can't be done in a flash, eh?" Harvey declared loudly with pride.

Fionna smiled, cup held in both hands, and took up the story. "I actually chose it. Sounded a quality place – several big names have stayed there. The Queen, Prince of Monaco."

"I think you'll find that the Rolling Stones and Sting

stayed there too at some time."

"Really?" Harvey asked, surprised more that Westward would know such information, "How'd you know that, old friend?"

Westward shrugged and chuckled. "Amazing what you can find out from old magazines in dentist surgeries."

Abigail's parents laughed heartily.

"Actually, Innsbruck is a lovely place," Fionna continued, waving her hands, "there's a wonderful coffee shop, Schmankels. Only a ten minute walk from the Europa." She sighed. "I do love Innsbruck." She seemed in a daze of happy memories. The smirk which she tried to hide, along with the glance which Abigail's parents shot at each other told Westward that the memory for each of them was to remain private.

"Ever been skiing, Jordan?" Harvey ventured, tonguing cream from his moustache.

Westward, drinking from his glass, shook his head.

"Too bad – great fun, you know. Provided you keep away from injuries I suppose!"

"I think that's what has put Jordan off, isn't it? He does have a rather badly injured knee," Abigail chipped in.

"Yes, we discussed that. Too bad about missing skiing."

Before any further details about football were enquired about, Westward took control of the conversation once again.

"Do you go anywhere in the summer?" Westward asked. The answer was kind of exactly what he had expected.

"Oh, heavens, Yes!" Harvey began. He munched on a biscuit, brushing crumbs from his crisply pressed trousers. His wife looked on, unimpressed. "Last year went to Nice. Terrific there – climate and atmosphere, good time had by all."

Fionna slowly shook her head. "Are you sure it was just that? Perhaps the half-dressed ladies added to the attraction, darling?" she smirked as she drained her cup.

"Hah! Well, you know!" Harvey looked away sheepishly, rubbing his hands on the arms of the chair.

Westward smiled quietly as a brief silence followed before Abigail interjected.

"You can meet my sister later – she's out jumping at the moment. Mum's convinced that she'll be a an Olympic Show jumper some day."

"Probably not today," Fionna announced, "lot's of training."

Fionna then spent ten minutes explaining the potential of her daughter who she was clearly very proud of. Her father then added his part of the conversation as Westward was happy to sit and listen. Abigail glanced at him every now and then. Her face showing her acute embarrassment at the natural boasting of her parents.

After an hour or so of mixed conversation, Westward announced that he had to leave to prepare for work. As they left the house, Harvey made a thumbs up to Abigail whilst Westward had his back turned. Having said their goodbyes, Abigail drove Westward back home. He remained quiet, pensive.

"What's on your mind?" she asked negotiating a right hand turn.

"I was just wondering what your Mum did with her time. Clearly, your Dad keeps busy, but what does your Mum do?"

She had never really considered such a question. She frowned as she changed gear, running her mother's day to day life through her head.

"Absolutely nothing, really!" She smiled at the realisation and turned to him as she slowed to a halt and pulled the handbrake on.

"She must do something."

Abigail shook her head as if a revelation of great consequence had occurred in her mind.

"She tried golf and tennis – not her thing. She knew that she could never improve at either enough to really enjoy them."

"Gardening?"

"Be serious!"

"Sorry, just asking!"

"Actually, she does appreciate a nice garden – but she does none herself. She likes designing them, but someone else would always have to do the work."

"Sewing maybe?'

"Nope."

Westward was clearly perplexed. "So – how does she fill her day?"

"She looks after my Dad – he is very happy."

"I could tell that. What about swimming?"

"Oh, goodness, no – she would say that it would destroy

her hair. Actually, she likes facials, massages, that sort of thing – but not sunbeds, funnily enough."

"Does she cook?"

"Oh, she'd like to think so. She does enjoy good nutrition, but she's not obsessed with it. No, come to think of it, she's not actually that confident a person – although you'd never know it. She does like to travel – but only with my Dad."

"So – does she help with horses?"

Abigail roared, putting an apologetic hand to her mouth. "I'm sorry, Jordan, I can never imagine my Mum actually cleaning horses out! Her idea of horses is Ascot in a Jaques Vert outfit with a very attention-seeking hat. It's as much as she would do to keep the living accommodation end of our horse trailer clean. She does like to flick through magazines though – the sort you don't have to lick the pages."

"Oh – I think I know what you mean. Horse and Hound? Country Life? The Field?"

Abigail smiled. "Well, you are catching on!"

"She really is quite a snob, isn't she?"

"And she enjoys it immensely! For Christmas she bought Dad this fantastic Burberry wax jacket – you should have seen his face when he unwrapped it. It was bought with one condition however - whenever he wears it, she always makes sure he keeps it open so that everyone can see the tartan inside so they know exactly what it is!"

"Unbelievable!" Westward grinned, folding his arms. "I get the impression that the outdoors are a big part of your lives?"

Abigail gave a knowing nod. "You could say that. Daddy's often threatened to take up shooting some day."

"What a character!"

They both looked through the windscreen as two boys on BMX bikes whizzed past the car.

She sighed. "So, see you tomorrow?"

Westward nodded, joyfully.

They drew close to each other and embraced.

"Sorry, I really must go."

"Sure, I know. Will you call me?"

Westward nodded as he jumped out, smiled, and tapped on the closed window and ran up the drive, a far cry, he thought, to the place where he had just been. But his emotions towards this girl were growing stronger by the moment.

So, it seemed, were Abigail's for him.

And God Himself, Westward considered, was looking down and smiling all the while.

****

Months later

"Of course you can, old boy! Actually wondered what took you so long in the first place. But, then again, you know how things are, can't be done in a flash, eh? There you go, darling – a wedding in the family to look forward to! Much to plan, eh? Church, reception, clothes. Big day to look forward to."

Abigail was conscious of Westward's nervousness which she could tell was edging towards anger. They looked awkwardly at each other before dropping what they knew would be a bombshell to her parents.

"Well, actually, Daddy......we've decided to have a very low-key wedding."

Fionna looked aghast, her cup chinking loudly as she placed it on her saucer. Her response was abrupt. "Don't be ridiculous, darling, I must get a new hat, you know, and matching shoes and handbag! Whatever's the vicar going to say? You know he's been waiting for this for ages!"

Abigail kindly smiled as she slowly shook her head. "I'm sorry, Mummy. There are so many implications here. We feel for all involved something quiet would be best for everyone."

Harvey shifted uncomfortably in his chair. "So what have you got in mind, sweetheart? Can't help feeling a bit disappointed!"

"I know. I'm sorry, Daddy. Perhaps you could explain, Jordan?"

"It's complicated. My mum and dad just don't get on at all, and to be honest I think they would be glad to not have the expense. I don't even know where my sisters live to send them an invite and I don't have that many friends who would really be bothered," Westward clarified.

Fionna scowled. "Well that's my chance to show off absolutely ruined."

"So, what do you want to do?" Harvey continued with a frown.

Westward popped his knuckles out of their joints as he battled to address the anger that was rising in him now.

Abigail and Jordan both went to speak at the same time.

"You go ahead, darling," Abigail conceded.

"Look. We have talked and prayed about this so much and what we want is a Registry Office ceremony, very private, here in Woodmouth - just two witnesses. Over and out. Then disappear to the Cotswolds for a few days."

Harvey and Fionna stared at each other, shocked at the harsh tones from their future son-in-law, as both searched for objections.

"I know it's nothing like what you would like to give us.......but it's what we want," Abigail added, frowning at Westward's aggression.

"Who would you have as witnesses?" Fionna chimed in.

Westward took a deep breath to calm down, aware of the effects of his sharply drilled comments. "I'm sorry. I knew this was going to be really hard. Stephanie and my boss John from work. I don't know anyone trustworthy enough to have as a best man and John's about the only guy with his head screwed on."

A lengthy period of uncomfortable silence followed. Harvey rubbed his moustache and stared at the floor. Fionna played with a crease in the curtains and huffed impatiently as she fidgeted, desperately gathering her thoughts. Harvey eventually jumped out of his seat, offering open arms to Westward and Abigail. "OK," he said resignedly, "if that's what's going to make you happy, that's fine by me!" He embraced the couple as they stood.

Fionna's compliance took a little longer. "Me too - I suppose," Fionna reluctantly agreed, "but what will you wear, Abigail?"

"Oh, Mummy, I've seen this lovely Wallis Collection dress. You'll love it! Let me get the picture to show you!" she replied, beaming, as she enthusiastically dived into her pile of magazines.

Harvey sniggered as he folded his arms. "Do you need another drink? Might be here for a while if those two have got their noses in wedding books – son!"

Westward gave a tight-lipped chuckle of relief and took a fleeting glance at his pre-occupied wife to be.

"Sure. Glass of water, please – dad!"

The click for once had not been given place.

****

"When I first met Jordan, a guy same age as me, he was a bit of a mess and he won't mind me saying so! All he needed though was someone who he could trust. There have been several events in my life that have bought real joy to me, none more so than finding out that Jordan got saved."

Jon Mcdermott,
Friend.

Chapter 5

Ten years later.

"So, as you can see," the speaker pointed his pen animatedly at the multi-coloured pie chart projected onto the screen, "the potential for the Genesis Operating System, with our current specifications and benefits could give WestTech, even with the current market and competition, a yield of at least 9½% within a year or so. Mr. Westward, do you have any questions?"

The presentation was slick, even if not entirely genuine. The speaker had gained the attention of the majority of those present by offering a very much *'quid quo pro'* approach, cleverly masking any possible gain for his company. Westward's thoughts however were divided as he doodled on an A4 lined pad. He underlined the pre-printed logo several times.

WestTech.

Westward Technologies.

His own creation some five years previous.

Westward's sigh and shuffle in his seat could have been

considered as disinterest. He continued to play with his biro, thumbing the lid back and forth. Inevitably, as had happened several times before in meetings such as these, the clip to the lid eventually broke, flying across to the centre of the light wood veneer table before dancing to an eventual stop. Embarrassed, he reached across to retrieve the item and remained quiet for a few moments.

He tutted several times, swivelling in the black leather chair as he looked around the room and finally back to his pad. "Gentlemen, I have to say I am impressed with the progress that you have made, but........"

The attendees scanned the room in disbelief.

"There's so much more to be gained here," he continued, pocketting his pen, "This is a starting point. I sense there is a whole lot more here than meets the eye. We just need to expand our horizons."

Clive Wilson, Westward's second-in-command leaned over to whisper.

"Jordan, this is a great opportunity," he began, "It takes WestTech to cutting edge! This product is totally unique. You must admit it could save us years of development on our own!"

Westward creased a gracious smile and nodded. "Clive, calm down, I can see what's going on, it's OK!"

"Then what are you thinking?" he surreptitiously mouthed, irritated.

Westward patted Wilson's shoulder and stood, buttoned his double breasted jacket and reached over to shake the hand of the presenter. "I'll get my marketing guys to get back in touch with you within the next few days. I appreciate your time: have a safe trip back."

The other four bemused men present stood to leave, collecting tablets, mobile phones and briefcases.

"Thanks everyone, let's get back to work. Clive, could I have a word please?"

"Oh, sure," he mumbled, collating sheets of paper into a neat pile.

As soon as the door had closed, Westward poured two glasses of water, handing one to Wilson. Through the office glass he could see the fruits of his labours over the recent years.

Two hundred employees developing custom software for a variety of major, blue chip clients. First, the county, then the country and now Europe. Westward however, was still not satisfied.

"Clive, I-," Westward was interrupted.

"Jordan, I can't believe you!" Wilson interrupted, vigourously shaking his head. "This is a gold mine for WestTech! and no gamble. You saw the numbers! We could really become a major player with Genesis!"

Westward rubbed the uncharacteristic stubble on his tired face and sat back, hands behind his head. Wilson meanwhile paced up and down, irked and unsure how to win over this situation. Still Westward remained silent and begun to calmly jot notes again on his pad. Wilson's frustration in the end got the better of him.

"Don't you have anything to say?" he asked thumping the table.

Westward continued for a few seconds, turned the pad around for Wilson to see, tapped the heading and regained his relaxed pose. On it was the word 'Revelation' in a bold, made up, 3D, handwritten font.

"That's what we are going to create. It's called Revelation. You just saw Genesis - we're going to create 'Revelation'!"

Wilson silently tapped his fingers through the headings.

PC... Mac... Multi-platform.

He glanced up as he caught Westward's nodding head as he smirked.

Wilson shoved the pad back to Westward. "It can't be done. It's not possible. And what's more you're crazy!" he screwed a finger into the side of his head.

"No, not crazy – just, what was it my wife says? visionally ambitious."

Wilson exhaled loudly as he shook his head. "No, come on, this is beyond the realms of insanity! This could take years, decades even...."

Westward nodded. "Do you have somewhere else to go?"

Wilson tried to hide a smile. "Ha ha. Do you realise the implications here? Copyrights? consider the grief that mobile phone companies have had from Apple over their supposed copying I-phone technology? Not to mention the development costs – man, they'll be horrendous!"

Westward tapped his pen against Wilson's partially drunk glass of water. "Clive, you are such a half-full guy, do you know that?"

"Maybe – but at least I am a realist! You are just off the scale with this one. It could cost you millions! Millions that you don't have!"

Westward raised his eyebrows. "I'd settle for millions actually if it were only that. It is likely to be billions actually – but think of the basic maths. How many units of Windows based machines are sold each year at the moment?"

"Off the top of my head?" Wilson shrugged, "maybe five hundred million."

"Macs?"

"Maybe fifty million – going up every year, though."

"Plus over a billion mobile phones and probably three hundred million tablets – but that would have to be later, I think."

"Wow, that's a relief. What's your point?"

Westward scribbled a few more notes. "Let's say Macs and PCs together, total sales five hundred and fifty million worldwide. What do you reckon the cost to develop the OS?"

Wilson slowly shook his head. "I would guess somewhere around ten billion – that's what a new version of Windows would probably cost - and the most recent versions were maybe a lot more, I don't know for sure."

"So, let's say fifteen billion. Divide that by five hundred and fifty million, gives you..."

Wilson punched the figures into the calculator on his mobile phone. "Just over twenty-seven quid."

"So, sell three hundred million units of 'Revelation' at say, sixty quid for the cut down, home user version, and two hundred and fifty million copies of the full business version at a hundred and twenty, the profit is...."

Wilson went back to the calculator. He took a sharp intake of breath and silently walked over to the window. Outside, the hubbub of activity amongst the partitioned areas of the R&D department continued in its usual methodical manner. Wilson folded his arms and shook his head – all these ants, moving things from one place to another. One pressed enter to send an email – moving things. Another walked from their desk to the photocopier – moving things. Two others stood either side of a partition engrossed in conversation, articulating over the diagrams on a sheet of paper - moving things.

"Tozer was right, you know, Clive," Westward allowed himself a small smile, "just moving things from one place to another."

Wilson thumped his head in frustration as he was recalling the writing of the deceased preacher. "Jordan, you are so annoying! How did you know that was what I was thinking?'

Westward grinned. "Because I often stand in exactly the same place and contemplate the same thing. All work is exactly that. Anyway, "Revelation" is what we are going to do – and you are going to project manage it for me."

Wilson spun round and cackled like a crow as he laughed.

"I don't know how you do it but God bless you, Jordan Westward," Wilson grinned as he shook hands with his boss, "He knows you are going to need it! Want some lunch?"

Westward stood and ran a hand through his hair. "I thought you'd never ask! Incidentally, what was the final figure?"

Wilson turned as he reached the door. "Home and business together, nearly fifty billion."

"How long to develop?"

Wilson again shrugged. "The last Windows, if that's anything to go by, five to six years, depends how many guys you have on it. Don't forget, Microsoft has over a hundred thousand people on the payroll. And what about the fifteen billion?"

"Then we'd better make lunch a quick one. Sandwich at BB's?" Westward grinned as he once again buttoned up his jacket and ushered a chuckling Wilson out.

****

Three weeks later.

Wilson and Westward, as per usual, were the last in the office. It had been two hours since the previous member of staff left. The pair poured over the huge pile of printouts of coding, looking for the clue. Wilson took another bite from his burger and turned the perforated paper over again. Westward again glanced at the clock – eight-thirty. The artificial light had long been straining his eyes, but still he had continued. For three hours.

"Anything on yours?" Westward ventured, taking a healthy bite from a flaky sausage roll, wiping crumbs from his lips.

Wilson chewed, shook his head and swallowed. "It might help if I knew what I was looking for."

"You'll know it when you see it".

Wilson ploughed through twenty more sheets before loosening his tie and twisting his head from side to side. Then, as he began the next sheet, his eyes were inexplicably drawn to the centre of the green and white lines. "Jordan," he said quietly, staring at the sheet, "come and look at this. I think I may have found it! I think I've found it!"

Westward rushed round and stared at the sheet. He turned over to the next page and back. He ran a finger over six particular lines, nodded and put a hand on Wilson's tired, stiff shoulder.

The two grinned at each other.

"You, young sir, are a champ. Nothing but a genius. Do you know what this means?"

Wilson looked back at the sheet. "That I can go home now?"

Westward tutted. "You part-timers, you're all the same. Go on, get out of here, see you tomorrow. I'll fix a meeting for tomorrow afternoon."

"Seriously, what does it mean? You understand this programming stuff better than I ever will. I know what it says, but – what does it mean?"

"Sheesh – do I always have to hold your hand, Clive? What it means is, when the programme was written, it was left with the tiniest hole for someone with an ounce of faith to join two dots together. Kind of like using the some strange ability to get Spanish and Germans to converse and understand each other."

Wilson gave a confused frown.

"Alright, Clive - all it says is this: it can be done!"

Wilson mockingly feigned being asleep on his feet.

"Go on – go see your wife while she is still awake!"

The two men high-fived as Wilson made his way home and Westward returned to his office. He worked out that he still had two hours of work to put together his presentation.

I ought to call Abigail and let her know.

****

"So you can see, what we thought was impossible is very much doable," Westward tapped the enter key on his laptop keyboard, "and finally, with this, we become the producers of the most innovative computer operating system for years."

Low tones filled the room as each person leaned over to the person next to them. Heads nodded.

Westward folded his arms. "To be honest, I don't even know why I invited you all here. You are supposed to work for me, remember?"

Westward was immediately pummelled with questions.

Anticipated time-scales before commencing development were debated along with how relationships with other major corporations were likely to be affected. Westward was also challenged regarding the required specifications for machines and how he envisaged potential compatibility with mobile phones and tablets. The biggest challenge was how such a venture could be financed. Westward's preparation was rewarded as no question was asked that he could not adequately answer.

Wilson got up, walked to the front of the meeting room and stood next to Westward. He firmly shook his hand.

"Ladies and gentleman, I would like to introduce you to Mr. Jordan Westward – the brains behind the world's first cross-platform computer operating system. We will have Microsoft Windows and OSX products applications running together - side by side."

Westward concluded the meeting. "Ladies and gentleman, this is truly exactly what its name suggests: it is a revelation. Let's go change the world!"

****

Westward was excited the next morning as he prepared to ring the list of companies that he intended to contact to raise money for the Revelation venture. His mobile phone vibrated in his pocket at exactly eight o'clock as he pulled the door closed on his car. He pulled the device out, and noticed it was a Bible app that he enjoyed announcing the new set of verses for the day. He tapped the screen to pull up the new verses.

The red text of Deuteronomy 7:22 slid across the white screen.

"And the Lord thy God will put out those nations before thee by little and little: thou mayest not consume them at once, lest the beasts of the field increase upon thee." Westward read to himself. He looked up at his house in front of him.

"What could that mean?" he asked himself, running his finger in contemplation across his lips before starting the car.

****

His excitement had soon turned to frustration as he drove home in a foul mood twelve hours later. He had not given the verses another thought all day.

He slammed the front door closed on his house and went straight to his study, ignoring everyone else in the house. He flopped into his chair, swivelled a few times before picking up the post. He flipped through each envelope and tossed them back onto the desk. He sat and stared into space until his thoughts were disturbed by a knock on the door.

"Well, nice to have you home – well, actually it is nice that you remember that you have one," his wife sarcastically began.

Westward got up and embraced his wife. "I was convinced that I had come up with an idea, Abs, an idea that would put us on the map. It would have made billions."

"Revelation?"

He nodded, gazing in to her smiling, caring eyes.

"I had it all planned out. All I needed was fifteen companies to give me a billion pounds."

"Oh, I see. not much then."

"Look, I know it's a lot of dough, but you know how much they could made on the investment?" Westward huffed as he returned to his chair.

She slid over to stand behind him and began rubbing his shoulders as she kissed the top of his head. "Sweetheart, are you sure that you were ready for something as big as this? Was the world really ready for it?"

"Why do people not see a great deal when it's put in front of them? I mean – do you know what the guy at IBM said when I called them? Trying to get them to see the possibilities was like asking a duck to bark. They said, and I quote, 'at the moment we are streamlining global markets and re-defining dynamic methodologies'. I mean what kind of nonsense is that? The guy had had a major charisma bypass."

Abigail remained silent.

Her next words went through Westward's heart like a spear. "Maybe it would have been too much, too soon. What is it my Dad loves to say – 'you know how things are, can't be done in a flash!'"

Westward chuckled as he remembered his first encounter with his father-in-law.

Then the voice from inside spoke. *Little by little.*

Westward jumped and grabbed his mobile phone. He pulled up the verse again. There it was. Little by little. He groaned inwardly at his insensitivity to the voice of God's Spirit.

"Read that – I should have known when God was talking to me." He thrust the phone out to his wife.

Abigail sniggered and covered her mouth in amusement.

"That's so funny!"

Westward smiled and playfully punched his wife on the arm. "What's so funny? I have been up to my backside in alligators for a couple of weeks and all you can do is laugh and say 'that's funny!'"

"It's obvious, Jordan, God is saying too much too soon will be harmful. It's very simple."

"Well, that's why you saw it and I didn't – you're simple".

"Thanks – but seriously, if you follow this thing through any further, at this moment in time, it will be like trying to catch a falling carving knife."

Westward bit his lip. "I'm hungry. What's for dinner?"

"Air pie without the pastry."

"Well, at least that's gluten free."

"No guarantee that the air is sanitary though – Matt cooked it."

"Oh, heck. McDonalds is it then?"

"No, Chloe gave me a hand making a rather nice vegetarian risotto dish."

Westward playfully scoffed. "Oh, whoopy-doo!' Right, I'm off to the fried chicken place, then."

"By the way," Abigail asked, kissing him on the lips gently, "how much do you stand to make from taking on the Genesis project?"

"About five million. Why?"

"We need a new washing machine, it packed up today."

Westward rolled his eyes but couldn't help but beam as the two opened the study door to be mobbed by very happy and excited children.

****

Five years later.

Westward was enjoying a rare, few minutes in his day to read from his Bible and also from a recently received business magazine. He had picked this up several times and been inter-rupted each time and consequently had not had a chance to read a single page. He casually flicked through it briefly to start with and then turned to the second part of an article which specifically dealt with management in the football world.

'The trouble with management of any sort,' the article began, 'is the all too familiar balancing act of trying to keep everybody happy. This is, of course, at best, a complex imposs-ibility. There are many relationships which can become strained because each party is attempting to obtain what they want with minimal cost on their part and as always this is at the cost to another party. The salesman will try to gain the biggest profit possible, but naturally at the cost to the customer. The department manager, eager to obtain promotion will achieve his goal by two possible means: by his own abilities or by making out that his competitors are not as adequate as he is.'

Westward frowned but continued on in the hope that he could glean some nugget of wisdom.

'In football management, it is no different. A top flight club manager, or even that of a boy's club playing park football on a drizzly weekend, has the same challenge harmonizing players, owners and fans. He must keep the first team, the reserves, their families and the club's supporters happy all at the same time. They all expect a return for their investment.'

He looked up and out of the window a few feet in front of him and briefly re-wound his mind back to playing years before. The injury. The heckling. The despising.

He continued to read. 'For some, the job is, as has been said before, almost impossible. For some, the best they can offer must be done with the attitude of allowing the discontentment of those involved on the other side to be simply water off the proverbial duck's back. One manager, an ex-player, once sarcastically said that football management was tough – he was sometimes still at the club at three in the afternoon. Another said that a manager was never complete until he had experienced being sacked.'

Again, Westward recalled the devastating emotion years before of being told that he was being 'let go' a month after he had just signed a lucrative year long IT contract with a multi-national oil company. He carried on with the article, everything resonating with him.

'Clearly, there are those also who have achieved huge success whilst others belong in the 'nearly made it but not quite' category. There are some who win trophies year after year, have millions to spend creating a 'super team' whilst others have to make do with whatever players manage to survive through the youth programme. Other than that, all your average division one or two club can rely on is the potential low cost occasional 'bargain buy' of a player near the end of his playing career or a free agent'

Westward immediately considered Brian Chambers, current manager of Woodmouth Albion. As businessmen and Christians, their paths had inevitably crossed many times and the two had developed an amiable relationship. Anyone taking a brief glimpse at his profile on Wikipedia would be forgiven the thought of considering him to be the classic 'also ran' despite the usual comments regarding lack of citations to back up some of the information presented. Born in a rough area of Glasgow in the era when men worked hard to scrape a living, women stayed home, and footballers, even though they made a wage higher than those in regular trades, were still sometimes having to drive taxis of an evening to supplement their income.

Chambers had been described by one of his school teachers as 'not academically minded. His father, James, a failed trialist himself at Arbroath had encouraged his son to 'play, play and play some more'. Success in sport at school was followed by a carpentry apprenticeship. St.Mirren saw prospects in him as a central striker, despite his slightly stocky but meagre five foot eight frame. Comparisons to Kevin Keegan were inevitable. His debut for the first team saw him score twice in a 3-1 win at East Stirling. Three seasons at the Saints attracted attention by bigger clubs and he was ultimately transferred for the then heady sum of £250,000 and received a pay rise which took him up the salary ladder and not far away from some of the glamorous elites at the time. Several hundred pounds per week and an initial three year contract at Aberdeen the reward for his consistency. Once again, for the five seasons he stayed at Pittodrie, he dependably scored, averaging a goal every three games for the 180 odd games that he played. He managed three appearances for the national side, all three games ending sadly in defeat with Chambers being substituted in two of them. Aberdeen managed a highest league position of third during his playing time at the club.

From Pittodrie he moved on to Motherwell, the club enjoying something of a revival in footballing fortunes due to cash injections from a variety of wealthy entrepreneurs. He played four seasons at Fir Park, once again scoring freely, mainly because of the attacking wing-based play adopted by manager Eddie Patterson. Once again, however, the chase for silverware eluded the club. Chambers' eighty-fifth minute winner in a historic 1-0 Scottish Cup semi-final victory over Rangers had set up a tie with Celtic, but this had ended, once again in heartache in a 4-1 defeat.

Midway through his fourth season, he experienced ankle damage during a training session and at the age of 33 had to hang his playing boots up. He had always had a modest lifestyle - no gambling, womanising or drinking - but was still left in a challenging position: return to his carpentry trade or try his hand at management. Because of his age, clubs showed little initial interest in him in the capacity of the latter. He was however taken on as a pundit by TV commentary teams and spent ten years in this role during which time he pursued a full FIFA coaching and management qualification.

At 43, he had dived once again into the management arena and signed a two year deal with St. Mirren. Following a narrow escape against relegation, Chambers took the club up to seventh place, followed by eighth a season later, a seemingly lack of reward for his and the team's efforts. The club did not renew his contract. He spent three seasons coaching youth teams but inside he felt that he had more to offer. He turned down lucrative offers by Aberdeen and Motherwell as coach citing a clash in 'differences of opinion on playing styles' between himself and directors. Chambers then applied for the vacancy at Woodmouth Albion following the untimely death of ex-player Harry Crowther, a larger than life character, loved by the fans, whose shoes he knew would be difficult to fill. He signed a three year deal which was extended for a further three following his leading them to two promotions. They now had hit the dizzy heights of the Championship which bought with it a jump in quality of opponent but also much more in sponsor money. He drafted in two big name signings: Magnus Gustavsson, Danish international defender for £2 million and also twenty-two year old German striker Gerhard Messen for £10 million. The anticipated success had not followed.

The fans began showing their disapproval as crowds began to slowly decline. In their first season in the Championship, they had attracted average attendances of 20,000 per home game. By the third season, they struggled to reach 12,000. Chambers knew his time was coming to a close with the club and, as he personally had financially succeeded, everyone linked with the club knew in his heart that he was counting his days to finish the contract. He knew that the club would not sack him as they could not afford the severance pay. He was, in fact, dangerously safe.

Westward on the other hand was at the top. Wikipedia showed that Westward Technologies had become one of the leading software developers not just in the UK but also in Europe. It had been a long process but his current tenure was not enough and so the world beckoned. He sat back and allowed a brief journey into the annals of his past.

Having held on to his bank job, by the skin of his teeth, he took the plunge, much to the disapproval of parents, to change career direction to I.T. Discontent after a few years with lack of promotion in his first permanent position, he again took a gamble and worked for a major corporation in the city of Manchester. A year later, tempted by the financial benefits of self-employment, he formed his own company, secured a long term contract with commitments for pay increases every six months. Within two years he had quadrupled his pay, effectively then ten times what he earned three years prior.

Still dissatisfied, despite his now married status, he had spent every spare moment studying business and finance and, anticipating the upcoming growth and demand for local area networks, scoured every conceivable manual on that subject too. Eventually, working independently became impractical and he took on initially three, and within two years, ten members of staff. Westward Technologies ultimately appeared, floated within a year on the stock exchange, enabling Westward to re-invest huge amounts of his profits to diversify into software development.

Westward, an 'entrepreneur and visionary extraordinaire', according to an article in a previous issue of the magazine that he tossed on to his desk, saw a huge chasm between the two major computing developments of the time. He wanted to bridge the gap with a software platform able to run on both.

Most said this was impossible, not just from a practical and scientific point of view, but also from the initial objections from the two companies whose products that he had hoped to annexe. Despite several attempts from Microsoft and Apple to block his progress, no copyright breaches were proved and Westward's goal, 'Revelation', was commenced.

The local paper had described him as 'the man that stopped at nothing'. He remembered smiling at that quote. But, even though he had enjoyed the challenge of the I.T. World, he missed playing football.

He sub-consciously rubbed his knee gently as if hoping some divine intervention would take the injury away. He stared at the plainly framed black and white photo on the wall to his left showing him lifting the trophy from victory in a locally competed tournament. His face said everything as did the joy on the players that surrounded him. He smiled to himself as he allowed the final few minutes of the match to play through his mind. Twice in the space of a few minutes he stretched to make goal-line clearances with his team's goalkeeper first stranded diving one way as a deflection from a fellow defender spun towards the goal, then, moments later, sliding in to just connect with his toe to push the ball past the post as an attacker had lobbed the ball goal-ward over the 'keeper.

Most local matches in those days produced a hat-full of goals – this was an exception - the only goal of the game coming in the opening few minutes from Westward himself. Having charged up at the last moment for a corner, he threw himself at the outward swinging, loping ball, tumbling to the floor as his torpedo-like header crashed into the net.

He sighed and inwardly shrugged with resignation that anything more than a kick-about with his children would remain a dream.

But, he began to count his blessings.

A thriving business, an exciting product development underway, a wife that many men envied him for, children of whom he was so proud – and he lived in a dream house outside his town of birth. However, despite their lack of consistency, there existed a football club that inside he still loved.

And how I would love to play again, he contemplated with a deep sigh.

****

Two years later.

This is a complete mistake. Westward mumbled under his breath as he once again pulled himself up off the turf. *What am I doing here?*

He now knew that he had been foolish to have offered to play but Middlewich Green, even though scantily supported at the recreation ground, seemed like an opportunity not to be turned down. Not only was he playing out of position at left-back, he was feeling it, both in lack of fitness but also in his knee. He withstood the player just in front of him, arms out wide, head and shoulders and more above him. The winger whom he had shadowed the entire match, a lithe, quick player, several years his junior, chested the ball and allowed it to drop to his feet. Westward moved nearer and pushed his chest into the player's back just as he slipped past him. Westward grimaced in disappointment of himself and swore under his breath as he was clearly beaten. The winger accelerated and got a couple of paces ahead of Westward who did his best to keep up on the soggy, muddy pitch. The little man blasted the ball towards goal but it curved away just at the last moment and skimmed past the post.

The winger leisurely jogged past Westward and commented under his breath about how slow Westward was.

That really doesn't help things.

Once again, a few minutes later, the winger had possession, this time running at Westward on the right-wing. He slipped the ball past Westward, sped up to catch it just before it went out of play. Westward again was too slow and angrily slid in and with the full force of both legs, chopped the man down with his studs painfully impacting the player.

Westward cursed at the slightly-built opponent as the winger lay clutching his ankle.

"Oh, come on ref, for goodness sake!" Westward retaliated as the man in black produced a yellow card for him. The rain poured down incessantly, the pitch becoming even more difficult to maintain footing. Westward still could not understand why the referee had not abandoned the match long ago.

"Son, I don't care how big you think are," the referee made comment to Westward's tall frame, "but you cannot carry on tackling like that."

"But ref, he's been having a go at me all afternoon! What am I expected to do?"

"Control yourself, that's what. Number please?"

"Oh, for crying out loud, you are an unbelievable piece of work, you are!" Westward muttered as he turned around revealing the number five on the reverse of his shirt.

"I beg your pardon? Right, Mr. Westward, I have had just about enough of you. Go take an early shower and cool off, would you?" he spoke in an efficient, clipped, business-like manner as he popped the yellow card back into his shirt

pocket and brought out a red one to the joyous raptures of the
scattered, sparse crowd. Westward swallowed another cuss in
as he gritted his teeth and shook his head in disgust. His side's
captain ran over just too late to intervene. He protested on
Westward's behalf, but the referee simply shook his head and
pointed to the sidelines.

Abigail, standing alone, looked down as once again his
temper had got the better of him. Westward lumbered his way
past the smirking player whom he had felled moments before.

"What are you smiling at, you...." Westward angrily
muttered through clenched teeth. For good measure he kicked
the player hard in the thigh with the toe of his right boot.

Immediately, the referee ran over and hollered at
Westward to get off the pitch. "Just pray, son, just pray that I
don't take charge of another game that you're playing in as I
can't guarantee that my leniency will be the same as today. A
sending-off is too little, but that's all I can do for now. But, be
sure, the authorities will be made aware of your antics today
and there will definitely be repercussions, alright?"

Westward again cursed under his breath and spat back at
the referee as he walked away approaching his wife.

"Jordan, I -" Abigail began.

"And don't you start, either!" he bellowed as he stuck a
finger out at his wife as he walked past. She took a deep breath
as her lips began to quiver in shock at his behaviour.

"Jordan!" she screamed, "get a grip!"

He turned, paused to stare at her and grabbed a bag full of
kit and drinks bottles and with all his fury threw it at her as
she stood no more than ten feet away. She jumped back,
protecting herself with her umbrella. He continued walking
briskly towards the wooden hut where a hot shower would
greet him. Abigail ran after him.

"Jordan, for the love of God, stop! What on earth is the
matter with you?" she pleaded. She attempted to stop him by
grabbing his shoulders. He simply shrugged her off and
continued his resolute march. She ran past him, folding her
umbrella up as she did so and resolutely stood in front of him.

"Please, Jordan, I want to help you," she gently beseeched.
He stopped in his tracks, the rain ever forceful over the two of
them, Westward's shirt long having stuck to his torso. Behind

them, in the distance a cheer went up as the opponents scored again, putting the game seemingly out of reach at 3-1 with ten minutes left. Westward looked down at her, took a deep breath wiping his nose and face on his forearm and the tears began. She embraced him as he responded in sobs of weeping. "Jordan, it's OK, it's OK."

In between fits of shaking, he mumbled "I don't know what's the matter with me. I just don't know. I don't want to be like this. It's like being the Hulk. One minute I'm fine, the next I'm so full of anger, I just want to hurt anybody and anything. I have prayed and - I just don't see a way forward! I honestly thought that I had conquered this thing. It's been ten years since anything like this has happened."

Abigail sighed and nodded in appreciation of her husband's predicament. "Let's pray, right now, shall we?"

Westward shrugged his shoulders, resigned almost to the fact that he seemed a lost case. "OK."

They stood in each other's arms as Abigail poured her heart out for her husband. "Heavenly Father, we know that you hear our prayers. Lord, I just lift up my husband to you right now and ask for you to intervene in this situation. Please show us a way forward, in Jesus' name. Who the Son sets free is free indeed. In the name of Jesus, set Him free. Amen."

Westward whimpered an amen in agreement.

Talk to Jon, came from the voice of love again.

"Go shower, I'll wait in the car, OK?"

Westward nodded, kissed her on the forehead and hobbled off to the changing rooms. He stood under the steaming, refreshing spray, wishing that water alone would release him from his troubles. As he prayed under the water, he simply said, "Help me, Lord, please help me," and the tears once again began.

Talk to Jon. There it was again.

As he turned the shower off, he was aware of the noise of studs on the wooden floor as other players returned from the game. He dressed in silence and left the room without a word.

He opened the boot of his car, threw the sports bag in and walked around to the passenger door and slumped into his seat.

They sat and spoke for several minutes before a knock was

heard on the steamed up window next to him. It was Jon McDermott who had arrived just before Westward's dismissal. Westward pressed the button and the window responded and he watched it glide slowly down. McDermott compassionately smiled in the most un-condemning way that he could.

"Jon – what are you doing here?"

McDermott smiled compassionately. "It's funny you know. I haven't been back to Woodmouth for months but just sensed the Lord wanted me here today. I heard you were playing and thought that I would drop by."

"Man, it's awesome to see you. Do you want to come by the house?"

"Wish I could but, you know, places to go, people to see. But listen, Jordan, I'm not here to have a go or criticise at all. I just want to help." He fished in his sports bag and pulled out a CD and handed it to Westward. "This really helped me. I used to have the same problem – you know, the anger thing. I know, hardly seems possible, does it? But this was the answer for me. Have a listen – I know it's going to help you."

Westward looked casually at the disc, smiled at his friend and tossed it into the glove box. "Thanks, Jon, I appreciate that." He had no real expectations of a positive outcome from listening to the CD, but wanted McDermott to know that his thoughtfulness was appreciated.

"Give me a call – soon – I know the message will help. OK?"

Westward nodded and slid the window closed as McDermott tapped his hand on the car roof. Abigail started the car and slowly left the car park. The rainy, wet gloom in the physical world seemed to match that in Westward's spirit as they drove home in silence.

****

Two weeks later.

Westward, having served his suspension, returned to the team as a substitute. His team led 2-1 with a quarter of the match left, despite being down to ten men as a midfielder had already been sent off, when the manager gave the nod for him to warm up. As Westward stretched, the manager explained his tactical plan. He would be going on as a third central defender and he would pull off a midfielder. His team were, at the time, sitting mid-table so he felt that the consequences of such an experiment, were in fact immaterial. Westward nodded in understanding as he scanned the activities on the pitch and jogged a few lengths of the pitch. A few moments later, having gained the referee's attention, Westward made his way on to the pitch, high-fiving Michael Ellis whom he replaced as he passed by.

With twenty minutes left, his job was to solidify the defence and contain the opponents for a win. He explained to his fellow defenders the plan. They looked confused but shrugged their shoulders.

The game re-started with a goal kick for the opponents, Westward moving forward and out-jumping an opposing striker several inches shorter than himself. The ball was eventually chested and controlled by a team mate in central midfield. He in turn slipped the ball between two unsuspecting opponents to a winger who pushed his way down the left-flank to the by-line as the full-back, committed up front, had left a hole in the defence. A central defender charged over to fill the gap, but was easily out paced and out-skilled by the winger whose cross swung away from the goal straight to a striker on Westward's team who half-volleyed the ball. It rose gradually, skimmed the cross-bar and eventually came to a stop behind the goal several yards away. At this time, Westward had pushed up to the half-way line and applauded the move.

He returned to his normal position as again a goal kick was taken. Westward again easily won the aerial battle but instead of keeping his defensive position pushed forward and encouraged his fellow defenders to do the same. The ball was swung wide to the winger who twisted and turned to confuse the opponent's full back. He eventually pulled back and slid the ball along the ground to Westward, ten yards inside the opponent's half. He could hear the screams of 'what is he doing there?' from the touchline which he ignored.

He in turn flicked the ball forward to one of the strikers who played a one-two with him. He found himself on the edge of the goal area with a precious few seconds to line up a shot. Just after he let fly a 'daisy-cutter', inches off the turf, he was tackled from behind, fell forward and immediately grabbed his knee as he gasped at the intense pain that followed.

Click.

He rolled back back and forth as the cheer went up to signify that he had in fact scored. The player that tackled him genuinely approached, crouched down and, as the referee took out his book to note the player's name for the poor tackle, Westward with what ability he had in his situation swung a right hook at the player's nose.

The player was clearly shocked as his face was pushed sideways as a spurt of blood curled its way out. He covered his face with both hands as Westward used his good leg to feebly, but nevertheless intentionally make contact with the player's shins, despite the pain. The referee, not oblivious to the activities blew several blasts on his whistle as players from each side approached the scene to calm the battle.

A stretcher was called for Westward as the referee showed him yet another red card. His face grimaced as he was lifted gingerly onto the canvas with his forearm covering his forehead. As he was carried off the field, his manager approached him.

"Jordan," he lent over and spoke so as no one else was aware, "I've been kind to you. I know how much you want to play and I know your knee is caned. Central defenders can get away with it. But you are becoming a liability to this team. You may play like a cavalier but you have an attitude and self control that stinks. To be honest, I am not impressed by your goals, your skill or your intentions. I want people who can play as part of a team instead of thinking they run the show."

Westward remained silent and looked away to ignore the lecture.

"In short, I don't want you around here any more. Find yourself another club. You are not welcome here."

Westward twisted around in disbelief. "You have got to be kidding! You what?"

"I said – you don't play for this team any more. We have no room for people like you."

Click.

Westward feigned an apologetic face and beckoned for the stretcher carriers to stop and for the manager to come closer to his face. When he was a couple of feet away, he motioned for him to come even closer. When he was six inches away Westward raised his head and spat into the shocked man's face.

"You can carry on now," Westward huffed as he lay back down and tried not to concentrate on the excruciating pain emanating from his knee. A few paces later, he raised his head to see his manager remove a handkerchief from his tracksuit bottoms to wipe his face. Their eyes caught and all Westward saw was the shaking head of a man clearly disgusted and outraged at his behaviour.

Westward, within moments had once again complete regret and remorse at his behaviour. He asked to speak and apologise to the manager but his request was turned down accompanied by a reiteration of the man's request to not see him around again. He was eventually ambulanced to hospital and diagnosed with yet more knee ligament tears.

Same old story, he thought.

And again, those familiar voices returned to taunt him.

You didn't care about anyone else other than yourself. And who, to be honest, can blame you?

Everyone hates you.

Even your wife.

****

Three weeks later.

Westward was at home in his kitchen, engrossed in a humorous conversation with his wife when the telephone rang. A male voice on the other end asked to speak to his wife. Westward was puzzled but handed the phone over. He left the kitchen but stood just outside the door listening to her giggling, but not quite hearing the conversation.

She's sweet talking someone.

"OK," he heard her say, almost romantically, "I'll see you tomorrow. Bye." The phone was then replaced on its cradle on the worktop. She started humming and busying herself happily.

Click.

That click. The angry click.

He stood and leant casually against the door frame and scowled. "Who was that?" he suspiciously asked.

"Oh, no one." she coyly replied, still smiling but not making eye contact with him.

Westward grabbed a glass jar of teabags and threw it forcefully to the tiled floor, the shards and contents flying in every direction.

"Don't 'no one' me, Abigail!"

He then reached for a soft broom and began banging the kitchen table with it, dents appearing on its varnished, wooden surface.

"Jordan! Stop it! What's the matter with you?"

"I'll tell you what the matter is – him! whoever that was, he is the matter! And you!" This time, one of the wooden chairs became the victim of his demonically enticed onslaught. With all the force available, he raised the chair above his head. The spotlight in the ceiling smashed in the process sending glass everywhere as he brought the chair down hard onto the table top, the chair splintering into spraying fragments.

Abigail stood motionless, wide-eyed, hands on her face in shocked horror as he bought the chair down on the table again and again. "Jordan! you'll wake the children up, please stop!"

She did not recognise the man with her, and was very, very scared.

"Children! Oh, yes, anything goes wrong, just hide behind them. Always the way, Abigail! Well, guess what? I don't care anymore. I'm out of here!"

He stormed out of the room and seconds later she heard the slamming of the front door and the gunning and screeching of Westward's WRX as it spun down the unmade driveway. She slumped onto a chair and burst into tears as her head fell into her arms on the table. Even if she had explained that the call was from an old school friend that she was just humouring, she knew Westward was in no place to understand. She threw a very quick prayer up to Heaven for her husband just as their oldest son Matthew appeared at the doorway.

****

Westward threw the car around several sharp bends at
increasing speeds as he made his way to the outskirts of town.
Commentary of Liverpool's home game against Borussia
Dortmund flowed out from the WRX's stereo as he raced
through the gears. Eventually, he pulled over into the entrance to
the deserted car park in a wooded area of Woodmouth's
country park. He pulled the car to an unnecessary, screeching,
grinding halt on the gravel and switched the engine off, the
radio following in automatic obedience. He breathed in deep
and let out a slow exhalation as he allowed his head to drop
back against the head restraint and closed his eyes.

He prayed for his wife, his work and his children and sat
in silence a while to collect his thoughts. Then a voice within
his heart, spoke.

Listen to the CD.

In the usual business of life, work and family, Westward
had completely dismissed the item given by his friend. He
stared at the glove box, an inner wrestling taking place.

*It's just a CD, it's nothing. What makes you think it will
help?*

Jordan, this will set you free. Listen to it.

*Let's face it, you've always been angry, you always will
be. Don't waste your time.*

Jordan, you will be set free.

You're a lost cause, you have no hope.

Jordan, I want you to be set free. Listen to the CD.

"SHUT UP!" Westward roared at no one, slamming his
hands over his ears, "just leave me alone, all of you!"

After several moments of deep breathing, he opened a bottle
of water and took a few sips before turning the ignition on.
Liverpool and Dortmund obliged their continuation just as
Dortmund went 2-1 up. Westward shook his head in disappointment and bravely took the CD from the glove box and
pushed it in.

The introduction of the CD revealed the minister and his
credentials before announcing the title of the message:
"Deliverance from evil spirits". Westward's immediate reaction
was to turn the stereo off but he decided to give the recording
a chance for a few minutes. A strange presence of peace and
love in the recording stopped him, his finger hovering over the

on/off button. He allowed the disc to continue and was engrossed for twenty minutes as the plain, unexciting voice of the British, well-spoken minister expounded on the various methods that demons use and how they can influence and possess a human being.

One of them caught Westward's attention.

Alcohol abuse.

He was confused to begin with. After all – he was free from alcohol, right? However, he had been unaware that, as the minister explained in clear, concise terms that one demon can be completely unrelated to another and so will not leave just because the other does. He stared out the windscreen at the gentle waving of centuries old oak branches as the dusk turned to night.

"Right now," the minister continued to the live audience, "I can tell that some of you here are wrestling with demons. Some have been there for many years and you were not even aware of. Yet God in His love and mercy has provided a way for you to be set free. It was never His will for them to be there, but it is His will for you to be free. The way forward is, as always is with the things of God, quite simple. The blood of the Lamb provides healing, salvation and deliverance. It is all inclusive. God has provided His way of life – nothing missing, nothing taken away. But it will take faith for you to receive from God. Faith in what He has already provided at the cross."

Westward sat aware that a wrestling was taking place inside his very belly as the minister began speaking in what appeared to be another language for a few moments, one that he had not heard before. He then continued in English. He briefly explained how salvation, healing and deliverance were all available with Jesus.

"Alright. Here is what we are going to do. You also need the presence of the Holy Spirit to take the place where those demons currently reside. A basic law of science is that no two things can occupy the same space, so by virtue of that premise, we need one to leave and the other to take up residence. So, what we are going to do is to simply breathe slowly in, and then breathe forcefully out. We will breathe the Good Spirit in, and we breathe the bad spirit out. It is that simple. However, make no mistake, the bad spirit will not want to leave, but by virtue of the Power of the blood of Christ, they cannot stay. James 4 verse 7 says 'Submit to God, resist the devil and he will flee'. This is not just a surrender to the Power of God, but an active wrestling with evil spirits."

As the message continued, there was the sound amongst the audience of people following the minister's instructions as the turning over in Westward's insides got stronger and stronger. The minister continued praying over the top of the breathing performances. "Satan, we come against you and all your minions in the name of Jesus. We bind you in the name of Jesus. We command you to leave, in the name of Jesus." For several minutes, interspersed with the strange language being spoken, the minister continued as several of the congregation on the disc began screaming. Eventually, calm was restored and the minister kept repeating "We praise you, Jesus, we praise You, Lord. Alleluia. You are King of Kings and Lord of Lords. Glory to your name. Alleluia! Alleluia!"

Westward wrapped his arms around his stomach as the pain increased. For a moment he thought that his appendix was about to burst. The CD came to an abrupt and unexpected end leaving Westward in a state of panic as he rewound in his mind to what the minister had said.

Just breathe.

He closed his eyes and took a deep breath in before forcefully breathing out. He began crying in pain but persisted in the breathing.

In between the grimaced fits of cramping, he was just able to mouth the name of Jesus and nothing more. For a full five minutes he wrestled with the demon. In between breathing, he began to simply, with all his effort possible, command the demon to leave – adding 'in the name of Jesus'. Eventually, he struggled out of the car, exhausted, and leant over the bonnet. After a few minutes he was aware of a lightness about him despite being more tired than having run several miles.

He stood up, took a deep breath in and this time slowly let it out. He raised his arms to the sky and yelled at the top of his voice, "Thank you, Jesus! Thank you, Jesus!" He then placed his head in his hands as tears came once again, not tears of defeat this time, but those of a monumental victory having been won. As he continued weeping, he pulled out his mobile phone and called Abigail.

"Abigail," he whimpered between sobs, "I am so, so sorry. But it's over now. It's gone. My anger. I know it's gone. You just got to believe me."

On the other end of the call, he heard her sigh. "I know it is. You listened to the CD didn't you?"

"Yes, I did and I feel like I've just done fifteen rounds with Rocky. But I won. Jesus won, Abigail. It's all over now. And I am so sorry. Please forgive me."

She quietly consoled him and confirmed her forgiveness.

"Come on home, sweetheart – we have some new chairs to pick out of the catalogue and you have a bulb to change," she laughed. He took one final deep breath in.

"I'm on my way," he stammered out in between sobs, a peace long forgotten returned to his heart as he took a much slower drive home.

****

Days later.

"You're doing that thing," Abigail commented as she glanced at Westward out of the corner of her eye.

He shot her a defensive look. "What thing?"

"That thing you do when you are thinking or planning something. The corners of your mouth go up and down."

He hesitated before replying. "You know something, Abs," Westward started without taking his eyes away from the football highlights on the TV screen, "I think I have finally got to that point where I never care if I play football again."

Abigail pulled away from his embrace and turned slowly with a face of mock horror.

Westward sniggered at his wife's humour before launching into a full scale tickle fight which left them both in fits of laughter. Eventually, when calm returned, during which time Westward had missed two West Ham goals against Everton, he continued. "No, I am perfectly serious. I am completely content. I have you, I have the kids and I can virtually pick and choose when I work. Life couldn't be better."

Abigail frowned, open-mouthed, not quite sure of the

truth behind her husband's unexpected words. In return, Westward smiled and slowly nodded.

"You really mean it, don't you?" she stated rather than suggested with a warm smile.

"Yep. I sure do. I don't even know if I'll even bother going to many Woodmouth games now. I might take Matt every now and then, but," he paused before continuing, "I have a strange feeling that God is about to do something really unexpected in our lives."

"Sounds ominous. What on earth do you mean?"

"I'm not certain really," he continued as Everton pulled a goal back, "but I think something big is going to happen for us."

****

"The first time I ever met Jordan Westward, he came across as an egotistical, self-centred, domineering brute of a man. As he proudly marched up on to the platform, flicking the back of his hair, the person next to me began quietly singing the words to that old Carly Simon song, you know, 'You're so vain'. He ranted about sin and hell – not what I wanted to hear on my first visit to church. But after he had spoken, he talked about the love and grace of God and how Jesus loved ME and how He wanted to save ME. He took time to speak to me personally and when he is up close to you – there is something different in his eyes. I can't explain it. And when he prayed for me, well, my body felt like fire went through it."

Barbara Dennis,
Attendee,
Mill Street Baptist Church,
Calverley.

Chapter 6

Two weeks later.

" Goodnight guys. Great work again today on that user interface," Westward encouraged through his open office door. Some co-workers picked up coats from the backs of their chairs and headed towards the end of the office.

He tossed the report onto his desk and exhaled wearily as he glanced once again up at the plain, white-faced clock. The second hand glided its way around as another minute past. It was now ten past seven and he was irritable. His left knee began to ache as it always did when he was under stress. Something was not making sense in the document that he was reading. He stared down at the small gold-framed photo of his family. He smiled as he remembered their treasured visit to Ireland the year before, he and his wife balancing on one leg, arms outstretched at the Giant's Causeway.

He sat back and stretched in the hope that his mind would be refreshed and picked the document up again. He turned back a page and placed the paper on his desk in front of him.

He continued reading as he placed his chin on his palm.
Then he heard the voice.

Buy the club.

It was that loud, it was almost audible, but he knew there
was no-one there. He jumped and looked around expecting to
see someone standing behind him. He frowned and slowly
stood up and walked outside into the empty expanse of the
brightly lit office. He scanned the room carefully, but as he
expected, there was no-one there save the distant drone of a
vacuum cleaner. Then, as he turned to return to his office, he
heard the voice again.

Buy the club.

He stopped in his tracks and shot round ready to attack an
invader.

This is like Field of Dreams, he thought to himself.

Westward shook his head and stood with his hands on his
hips. Then he realised who the voice was and he began
trembling.

Yes, Jordan, it is I am.

There was no physical body there, but once he recognised
the voice, he felt the familiar presence. Westward could no
longer stand. He crumpled, spread-eagled with his face to the
carpet-tiled floor. He was unable to speak, such was the
awesome nearness of the invisible person. Had anyone
remained, he would have looked altogether foolish.

*"Will you buy Woodmouth Albion for Me? I can use it to
change this town and this country. Will you trust Me to be with
you? I will bring glory to My Father and you will play and
manage the club for Me."*

The world around him gradually faded as those two words
echoed around in his mind.

Play....Manage....Play....Manage....Play....Manage....

He thought that there must have been at least a hundred
angels singing around him such was the volume of the
breathtaking sound that began to fill the room. He still could
not open his eyes to take in the events around him. Somehow,
he was totally enveloped by the ensemble. Even a choir of the
greatest human capabilities could not have sung in such
beauty, harmony and truth. It emanated from every corner, in
front of him, behind him, to the left, to the right.

Inside him.

Then he felt the arms around him. He was being lifted, up, up, up. He watched as his body remained prostrate on the floor in the office. He saw the last dregs of employees exiting from the main doors out to the blustery expanse of the car park. Then he could see the town, his beloved town of Woodmouth, then the county and then the familiar outline of the United Kingdom as he flew, spread-eagled above the Earth.

Then, all of a sudden, he was in the place where he knew was safety, love, compassion, joy - and reverence. Despite the safety, he did not want to be there. Despite the reverence and powerful presence of this man, he did not want to leave. Finally, he raised his head to briefly take in his surroundings. There was no floor, no ceiling, no walls, no windows, no doors. Just white. A bright, shining, clear, untainted white. Then another man appeared from the distance and walked purposefully towards him. He was even whiter than the surroundings. Westward could do nothing but bow and look away. The man towered above him.

He must be ten feet tall, Westward considered in awe.

He was also broad, so strong-looking. He approached Westward and stopped a few feet from him.

"Jordan, arise, I am merely a servant like you. Do not worship me, only He that sent me."

Westward tried to get up. With all the strength he could muster, he got to his feet like a new-born lamb, stumbling, faltering. He placed a hand in front of his face to shield himself from the glare. Then he saw the wings. Huge wings. And the man's hands. He remembered his father's, they were big as he thought back to the past, but these were so, so much bigger.

"Who...who are you?" he stuttered.

"It is not important. But you must listen."

Westward gradually lowered his arm and took the risk of looking the man in the face. His eyes burned towards Westward, but in loving power. Westward's initial fear was leaving as he closed his eyes for a few moments to adjust to where he was. He looked about him and his mind took him back to his salvation.

This is the same place! That place!

"Jordan, the Lord has a task for you. He has decided that you, and only you, are the person who can do it. As always, it is your choice. Each person the Lord chooses to create, He has a plan for that person's life. Your time is now. If you will use faith, you will succeed. The Lord also knows of your pains, frailties and fears. If you allow Him, He will overcome them with you. The Lord would like you to buy Woodmouth Albion Football Club. He would like you to play for it and manage it."

Again, those words reverberated around in his mind.

Play....manage....play....manage....play....manage....

All at once, he felt like Gideon at the threshing machine and many excuses battled their way to the front of his thoughts.

"But..... my knee, my family, my work, my...."

"Jordan, it is a time for you to trust deeper than ever before. It is a time for you to truly walk by faith - and not by sight. Just remember what the Lord has said. There is nothing that you will go through that the Lord has not gone through Himself and there is nothing that you cannot do if you remember that He is with you at all times. Wherever you go, He goes with you."

At that moment, the man knelt down before him and touched his left knee. Liquid warmth flowed through him, emanating up his thigh, down to his toes, up through his torso, neck, head. He raised his hands and closed his eyes. He knew this feeling, rejoiced in its memory and despite his futile efforts, he began to weep. His body convulsed as the power worked its way around his body. He shook his head as the tears began, joyful, gladdening, releasing tears.

"I'm sorry.....I'm sorry," he wailed. His fears were being over-run - not removed, but over-run. They remained, but the power would prevail.

After what appeared to be several more minutes, not that time seemed to mean anything here, the man stood and placed his hands on Westward's shoulders as his tears subsided. He smiled as Westward gazed up at him.

"You have been empowered. All you need do now is listen and obey. You will have great success. Much will happen. There will be much joy, but much sadness too. Not everyone will understand. Remember what the Lord has said, 'If God be for us, who can be against us?' The Lord is with you...The Lord is with you...The Lord is with you..." The words tapered off into the distance as did the man, the place, the love. His body began falling, falling, yet he felt no fear. Then suddenly, he was back on the floor of the office. It was as quiet as it had been all that time ago. He sat up and shook his head as he glanced at the clock and frowned.

Three minutes.

He pushed his hands through his hair and wiped his eyes.

He slowly walked back to his desk and collapsed into his chair. He stared at the carpet as if answers were there. What had happened? Did it actually happen? He picked up a pen and began tapping it on his desk with no particular rhythm as he stared on. Fifteen minutes past as he thought carefully, trying to put his own thoughts into what had occurred.

Buy the club....Play for the club....Manage the club.

He grabbed a piece of scrap paper and began frantically scribbling notes, whatever came into his head. Players, positions, money, opponents, the ground. Then he stopped and threw the pen down.

"What on earth am I doing?" he muttered to himself.

Here he was.

A company director with a wife and five children.

He was thirty-seven years old and had a long-standing knee injury.

Then it dawned on him.

Before the man appeared, his knee was aching. He gently rubbed it and realised it was no longer causing any pain. He jumped up and walked with pace and halted just outside his office. There was a long corridor between the glass fronted offices and the computer-clad desks of the software designers. He ran towards the water machine, about a hundred feet away. Even though he was only in his work shoes, he ran, back and forth, back and forth. Finally he stopped, hands on hips and smiled. He chuckled and finally laughed out loud and clapped his hands.

There was no pain. Nothing.

He ran up and down the corridor for the next ten minutes, smiling all the while. Finally, he stopped, jumped up and down with his hands in the air and began to shout, "Yes! Yes! Yes! Thank you, Jesus! THANK YOU, JESUS!"

He cupped his hands over his mouth and walked back to his own desk. He glanced once more at the clock. It was now seven-thirty. He remembered it was Wednesday evening. He could still make it to the meeting at the church if he dashed.

He quickly called Abigail to inform her of his unusual intentions, without giving any indications of the events of the evening. As always, she understood and simply said that she would see him when he got back.

She's so awesome, he thought to himself.

He grabbed his jacket from the back of his chair and his briefcase. He stopped abruptly and stared at the document on his desk that had caused him so much anxiety that evening.

Tomorrow! he thought to himself with a broad smile. At one minute to eight, he hurried into the sanctuary of Woodmouth Christian Fellowship.

****

One hour later.

The hundred or so attendees were just finishing the final chorus of one of the church's favourite songs, many still with hands in the air and eyes closed as Westward crept in and took a seat at the back. He waved at Chris Lewis who as usual sat behind the PA desk. He had hoped that the Pastor, John Rogers, had not seen him yet.

"Bless the Lord, oh, my soul and all that is within me, bless his Holy Name!" Rogers spoke clearly and loudly with the aid of a lapel microphone attached to his customary open-collared, long-sleeved, blue shirt. The final resonance of the acoustic guitar chords and keyboard faded as Rogers bid the congregation to sit.

"Welcome one and all once again," he began as he paced up and down on the stage. He prayed quietly to himself before he returned to his perspex pulpit.

"I have to confess something. I had a message which I was going to bring tonight but I firmly believe that the Holy Spirit has something different in mind." Once again, he continued his wandering before coming to a halt at the edge of the stage. He knelt down, closed his eyes and raised his hands. "Everybody pray, please. Every head bowed, every eye closed."

At once the hall was full of the sound of a unified body of people seeking the heart of God, calling at the door of the throne-room of Heaven itself. Westward bowed his head and joined in.

"Almighty God," Rogers began, "we thank you for your presence here tonight. We praise you not to bring you down, but because we know that you are here. Lord – I simply ask that you have your way here tonight. I commit this whole meeting to you. I lay aside all my plans and ask that you do whatever it is that you need to do. We know that you are a God who loves. We know that you are a God who heals. We know that you are a God who saves. We know that you are a God who delivers and cares. Have your way, Oh, Lord, have your way. In the name of Jesus we ask, amen."

The hall reverberated with a hushed but unanimous "Amen" as Rogers stood back up and returned to his pulpit.

"I had planned to speak on the end-times tonight, but I believe God has something very unique to show us. By the way, welcome, Jordan," Rogers stared at Westward and clicked his fingers, "I believe tonight is about you."

Several gymnasts tumble-turned in Westward's stomach in anticipation as Rogers began.

"In all of history, I firmly believe that no one has seen such a drastic change in a character than that of the apostle Peter. Here was a man who walked with Christ, ate with Christ and lived with Christ for three years or more. He witnessed, first hand, miracles at the hand of Jesus. And yet, when it came to the crunch, in the flesh, he denied ever knowing Jesus – an event that Christ Himself even foretold just before it took place. This broke Peter. Yet in just a few short weeks, he stood up in front of an immense and puzzled crowd of Jews from all over the surrounding areas and preached a message under the anointing of God's Spirit and thousands of lives were impacted for eternity."

Rogers continued, no notes, but simply allowing the Holy Spirit to speak through him. For an hour he expounded on a message about second chances. He then came to silence as the congregation, some in tears, some in sheer wonderment, sat considering how this was to be concluded and how it may be relevant to them. Westward tried with all his might to hold back yet more tears.

All of a sudden, Rogers spoke. "Jordan Westward, come up would you please? I know that the Lord is dealing with you."

Westward wiped his eyes, pushed his chair back silently on the well worn, green carpet and made his way to the stage where he was handed a microphone. He took a deep breath and turned to Rogers, a full head and shoulders below him. Rogers closed his eyes and laid his hand upon Westward's shoulder.

"Jordan. God has touched you tonight and wants to finish a job. He has laid before you an opportunity. He is the God of second chances. Whatever that maybe, He is saying trust Him! He is not ordering you to do anything, rather He is simply asking 'are you willing?' All the resources will be there as you need them. Whatever you have at any one time will be enough. Do not try to work this out in your own understanding. Simply believe. There will be a victory that you never thought possible. And this has nothing to do with computers or technology. This is to do with sport." Rogers nodded to the musicians who began to ad-lib instrumental music to cement an atmosphere. "Would the elders come up please?"

Three men, all of different ages made their way to the stage and stood surrounding Westward and began silently praying. Westward sank to his knees, hands out in front of him in a receiving attitude.

Rogers continued. "I, the Lord, know your disappointments. I am now making appointments for you, Jordan. You will travel in the name of My Son and share His name with those you meet. I will glorify my name in this town and many, many others. The road will not be easy – there will be many who you should not trust, because they do not trust me. But I will pour out my love and my Spirit on all who are open. I will give you discernment. Do not be worried about your business – that too will bring glory to my name, but in my time."

Westward began to shake irrationally. He found himself, simply saying over and over again, "I receive, Lord, I receive! I receive, Lord, I receive! Lord, I love You, Lord, I Love You!" He then began to utter words in a language that he did not know. As he kept his eyes closed, he saw a vision of a sky covered in grey clouds, which parted like curtains at a theatre to reveal a new backdrop, so blue, so fresh, that no paints in the world could humanly recreate – because it was a unique creation from God Himself. Westward was caught up in the love of God, totally unaware of time, unaware of anything in the physical realm around him. The tears, floods of pain and anguish, that even he didn't realise he was still carrying began evaporating. Then he was conscious of a joy that he had not known before. Even his salvation, many years before seemed ordinary. This seemed to take things to another dimension, not arrogantly, not in a way that he was superior, but he was now empowered in a new, fresh way to serve God effectively.

He had not only received all of God.

God had finally received all of him.

****

Westward checked his watch having been prostrate on the stage for what seemed like eons.

Eight-thirty. Just twenty minutes.

As he stood, he saw several others in a similar position.

Then the voice spoke in his heart once again.

"Will you go and heal them for me?"

Westward stood and scanned the room. At the back of the auditorium was a woman in her forties in a wheelchair, quietly praying and reverencing God. Westward did not recognise her as a regular attendee and boldly walked up to her. He held out his hands as she looked up and gently smiled at him.

Westward spoke, simply and clearly. "Jesus has sent me to offer you healing."

The lady's sigh spoke many silent words as she closed her well-wornBible.

"Do not doubt, only believe!" Westward smiled, gesturing with his hands for her to come. "In the name of Jesus, stand!"

At first, the woman resisted but Westward stood firm and

repeated the words, this time with a firmness that surprised even him. "In the name of Jesus, stand!"

The woman lent over to carefully place her Bible and notebook on the table next to her as Westward graciously and tenderly smiled again, motioning with his hands for her to leave her wheelchair. She placed both her hands on the sides and found that she could move her legs voluntarily without assistance. She placed them on the floor and pushed the weight of her body up on her arms. At first, the movement caused her anguish as she felt nothing in her upper legs to give her strength.

"It's OK," Westward encouraged, "you can do this. God has enabled you. Just accept by faith and trust him." He automatically went to place hands on her arms to help but then the voice spoke.

No, she must do this by herself. I will do it with her.

The woman once again strained and pushed as if giving birth and found that she could stand, unaided, for the first time in ten years. She placed her hands over her mouth in shock and shakily balanced herself, expecting to fall back onto her wheelchair any moment. By now, a crowd of several people had gathered around and began praying in the Spirit as Westward took three steps backwards and again motioned for her to come to him. "In the name of Jesus Christ of Nazareth, walk!"

The woman put her hands out in front of her as if to get Westward to give her balance. He shook his head and again gestured for her to come to him. Shaking, the woman took one step. Then another. Then a third. All the time, Westward moved one step further away. She stopped for a moment and he cried "No! Do not stop! Jesus says come!" She was breathing heavily and swallowed hard as she took two more steps, this time a little faster as once again Westward stepped away. Then she began to go faster, all the time remaining a few steps away from his arms.

"Alleluia!" Pastor Rogers said under his breath as everyone began clapping and encouraging her. She began a brisk walk as Westward walked as fast as he could backwards towards the stage. He glanced back, his hands still out in front as he stepped up. She followed, amazed, joyous and free. Westward looked back as he began a gentle trot, all the time the woman following him. He trotted down the steps at the far end of the stage when he himself became aware of his own ability to run without knee pain. He sped up as the woman followed and began circling the rows of chairs that filled the hall. He finally finished in front of the stage as the woman fell into his arms as he punched the air, staring at the giant cross suspended on the angle of the ceiling.

"Jesus is Lord!" he roared at the top of his voice to a huge resounding 'amen' from the rest of the those looking on in amazement. The woman released from his embrace and wept tears of joy. At that moment an old man gingerly approached him, hobbling. Westward, still beaming, placed his hands on the man's shoulders and simply said "In the name of Jesus, be healed!" At first the man turned and walked away in the same way that he had arrived and then within a few seconds, then Westward clapped his hands. "Stand up straight in the name of Jesus!" Still the man saw no change and glanced back in disappointment and shrugged his shoulders.

Westward frowned, unsure why the woman walked and this man saw no chane. Then, once again, the voice spoke.

Infirmity.

He then called the man back and once again lightly laid his hands on his head. "Spirit of infirmity, I command you to leave this man, now, in the name of Jesus!"

The man jumped at Westward's commanding voice, but as he jumped, he recognised that his body felt different. He straightened his back and walked away with his hands held high. The whole crowd cheered again as he too began running around the hall as a seven year-old child with glasses approached him, one lens of her glasses frosted. He knelt before her and with all the love that he possessed, smiled and gently asked, "Do you believe that Jesus can heal you too?"

The girl simply nodded, with quivering lips.

"Then be healed, in the name of Jesus!"

At that very moment, she was aware that her right eye was able to see but everything was blurred. She looked around as Westward gently removed her glasses as her eyes widened in surprise. She could see clearly through both. Her mother and father embraced her in tears. "Mummy, Daddy, I can see you! I can really see you!" Westward looked her parents in the eye as he snapped the glasses in pieces before them as the mother, in tears, simply mouthed, "thank you!"

At that moment, Pastor Rogers approached Westward and embraced him. He cleared his throat before beginning.

"Jordan, bless you, bless you, bless you! But now you must pray for me." His attention was gained as he still had his lapel microphone switched on. He raised his arms wide to gather everyone towards him.

"Today," he began, stuttering, his mouth quivering, "I went to the hospital." There was a quiet expectation amongst the congregation before he continued. "Apart from my wife, you are the first to know of my situation. For several months now, I have noticed a number of lumps growing on various parts of my body. At first, I took no notice of them but in the end, my wife encouraged me to see the doctor. He immediately referred me to the hospital for tests, for which I received the results back today."

Rogers placed his hands on his bowed head. He took a deep breath and concluded.

"I have cancer."

The crowd took in deep breaths of shock.

"It has spread to some vital organs and the doctors have said that it is past considering therapy of any sort. I have, according to them, a matter of weeks to live."

"No!" Westward bellowed as Rogers jumped as if several thousand volts had gone through him. "Speak those things that are not as though they were!"

Rogers compassionately shook his head at Westward. "Jordan, I appreciate your concern and what God has done tonight, but I...," he cut short as he lowered his head again, "I have sinned and deserve what I have."

Westward stormed up to him. "You're our pastor! We look up to you! Why all the unbelief? NO! Nothing shall separate us from the love of God - nothing!"

Rogers looked up out of the corner of his eye at those watching him. "I have bought this upon myself and deserve it. I have lived a life of total hypocrisy for many months. I am now £100,000 in debt from a gambling habit which I have kept hidden from everyone. Everyone it seems apart from God and the devil. As soon as I get home, I have to hand over the keys to my house to men who I owe the money to or they will break me limb from limb. I have preached so many times about not giving place to the devil, and here I am, a victim of the very action which I have condemned others for. My wife is not here tonight as she is two hundred miles away at her sister's house. I am ashamed and feel disgraced and have failed you. God is dealing with me."

There was a hushed silence all around as Westward stood before him, Rogers' arms wide open as he broke down and sobbed. Westward enveloped him as others simply prayed. Westward began praying in the Spirit as God began to speak through him.

"My forgiveness knows no bounds, but you must surrender to me. Step down and set your house in order. I am the God of reconciliation and healing. Trust in Me, allow Me to love through you. Repent to those you have hurt and I will restore you."

Westward continued to prophecy for several moments as the love of God fell upon and into Rogers as he continued to weep. Eventually, Rogers calmed and with an air of resignation simply said, "Have your way, Lord, as I said at the start of the meeting."

Westward gently looked Rogers in the eye. "Where were the lumps, Pastor?"

Rogers through fear fogged eyes delayed a response.

"On my back and on my chest."

Westward placed his hands on the shorter man's shoulders. "Unbutton your shirt," he commanded.

Rogers shook his head but Westward smiled as he persisted.

"Unbutton it."

Embarrassed at first, Rogers obeyed. He looked down at his bare chest. There were no lumps present. Westward turned Rogers around to show his back to the congregation.

There were no lumps.

Westward simply smiled and nodded his head over and over.

"Praise the name of Jesus!" Westward turned and roared.

The musicians began praising God once again and to avoid any attention, Westward slipped a folded piece of paper into Rogers' shirt pocket and then quietly left. Upon his return, Abigail was already asleep and Westward decided not to wake her. Upon Rogers' return home, he unfolded the piece of paper.

It was a cheque for £100,000.

****

The next day.

The calming presence of the early morning radio presenter's voice had appeared in the main bedroom of the Westward residence some half an hour earlier at Westward's customary six-thirty. It was now seven am and Westward was still laying, unrested, in bed. As always, Abigail had not heard anything when the alarm clock had sounded. He smiled to himself at what to him was the most uncomfortable position to sleep in, her arm seemingly bent unnaturally under her pillows. Westward could hear the quiet sound of the children who had gathered to play in the bedroom next to his. He enjoyed listening to a few moments of clicking bricks, animated noises of planes flying and cars driving at breakneck speed along the plastic mat with the outline of a city road system.

Westward sat up on the edge of the bed.

I must get a new mattress, he thought to himself, gently bouncing on the ever softening edge, remembering his wife's reminder of the need several weeks before. He stood, stretched, and walked over to the window and neatly tucked the dark blue curtains behind their ties. He leant on the windowsill, quietly thanked God for another day and gazed out with wonderment at the sun, its gradually increasing gentle warmth announcing the arrival of a new day. In the field on the back of the house, an ever growing herd of sheep, occasionally bleating, were busily munching away on the grass which was beginning to grow steadily again. A very quick mental count showed another few lambs had joined the flock outside.

At that moment, Abigail stirred and sleepily opened her eyes before sitting up with a startled expression.

"Jordan, what are you still doing here?" she quizzed with a hint of concern in her voice.

"Abby, I'm not going in today," he replied without taking his attention from the sheep. "Do you fancy a picnic out somewhere?" he asked, finally turning to his wife and folding his arms.

She did not need to speak, her face showed her surprise.

"Oh, oh, what's up now?"

Westward looked everywhere but in her eyes. She knew something was not normal. He stood for a few moments before returning to sit opposite her on the bed. He sighed and took her hand in his. He finally looked into her gaze and smiled.

This is big, she thought to herself.

"There's some things that I need to explain," he started, "big things. Our life is going to change a fair bit over the next few years."

Abigail leaned forward slightly and squeezed his hand, a frown of concern hovering over her.

"What do you mean? Jordan, what's happened?" she spoke gently in an understanding voice, then joked "it's not that woman at work again is it?"

Westward quietly chuckled, shaking his head and continued, "I had an encounter with God last night before I left work and then he spoke to me last night in a dream. I know it was God - some would doubt me," he paused before continuing, "but Abby, you know in the past I have had some crazy notions and ideas but most have worked out? Well this is the craziest yet and I can't do it justice here and now. Let's go out for the day and I'll explain."

"You're going to take the day off work?" she asked with a smile along with a sarcastic hint of incredulity. "This must be big!"

"I know at first you won't believe me but I have always so appreciated your support for me; your trust and the freedom that you give me. I look at so many other wives who seem to run the show at home and hinder guys from progressing in life. You're so different and I guess that's why we've got such joy in our lives." He leant forward and lovingly kissed her forehead.

"Well, if you keep me in diamond rings and fur coats," she teased before yawning and stretching again, "I guess you can stay a while longer. Oh, and a bowl of bran flakes and a cup of coffee seem to work really well this time of morning as well!"

Abigail elegantly pulled back the quilt and swung her long legs to the floor, without taking her eyes from his approving gaze. Westward grinned. "I don't deserve you," he spoke shaking his head, "No, I deserve much more, but you'll do for now." She screwed her mouth up and threw a pillow at him which he ducked from and watched it hit softly against the curtains and then landing without consequence on the floor behind him.

Westward straightened his six foot four inch frame as he put on his fake, exaggerated North Yorkshire accent. "Eh, I know how to take care of lasses, you know."

At that moment, a very lively, six year old Chloe crashed into the room. She had taken in a deep breath and was about to spout out her complaint about her twin brother having impounded her toy Ford KA when she realised that her father was still there.

"Morning sweetheart," Westward and his wife chimed in unison before looking at each other with mutual smiles.

"Daddy, what are you doing here? You supposed to be at work!"

"Daddy's not going in today. How would you like to go out for a picnic?"

Chloe's eyes lit up and being lost for words she rushed back to the her bedroom with the traffic jam to joyfully announce the news.

"I need to shower," Westward quietly spoke and got up from the bed.

"OK. I'll get the kids organised. I'll shower later. Let me guess: Wallingford Dams is it?"

Westward's shoulders dropped. "How did you know?"

"Hey. You're my husband, remember?" she kissed his head and left to organise very excited children.

Within minutes, Westward was standing under the refreshing warmth of the shower's flow, contemplating the fors and againsts of the incredulous activity that was about to begin. A few minutes later, 'satisfied and invigorated' in accordance with the label on the shower gel, he towelled himself dry. He made a quick call to his office about his 'unprecedented', 'unscheduled', and 'totally unexpected' day off, as was described by his secretary. By nine-thirty, the family were driving down the narrow, private drive from their hidden farmhouse.

An hour later, having stocked up on all the usual Westward picnic refinements from the supermarket, he gently took the people carrier down the steep slope into the near empty car park overlooking the reservoir. He pulled into a marked space, handed two pound coins to Matthew in the centre of the row of seats behind him and instructed him to get a ticket from the nearby machine.

"Can we get out now, Daddy?" an excited and wide-eyed Chloe beamed.

"Sure, sweetheart. Stay near the path and we'll catch up with you. Have a run around for a while and then we'll have some food.

"OK, come on Caleb, let's chase the ducks!" Chloe squealed with delight.

"Jason, Matthew, please keep an eye on the twins," Abigail firmly instructed, smiling at the ready energy of her youngest children.

"Sure, Mum! See you later."

"Rachel, please take the sun hats, it is quite warm today!"

"OK, Mum," she groaned at the delay in catching her siblings up. Eventually, she slammed the rear door down on the back of the van and sprinted off in the direction of her brothers and sisters.

As they watched the five children charge off into the woods away to the left, Abigail smiled. "Jordan, we are so, so blessed." Then she sighed. "But how wonderful it would have been to have had more children. Just look at them. Free to come to places like this when no one else is here. Oh well, never mind." The children ran between trees, soaking up the spring sunshine, scrunching their way through the remnant of the leaves from the previous Autumn.

Westward was silent for a moment, aware of the often silent heart's desire of his wife, the unexplainable emptiness which he shared too. He stared out of the window, again wondering why there had been no more children. He recalled each birth momentarily. Matthew, now 16, had been followed a little over two years later by Jason. Rachel had just turned 10 and the twins would turn 6 later that summer. Miscarriages in consecutive years just after had left an emotional mark.

Oh, Lord – you know our pain! Our family size is your choice – but more sure would be awesome! Westward silently prayed.

"Doesn't seem nearly six years since Chloe and Caleb were born does it?"

Abigail silently nodded, enjoying the view of the children. "I have few regrets in life, Jordan, but the biggest has to be having the gap between Jason and Rachel. How many children might we have had in that four years? And I often wonder if the hurts of the two miscarriages will ever pass," she bit her lip to control the tears.

Then, before her melancholy moment seized her thoughts for longer than necessary, she changed the subject.

"So, Westward, what have you dragged me out here today for?" she asked, her gaze following a duck as it waddled contentedly past the front of the van, stopping to peck at a piece of bread left by an earlier visitor.

Westward exhaled heavily. "Man, where do I start? OK, you know I was in late last night. I should have woken you up."

Abigail's face showed a different opinion.

"OK, you're right, I should know better than to do that," he conceded.

His wife turned and smirked. "It's never stopped you before, seeing me asleep. If I remember rightly, that's how the twins got here after that so called 'meeting' you went to and got home at two in the morning."

Westward chuckled and reached for his hot chocolate and muffin. He peeled back part of the wrapper, offering some to his wife. She pulled another face – this time disapproval.

"Jordan, I don't know why you bother with those things – all they are is a packet of crumbs."

He bit into it, relishing the tangy taste of the blueberries, but failing to stop several large crumbs falling into his lap.

"Told you so!" she commented, shaking her head, her eyes returning to the children.

"What?" he replied with a mouth full of muffin, brushing the crumbs from his legs with an elbow.

"Like I said, a packet of crumbs! Oh, please, at least put one thing down and clean yourself up properly, man!" she playfully exclaimed.

He chewed, exaggeratedly, moving his head up and down, until he finally swallowed with a huge forced gulp whilst licking his lips.

She turned her gaze back to the scene of nature in front of her. "You are just simply disgusting!" She remarked, folding her arms and holding back a mischievous grin.

He took a deliberate loud slurp of the hot chocolate as she let the smile out and gently slapped his arm.

"OK, when you've quite finished your little moment of criticism!"

She reached over to kiss his cheek and lingered as shewhispered "I love you," before placing a graceful hand on his thigh. He finished the rest of his muffin and downed his drink watching Caleb weave his way in and out of the trees, arms outstretched like an aircraft.

"Abby, seriously, for a moment, hear me out." He paused and sighed. "Something happened at work last night. I can still hardly believe it myself. God really showed up. Come on, let's catch them up, I'll tell you on the way."

She frowned in frustration, the suspense becoming more unbearable. "Oh, come on," he said, pulling the handle on the door to get out. He motioned for her to follow. They joined hands in front of the van as he pointed the keys back to lock it. He gestured to the path, surprisingly dry for the time of year, and they began a slow walk.

"Abby, my knee got healed."

She stopped dead in her tracks. "What? Are you serious? You have no more pain?"

"Nope. None. It's amazing. It's like new." He trotted up and down on the spot as if to demonstrate, before continuing their walk.

"So – you've dragged me over here, as nice as it is, just to tell me that?"

"Well, as if that is not enough, God showed me some other stuff – big stuff. You know you love a challenge?"

She pulled a faked face of fear.

"Well, you're soon to be the wife of........," he left his

sentence hanging, wondering how to break the news.

"Oh, come on, Jordan, spit it out!" she slapped her sides, a mixture of impatience and anxiety.

He waited a few moments. "A player/manager of a professional football club."

She stopped once again in her steps, frowned and closed her eyes.

"Did I hear you right?" she replied, clearly unimpressed.

He nodded and gave a childlike grin. "God told me to buy Woodmouth. Buy it, manage it and play," Westward continued, casually flicking a small rock onto the grass with his right foot. They began walking again, Abigail staring at the ground a few paces ahead of her steps, aware of the joyful sounds of her children playing.

"Look, I don't want to burst a bubble here, but – you've not played properly for years. You're - dare I say it - thirty-seven. No, come on, what's going on?"

Westward swung her arm back and forth. "I knew it would seem wild to you, but I was up praying for ages last night. I wanted to get confirmation from God that I had heard right. I waited until I got a scripture. Then, at three o'clock this morning, I got it."

At that moment, the Spirit of God spoke to Abigail's heart. *"Trust me, obey me and all will be well."*

"It was Joshua one verse eight, wasn't it?"

Westward now stopped this time. "Yes!" he exclaimed excitedly, "but how on earth did you know?"

They began walking again. "My Bible reading last night. Joshua one eight."

"That's incredible! It must be from God! What did it say? Tell me, What did it say?" She paused and then recollected the verse and began, "This Book of the Law shall not depart from your mouth, but you shall meditate in it day and night, that you may observe to do according to all that is written in it." Then together, they finished the quote. "For then you will make your way prosperous, and then you will have good success."

"Yes! That's it! As long as God is put first, this thing will work!"

Struggling to take everything in, there was a brief silence

before Abigail spoke again. "You read another verse as well, didn't you. The other key to this is -"

"Yes!" Westward interrupted, "Unity! Behold, how good and pleasant it is when brothers dwell together in unity! Psalm a hundred and thirty three!"

"Oh Lord!" she smiled, again shaking her head, "this actually could be real!"

At that moment, a breathless Caleb came running up to them. "Is it lunchtime yet? I'm really hungry!"

Westward and his wife grinned at each other. He pulled back his sleeve and revealed his watch and gently asked Caleb what numbers he saw.

"Erm, eleven-fifteen."

"Does that sound like lunch yet?"

Caleb, bit his lip in disappointment. Westward winked as he produced a bottle of orange juice and a packet of fruit sweets from his jacket pocket. The young boy beamed, thanked his father and ran back to his twin sister, holding his booty up high as if he had won a major trophy.

They continued their walk as the path curved away through the woods towards the giant dam which was beginning its spring obscurity as the trees had begun to blossom and block the view.

"What does it mean to the business?" Abigail ventured.

"To be honest, it seems to be taking care of itself. Revelation which we never thought would see the light of day is actually now ahead of schedule, sales of the other stuff is all in hand," he shrugged his shoulders, "there's no real concerns. Clive is in control."

"What about your fitness? running the club is one thing but, how can you keep up with the pace of men fifteen years or more younger than you?" she patted his stomach, "you've got some work here to do."

He nodded in agreement. "That's where I just have to trust God and do what I can. At the church last night, you should have seen it. There were miracles. Lots of people got healed. It was amazing. Pastor John by the way had cancer and got healed, and he's been really humbled about a gambling problem. I told him about what happened to me at the office and loads of people prayed for me. I'm sure they didn't really understand properly, but they love us and prayed anyway. One of them, you know the old lady who sits at the back?"

"Oh, Vera, the prayer warrior?"

"Yep, that's her, well, she gave me a word as well." Westward let go of his wife's hand and fished out his phone and tapped the screen several times to open a Bible app.

"Here it is, you know the story of when Peter and John healed the crippled man in Acts chapter three? He showed his wife the screen, which, as it usually did when he showed her something on his phone, went black, causing her usual face of frustration. He smiled. "Sorry, here it is. Vera said, in the same way that faith in the name of Christ healed him and made him strong, I will be made strong as well." He tapped the screen to lock it and replaced it in his back pocket.

"Oh boy, this news will certainly make your Dad's day, won't it?" Abigail commented after a pause, raising her eyebrows. Westward had not given thought to the reaction of his father, whom he had not spoken a word to in over three years. He sighed heavily and nodded in agreement. "Hmm, won't he be shocked. I don't suppose I'll hear from him though."

Momentarily, Westward's memories took him back to a rare park visit. He remembered his father kicking a football so high into the air that to him, a five year old, it disappeared into the sky completely out of sight, only to plummet to earth with a resounding bounce, seconds later.

So few memories, though, Westward thought.

Just then, they reached the gate of the enclosure to the dam. Abigail called the children to follow them. Westward pulled back the metal lever with a screeching clunk, swung open the creaking gate and held it open for them all. Above them, at each end of the dam stood two towers, stalwart guards over the huge body of water hidden at the top of the huge concrete structure. Westward could only imagine the devastation that one tiny brick out of the seemingly impregnable wall in front of him would cause.

The children made a dash to the steps to the right, their usual way up to the higher levels and out onto the road. From there, they would cross and take a footpath up to the high moors which overlooked the water held back from the dam and the hills behind where the van was parked. Momentarily, the sun hid behind a small, white cloud, but almost immediately returned to bring the glory back to the day.

"Can you see success for the club? I mean, you know how much I dislike football. I don't know much, but how do you propose to lift them up? Last I heard, and that was early this season, was that there was prospects of the club folding unless they got a shed load of money together. Has anything changed?"

Westward was quiet for a few moments. "To be honest, I have to come up with a lot of money. I have some, but I'm going to have to persuade some others to come aboard, and then further persuade some of the major share holders to let their shares go - and more importantly their control of the club."

"That shouldn't be hard, should it? Let's face it, would you stay onboard a sinking ship?"

"Well, you would think that they would be more than willing to let go, but, I know from the past, even directors of failing businesses can be so full of pride and they do not want to accept the inevitable." They reached the old, concrete steps, and walked single file up, holding on to the cold, metal hand rail, aware of the children who had sensibly stopped at the top.

"Well, Westward, I've always admired your ability to make money from money. Let's face it, I didn't marry you for your looks. And remember, I have always had an appreciation for the finer things in life."

"Well, like I said, you can stay for now! No one else has made any offers. Well, maybe the woman at work..."

"Jordan – enough!" she playfully interrupted.

They continued, hand in hand again on a wider part of the stairs, Abigail's mind turning over all the potential challenges which could come.

"So how long do you see this happening for? Like I said, you are thirty-seven, there are not many players still at the top much past thirty-five. I know one or two made it to nearly forty – but they were goalkeepers...."

"I haven't told you the half of it yet. People are going to get saved - by the hoard. Revival will come to our town." He then briefly outlined the events from the night before. There was a quiet moment as Abigail pondered sky-ward and considered once again all that had been presented to her before continuing.

"Jordan, you have always said that God judges our heart

motives, not necessarily our actions." She paused as she stopped walking, enjoying the faint earthy tang of the gentle breeze. "Why do you want to do this?"

Westward bit his lip as he gazed at the children as they sensibly moved over to allow a colourful parade of cyclists to whizz pass unimpeded as they expressed their thanks. "I have to confess," he began, "I had hoped that I could manage and play for Barcelona, live in a fancy mansion in San Cugar or Sitges, you know, somewhere on the Costa Brava and chase lots of dark-haired Spanish beauties on the beach."

Abigail, aware of his humour, impishly thumped his chest as he mocked a painful reaction. "For the glory of God is what your heart may say – but I know how you can get sucked into the narcissistic arena. You're like a gladiator whose never satisfied until he is the last man standing."

"And you'll be the one shouting to give me a shirt, I know!"

"Just for once, Jordan, be serious: examine your heart. Why do you want to do this? What is your true motive? What do you hope to achieve? That's all I ask. Are you willing to sacrifice even more time with me and the kids for a pipe dream?"

"Abigail – this is no pipe dream!" His voice was a little more than a raised whisper. "Look – if it had not been for God's presence and my knee being fixed, I probably wouldn't be standing here having this conversation. I fully acknowledge my weaknesses, the commitment that is involved and the potential impact on the family, but I also acknowledge that if we simply trust God, take each step at a time – well, look, let's just do that, one step at a time, OK? Can we do that?"

She smiled, albeit half-heartedly. "OK, yes, alright, one step at a time. Could we please make lunch the first one? I never did get my bran flakes this morning."

She called after the children to wait as the couple linked arms and joined them by a gap in the wall protecting the huge mass of water from the road. A blue and white Land Rover trudged with some effort past them and disappeared around the right hand bend ahead of them as they took the three steps down on to the sandy bank. Despite the fullness of the water above the dam, there still existed, much to the children's delight, a sizeable area of sand between the wall and the water's edge.

Each child began its own search for a batch of perfectly shaped and weighted stones for skimming. Within a short time, each was joyfully launching their artillery, boasting of how many jumps each stone made. After a few minutes, the parents noticed that Caleb was not within sight, but behind them to their right came a small child proudly brandishing a clearly troubled duck as it flapped and struggled in his grasp. Once he had gained his parents' attention he simply threw the bird into the air and enjoyed its aerial display as it flew off to find its compatriots below the falls.

Having given the children several more minutes, Westward called them together and the family made their way back to the car park for lunch.

Upon their return, Westward ran a hand over the rugged wooden totem pole structures flanking the entrance to the toilet block. He could not help but think how out of place they looked as he entered the unusually clean and odour-free building. He washed his hands and shook his arms vigorously after discovering that the hand dryer provided only negligible heat before accompanying his children back to the vehicle.

His wife approached him as the children fished around the picnic items in the boot of the van for their favourite crisps. She embraced him and smiled. "Jordan Westward," she whispered as she kissed him gently on the lips, "you go buy your football team. I know this must be God. Do you know why? A few days ago, I know you had laid it down when you said you didn't care if you ever went to a game again. You go ahead. Get lots of people saved and change this town of ours. You seem to have Midas hands. Go use them."

Westward's smile widened as his heart leapt. How many times he had enjoyed this: the empowering of a man through a wife who supported her husband's goals – even if, he reasoned to himself, they seemed totally illogical at that moment.

****

Two days later.

Westward took a seat in the reception area just outside Brian Chambers' office. Kayley Porter, a slim, attractive secretary in her twenties announced his arrival in clipped efficiency through an intercom on her well organised desk. She returned to her typing whilst Westward tried to look interested in the contents of a three month old issue of 'Camping International', a magazine which somehow seemed totally out of place in a Professional Football Club.

The door handle to Chambers' office rattled. It opened, revealing a player dressed for training, followed by Chambers himself. He looked perplexed as he bid farewell to the track-suited visitor and patted him on the shoulder. The man stood a good four inches taller than Chambers and Westward recognised the player as Gerhard Messen, the German signed two seasons previous. He had failed to meet expectations, barely managing double figures on the goal scoring charts in each of his two seasons at the club. He blamed it on the playing system adopted by Chambers – this involved playing no wingers, players which he considered essential for him to perform his function as a striker. He became frustrated and disillusioned with the future of both him personally and also that of the club. This led to several incidents off the pitch that did not help the cause of his reputation.

Naturally, he handed in a transfer request, but even the reduced £5 million price tag, his attitude and scoring inability had not made him a palatable choice for big clubs. On top of this, his £20,000 per week wage demand did nothing for his cause. The headline on the back of the Woodmouth Gazette after the previous weeks' 2-0 home defeat by mid-table club Plymouth was simply "Stop Messen About!"

Chambers stood, arms folded, watching a heavy-spirited Messen turn the corner to the stairs. Chambers slowly shook his head in wonder at the man's future. When Messen was out of sight, Chambers turned to Westward and his countenance changed immediately. He smiled, opened his arms and embraced him. He invited him into his office, and whispered "no calls" to his secretary. She nodded and smiled without taking her eyes away from the computer screen at which she was working.

Chambers walked around to his side of a large oak desk, inlaid with green leather. Compared to most clubs of this level, this was a more than comfortable office. He placed his paunchy figure into an over-sized leather chair and swivelled around to face Westward who took his seat in front of him.

Chambers rolled his sleeves up, undid his top shirt button and loosened his tie. Westward, as always, remained smart and ready for business in his suit jacket. He relaxed his arms onto the sides of the chair and tried to look comfortable.

"So, Jordan", Chambers began with a smile, "what's my Joseph been dreaming of, eh? Must be important for you to take time off work and not be at home with Abby and the tribe!"

Westward smiled at Chambers' reference to the prophetic dreamer from the book of Genesis in the Bible as Chambers swivelled round to a small fridge on the floor next to a half-filled bookcase behind his chair. Here, as was his custom, he kept a supply of readily available cooled mineral water. He took two bottles out and offered one to Westward who nodded in grateful acceptance. "You have my mother-in-law's taste – fizzy water in glass bottles."

"Seriously, Jordan. This must be big. A weekday morning, you're here and not chasing competitors' customers. I'm all ears!" Chambers picked up a pen and began to doodle, rather rudely, Westward thought, on a large notepad on his desk.

"Brian, I'll cut to the chase. I had a visitation from....."

"God? Now how did I know that?" Chambers interrupted, sarcastically, despite his sharing faith with Westward and often both attending the Woodmouth businessman's fellowship.

Westward sat uncomfortably for a moment or two, still not sure how to break the news. He decided the best approach was to be totally direct.

"Brian, I've come to buy the club."

There it was, he thought, *best way to do it - no messing.*

The words were out just like he would have done in a deal with a troubled company that needed his technology. Chambers had placed his pen on his desk and raised his bottle to his mouth, but stopped. After a hesitation, he took a swig before speaking.

"Jordan, what did you say? Did I hear you right?" he asked, his soft Scottish tones accentuating his astonishment.

"I want to buy the club. God has told me I am to do so."

Chambers sat at first in silence, and then he let out a

hearty laugh and threw back his head. After a few seconds, he looked at Jordan and saw that he had not joined in his enjoyment of the moment. Westward stared, his face straight and unmoved. Chambers' face dropped from a smile to a serious look that changed the atmosphere totally.

"Brian," Westward began, "You know as well as I do that the club is in trouble. It is almost certain, unless you listen to me, that next year they'll be in League One – that's if it is still in existence. On top of that, you'll probably be out of a job and most of your semi-decent players would move on."

He could not deny that such issues existed. His eyes narrowed as he stared at Westward.

"Jordan, did you say buy the club? As in Woodmouth Albion, this club?" Chambers articulated each syllable clearly.

"That's pretty much it," Westward nodded in agreement.

The silence returned as Chambers tried to take in the situation. "Look, my friend," he said, shaking his head, "You can't just come in here off the street. I know that you're doing well with computers and stuff, but please excuse me if I am just a little sceptical. I mean….," He broke off as he stood up and slowly paced around the room. Westward remained as calm as ever and stayed silent to allow Chambers to regain his lost composure.

Chambers turned to watch the reserves training outside the window far below. He shook his head and drank again. He returned to his chair and putting his hands together on the desk, focused his gaze on them.

"OK, Jordan", he resigned with a clap, "what's actually on your mind? This is the most crazy thing I've ever heard."

"Brian, I have had dreams, visions, instructions if you like - from God. But, maybe you could start anyway. What is this about the winding up order on the club?"

Chambers' expression changed. "How on earth did you know about that?" He enquired sharply.

"Don't worry", Westward defended, raising his hands, "there's no mole at the club. You will find it hard to believe, but God showed me in a vision a few nights ago. I made a few calls back to the States and I've got some guys who are willing to come in with me and make a purchase of the majority of Woodmouth's shares."

Chambers was silent but thoughtful. He then questioned about Jordan's knowledge of the club's overall debt.

"By my calculations, it must be around £43 million taking into account the money wasted on Messen a couple of seasons ago, right?" He quizzed rather than stated.

Chambers rolled his eyes in distaste at the mention once again of the player who had just left. He paused in surprise at the accuracy of Westward's data.

"Well, I just had the figures in because of the winding up order. It's £40 million."

"OK, there you go, not as bad as I first thought."

"Thing is though Jordan, we cannot carry on with the current staff. We need new blood, some names who will bring in crowds."

"No problem there – I estimate we'll have an extra £15 million to spend on players."

"Hold on – you keep saying 'we'. What...., what do you mean?" he frowned as he flopped back.

"I'm going to manage it."

"What?"

"Well, with you. That's to start with. If you want the club to succeed, there will need to be wholesale changes in many areas. I'll bring my business knowledge."

"And have control?"

"As well as play."

Chambers face creased into a smile before letting out a hearty chuckle.

"Play?" He probed, caustically in unbelief, eyes widened.

"Yep. I'm gonna be player/manager."

Chambers silently looked into the distance of the corner of the room, contemplating how sensibly to reply.

"Jordan, you're nearly 37 years old, manager of one of the biggest companies in this part of the UK and you are married with five kids. You can't be serious?"

Westward simply slowly nodded in a manner of total control and calm that surprised even him as Chambers leant forward over his desk.

"You haven't even played park football for so long, your knee is hammered and most players are retired by your age. What makes you think....?" he paused and continued, "Oh come on Jordan, this is ridiculous!"

"Brian, I agree with all that you are saying. But, my knee," Westward tapped, "is completely healed. My old anger is gone and God showed me a glimpse into the future of this area and this club. Mass revival. Success on the pitch that you could not imagine."

"Jordan, you know I have utmost respect for you and what you've achieved, but as you can imagine, I am really struggling with this one."

"Look, Brian, I would be too," Westward replied compassionately. "I've sat on this for a number of days, but I am convinced it's real. You know me, I always wait on things to make sure that they are from the Lord. I don't even book a holiday until I give God a chance to fill the Hotel first! God showed me a plan that will open this town to the Gospel."

Chambers relaxed again and picked up his pen to play with. "I have to confess that the stresses here often drown out my relationship with God. And I really don't like it. Go on then, what's the plan?"

Westward glanced each way in mock secrecy before leaning towards Chambers. "How about three years time, Woodmouth will be European club champions."

Just as he had reached the point that nothing else that day would shock him, Chambers' mouth visibly dropped in shock, then he smiled. Then he roared with laughter and slapped both hands onto the desk.

Westward continued. "I saw miracles on and off the pitch. I saw the ground filled for Gospel meetings."

Westward reached down for his case, twisted the combinations to open it and pulled out a document of several pages outlining his ambitious three year plan. Survive the current season, promotion to the Premier League the next, then qualification for Europe, then win the Champions League. He handed a copy to Chambers who pulled out a pair of bi-focal glasses which he placed firmly on the end of his nose before tilting his head back and scrutinizing the papers.

"Corporate Purchase of Woodmouth Albion Football Club," Chambers mumbled under his breath.

Westward clicked his case shut and returned it to his feet. "I thought 'purchase' had a little less aggression than 'takeover'!"

He took the last few sips of water before placing the empty bottle on the desk in front of him. A few silent minutes later, Chambers tossed the document onto the desk in front of him, took off his glasses and shook his head.

"I can see you've done some homework, and I don't want to pour water on your ardour, but let me just spell out the facts to you how they stand. We are just off the bottom of the league and our crowds are striving to top a very meagre 15,000. The players morale is at an all time low. The wage bill is spiralling. But money alone does not change attitudes. What do you propose? And come to think of it, where is the money coming from?"

"Oh, let's just say a friend in the States".

"No.....surely not Casey Wallace?" Chambers sighed as he recalled the ex-professional footballer.

"The very same!" Westward smiled, jokingly.

"I don't believe it. Well, has to be said, ending his playing career in Los Angeles was a stroke of genius. He's a household name now and probably not short of a bob or two."

"He thought it was a great idea. His words were 'cool, sounds fun'. I'm waiting for a text message from him this morning after he has made a few calls."

"Don't tell me he wants to play?"

"He considered it."

"Oh, come on!"

"Don't worry," Westward cut in with a grin, "his wife won't move back to England. The cold weather would ruin her tan!"

Chambers grunted and returned to the document and began scanning several paragraphs about players. "Jordan, what happens to current player contracts?"

Westward cleared his throat as he shuffled in his seat. "Well, technically, Woodmouth Albion as a separate entity will cease to exist, so all players would be unemployed. It is a perfect opportunity to see who the serious players are - with the club in mind, if you see what I mean. They will all have the freedom to leave, no commitments on either side to be fulfilled. No compensation from us, no commitments expected from them."

"What about if players like Lincoln leave? You more or less say goodbye to potentially millions worth of assets!"

"Pray he sees our vision and wants to stay. There is no

other way from a business point of view."

"And new contracts?"

"Easy. Maximum five grand a week. Bigger bonuses based on performance both as a team and as individuals."

Chambers shook his head. "I can't see our German friend getting out of bed for that money. He'd be on the first plane home."

"Good. He's a donkey. Overpaid and overrated. Mind you, I did agree with his criticism that you play the wrong formation. He needed wingers. But, all that aside, I don't have time for him. He'd be out. And, to be honest, Brian, you have never gained his nor some other players' respect. You've been too soft. I cannot abide the way they trash the reputation of themselves, the club and most of all - you." Chambers was shocked at first at Westward's contempt, but, having known him for so long, had gotten used to his forthrightness.

Chambers swallowed hard as he shot a glance at the cabinet in the corner of the room containing a few pieces of silverware and old photos of winning teams. He looked back at Westward. "How do you expect to attract players if you will only pay them such low wages?"

"Brian, five grand a week is a quarter of a million pounds a year! Surely blokes can live off that if they're sensible? Educate these guys to respect their career and not just automatically assume that they are worth a stack of cash just because they play football. They need to know that this is a privilege." Again, Chambers looked away, pensively.

"OK, what about transfer fees. Decent players cost money – lots of money."

"Don't pay it for starters. Look at Pierre Labosche going to Chelsea for £32 million. I wouldn't pay it. Go for freebies or guys from lower leagues. Let God take care of the rest."

"And how about you, Jordan. What's in it for you? Surely you aren't doing this for King and country alone?"

"Sure am. I don't need the money, Brian. But, I'll need you. You'll get £100,000 a year plus fat bonuses. You're a good manager, Brian. You have just needed some decent players with confidence and vision. If we can get ourselves into the Champions League, I'll double it."

Chambers shook his head and returned to the papers.

"You mentioned changing the playing system. What's wrong with 4-2-3-1?"

"Come on, Brian! Be serious! Your system has got the club where it is – close to relegation."

"OK. So, what do you change?"

"Play 3-5-2. With a sweeper and one or two stoppers in front of the back three. Two wing-backs - ultra fit - and quick, lively strikers, not apes like Messen. You can vary it according to opponents. 3-3-2-2 or 3-4-1-2. I had my pal Torenson in Sweden go watch Malmo last week now that they have this new manager. They played the top side and hammered them five-nothing playing a similar system. And this is a side that's in the bottom three of the Swedish League. I tell you what – watch how they move up the table now."

Chambers blew out a slow breath. "You realise that we don't have the right players for this system. Would we get them for next season with the money and time that we'll have?"

Westward sat forward, opened his hands and began to speak with passion. "Some guys are just playing out of position. I would suggest pushing Magnus into a midfield role, just in front of the defenders, kind of like a safety gap filler. Move Chris Haynes up front and drop Rudi to attacking, central midfield. We do have the players!"

Chambers eyes widened. "Jordan, today is Monday, we play Rotherham on Saturday. How can we get all this in place?" Just then, Westward's mobile phone buzzed.

"Casey?" Chambers enquired over the top of his glasses as Westward checked a text message.

"Yep. All systems go," Westward replied with a sly grin.

Chambers again closed the document and sat back, his hands behind his head.

"Jordan, I have to hand it to you. As always, a thorough job. Money's there. The plan's there - albeit ambitious. My main concern would naturally be your fitness."

Westward nodded in appreciation of the concern. "All I can say is that when God calls his people, he equips them. Who would have thought that Gideon would have wiped out the Midianites with 300 men? Some things we do in wisdom, others we do by faith."

Chambers once again stood and observed the match below through the large window behind him. He crossed his arms and nodded slowly. He turned back.

"There is one final barrier – you'll have to persuade the directors. We'll need a meeting set up."

Westward smiled. "All done, Brian. They'll be here in an hour".

Chambers sniggered. "You're totally serious aren't you?"

Westward nodded with a smirk.

Chambers slowly walked over to a glass fronted cabinet, above which stood framed monochrome photos of events from famous matches played at Wiltshire Park. One was taken from behind the goal in which Johnny Macnamara had scored the penalty which beat Chelsea. Chambers stared a while and Westward joined him.

"I remember that night so well, Jordan. The passion, the excitement. I was playing back home at the time but came down as we didn't have a mid-week game. Oh, it would be really something to have that back here."

Westward joined him and nodded in mutual appreciation. "I was there too. It was the first match that my dad ever took me to. You can imagine what it was like for a little kid like me. I was stood just there." He pointed to a location in the east stand.

Chambers stood back and looked in admiration at Westward. "Jordan, if you bring to this club the success that you've had in I.T. then this might just work. Let's see what the directors have to say."

"How about we pray?" Westward suggested.

"Of course!"

The two men stood, arms around each other's shoulders, heads bowed. Westward believed in simple, direct prayer, no fancy hypocritical words. Chambers smiled and echoed an "amen" as they ended.

Westward retrieved his case and paused at the door.

"One more thing, Brian."

"What's that?"

"The club has never had a motto, has it?"

Chambers paused and frowned pensively.

"No, it hasn't, come to think of it."

"Now we do – 'Per Unitatum Vis'. Look it up – it is the key

to this club's success."

In the remaining time before the directors arrived, both men sauntered around the training area and watched the senior side in motion. Westward watched with shock at the lack of understanding between some of the players as they passed the ball around. He looked on in consternation at the lethargy of the experienced players. Overhit crosses, inaccurate passes, lazy heading.

The two stood on the sidelines and talked back and forth between themselves, pointing out different positives and negatives from the various players. Occasionally, they laughed, several times Chambers shook his head and wondered if Westward truly knew what he was about to get himself into. Chambers saw out of the corner of his eye James Nelson, chairman of the club striding towards them. Westward noticed him too and leaned towards Chambers.

"Who's this, Brian?" he whispered, gesturing discreetly towards the man in his early sixties approaching them.

"James Nelson, chairman of the club. Nice guy. Not a Christian but a likeable chap." Chambers replied. Nelson held out his hand as he arrived offering an unexpected greeting before the official gathering.

"Hello Brian!" he smiled as they firmly shook hands.

"James, good to see you again. Have you met Jordan Westward?"

"No," he tilted his head, offering a hand, "Pleasure to meet you Mr. Westward. My wife passed your message on about this meeting. I must say I am fascinated. What do you have on your mind?" Despite the cheer as one of the sides scored, he did not take his attention off Westward as he spoke.

"Mr Nelson, the pleasure is mutual, Sir. I have a proposal which is likely to be of interest to the board and would appreciate time to share it."

"A proposal, eh? Well, now you have got me intrigued," he growled in a friendly way as his thick, white moustache twitched.

Westward was aware that if he could persuade Nelson, he would have a platform to conclude the take over of the club. Nelson, for all his jolly manner, was not a man to be walked over.

"Mr Nelson, I am aware of the financial plight of the club. I am also aware that relegation would only make this situation even more grave. I have been a supporter of this club for many years and want to see success here. My money and the business ideas that I have gained over the years, I believe, could see the club progress to where it deserves to be. Admittedly, there are a lot of changes that would need to happen, and this is where we need the directors to catch sight of the vision that I have."

"Is that right, old fellow? Well, Mr Westward, I have loved this club and have been saddened at its demise over the years. I'll listen to what you have to say." He cupped his hand over his mouth as if to whisper. "Anything to wind Marcus up, eh?" he chuckled, referring to another director of the club.

"I have not had the privilege of meeting the others before, but I know that Mr. Leworthy is quite a character, Sir."

"Ha! Now that's an understatement! Mind you," he paused nodding towards a tall, slim man fingering invisible dust from the bonnet of his Jaguar, "better look lively, here's the fellow now!"

This will make very interesting reading in the press, Westward pondered.

A few minutes later, the trainer called an end to the session and the players jogged back to the changing rooms as one by one the cars of the other directors began to arrive.

****

"When we heard that Westward had bought the club we thought 'what on earth?' OK, the investment would be great and he was a household name in Woodmouth when it came to IT and stuff, but what did he really know about football? And when we heard that we was going to be playing, we all just laughed. 37 years old and just starting a career in football with a dodgy knee! My dad was there the night he got his knee wrecked in the friendly at Calverley. He said he thought he would be lucky to walk again, let alone kick a ball. It must be a miracle, that's all I can say."

David Walker,
Supporter,
Woodmouth.

Chapter 7

2:30 the following afternoon.

REPORTERS FROM NEWSPAPERS, local and national, and more surprisingly to Westward, even TV crews assembled in a huddle on the pitch at Wiltshire Park. There was much low toned conversation as all eagerly awaited the arrival of Jordan Westward, Brian Chambers and Chairman James Nelson. A handful of lower division clubs had gone to the wall in the last couple of seasons and some reporters wondered if Woodmouth were about to join them in the same fate. Jamie Southgate from the Woodmouth Gazette was among the journalists. He stood alone, notepad in hand. He was not confident of the outcome of this meeting.

Westward, Chambers and Nelson walked onto the pitch from the player's tunnel and took a seated position behind a large table in the centre circle against the backdrop of the seating area of the stand with seating had been coloured to show W.A.F.C. The crowd and cameras followed them. Westward, as always, immaculately dressed in a double-breasted suit, Chambers preferring his track-suit and carrying a sports bag. Westward took a sideways glance to his left and smiled at Nelson's usual leather elbow patches on his checked jacket.

Chambers raised his hands to gather attention and waited for the chatter to cease. "Gentlemen, ladies, thank you for coming. We do not intend to keep you long but we wish to make a formal statement regarding the future of Woodmouth Albion Football Club......."

Jamie Southgate pulled a pen from his jacket pocket and bit the lid off with his teeth whilst holding his spiral bound pad.

What on earth was Jordan Westward doing here? he thought to himself.

"...........and all those associated with it, both players and supporters alike."

Heard all this before, Southgate mumbled to himself under his breath as he began to scribble in shorthand. Can't wait to hear. Messen is leaving? Chambers is being sacked? Lincoln sold for ten million? Hmm, no chance!

"Recently there has been much speculation with respect to the club's finances. It is true that there have been issues which had put the club in jeopardy but we are delighted to announce that the immediate future of the club has been secured. I will hand you over to club Chairman James Nelson to continue." Chambers sat down as cameras clicked, reporters scribbled and TV cameras rolled. Nelson rose slowly with an uncharacteristic stern face and took a typewritten piece of paper from the inside of his jacket. He cleared his throat and began to read.

"Woodmouth Albion Football Club wish to make an official declaration of the following information. The Woodmouth Albion board have agreed a deal to sell a majority share stake in the club to local, private businessman Jordan Westward, owner of the the Westward Technologies Corporation." He paused as a few whispers around the group began.

Nelson continued. "The proposed investment will see Mr. Westward purchase the club's approximate £40 million debt, as well as investing a further initial £15 million through the issue of new shares to invest in the purchase of new players and club infrastructure." Once again he paused before continuing.

"The club this week were on the verge of filing for bankruptcy and Mr. Westward's investment is potentially great news for the club." The members of the paparazzi looked at each other and there were several sharp intakes of shocked breath.

"What this means is that the club will effectively be sold to Mr. Westward. He becomes the majority shareholder and will have overall control of the running of the club which will become a subsidiary of The Westward Technologies Corporation. Brian Chambers, who will remain in his post as manager, will become assistant head coach under the guidance of Jordan Westward. Mr. Westward believes the deal will help the club return to the success that he believes has been long overdue." Again, a pause as several hands were raised to ask questions. Nelson raised his hands as if to hush the demand before continuing.

"The whole deal has been struck within a few days in order that Mr. Westward can take his post for this Saturday's game at Rotherham."

"The club firmly believe that with this investment that Premier League football at Wiltshire Park will not just be a possibility. It will be a certainty. As you are aware, the club is currently second from bottom in the Championship table ahead of Saturday's trip to Rotherham, knowing that anything short of victory will virtually seal the club's relegation. There is much preparation to be made so that is all the board have to say at this moment in time. I will however hand you over to Mr. Westward for a brief opportunity to answer any questions."

Southgate shook his head in disbelief and ignored Westward's gaze. *How is this proud, arrogant guy going to offer anything to promote this club? Yes, sure, he's been a supporter for years, but what does he think a few million is going to do? It is just staving off the inevitable for a couple of years. And knowing him, dragging a few quid out for himself!*

Westward straightened his tie as he stood and scanned the crowd as he placed his finger tips on the table. He noticed Jamie Southgate and nodded as if to acknowledge his presence. Westward began.

"Thank you, Mr. Nelson," He stood upright, hands behind his back, "it is a pleasure to at last be able to offer this club the resources to fulfil its potential. As you are aware I have been a very keen supporter of this club since I began watching them play when my father brought me here many years ago. I have seen it prosper and I have seen it survive by the skin of its teeth. I have seen players raised up and then sold on for a profit that was soon swallowed up in an effort to simply keep going as supporters' loyalty has waned throughout the years."

Southgate furiously scribbled some shorthand as he glanced between pad and Westward.

You have to give it to the guy, he contemplated, *he does have a commanding air about him.*

Westward continued. "I believe that Woodmouth has always had great capability to build on its rich footballing heritage. The club has always maintained an excellent reputation, both off the pitch and on it. There are many current members of the playing staff that, with the correct motivation and tactical planning, will grow to become distinguished names. Others may need to move on in order that they, how shall we say, best enhance their career opportunities. The board has done an excellent job under difficult conditions thanks to the stewardship of Mr. Nelson," Westward glanced at Nelson and motioned a hand in his direction, "who will continue in his role as chairman. Brian Chambers and the squad have my full support."

All went silent for a brief moment as he placed the sports bag that Chambers had carried onto the table. He then pulled out a shirt which everyone present immediately recognised as the white with red trim worn by the Woodmouth team when playing at home. He revealed the reverse to the crowd. It read "WESTWARD" along the top with a large number thirty-five underneath. Westward proudly held the shirt up over his jacket, looked briefly down with a smile and continued once again. "I look forward to my duties for the next few seasons as player/manager!" The whole crowd erupted in turmoil as cameras clicked all around and hands were raised with questions firing from all angles.

Southgate paused his writing mid-sentence.

PLAYER/MANAGER! THIS GETS WORSE!

A few moments later, Westward sat down, casually crossed his arms and awaited the barrage of inquisition. Above the cacophony of voices, Nelson stood and again raised his hands for attention and silence.

"I am sure that there are many questions which we will

attempt to answer. Please be brief and to the point."

Southgate promptly raised his hand and Nelson nodded to him for the first question. "Mr. Westward," he began with an air of disbelief and evident sarcasm, "I am sure that your lifestyle is already full with a major corporation to run not to mention your wife and five children. Adding the responsibilities of managing a football club is one thing – but how do you expect to play as well?"

Westward waited a moment before responding. "Thank you, Jamie Southgate, Woodmouth Gazette." Southgate lowered his head in embarrassment.

OK, advantage Westward! You're supposed to say who you are and who you represent, idiot! He rebuked himself.

"As you all know, Westward Technologies has, over the years, grown and prospered by God's grace."

Oh, here we go, Southgate inwardly groaned, *his God again.*

"The company has succeeded not due to one person but to a team of dedicated, committed professionals who have worked incredibly hard. I have several technical and financial advisors who will easily take on my current share of the workload. I will of course continue in overall authority and I have the full support of my wife and family. Next question."

He pointed to a short, stout man dressed in a hooded sweatshirt, standing at the front of the crowd.

"Mr. Westward, Kevin Halligan, Daily Mirror. Erm, briefly, I understand that you are now thirty-seven years old….."

"Thirty-seven in a couple of weeks, Mr. Halligan, please do not wish my life away!" Westward interjected in a humorous manner. There were a few low toned chuckles out of politeness.

"OK, at your age, how do expect to keep up with the physical demands of professional football? Also, I read somewhere that you have a long term knee injury?" Was it more of a statement or a question – Westward could not tell for sure.

"Thank you for your question, Mr. Halligan. First, I am going to have to deal with the demands of the Championship then the Premier League in a couple of years time, as that is our ambition. Yes, my knee has been a problem, but now I am glad to say that God has given me a total healing. Many will scoff at this, but that's OK. It has been an absolute miracle. I understand that I will have to work much harder to sustain suitable fitness levels than say the lads in their early twenties. This I will endeavour to do to the best of my abilities. In fact, I will be enforcing a training regime that will be demanding on all players of all abilities. At the present time, the players are clearly not as skilful as others in the league. To combat this to start with, we will concentrate more on overall fitness to deal with the shortfall of skill."

Westward then pointed to another reporter, an attractive brunette woman in her early twenties in a blue trouser suit and white blouse. She fluttered her eyelids and spoke in a quiet, seductive tone.

"Jordan...., sorry, Mr. Westward, Layla Park-Simmons, Daily Mail. The temptations that go along with the privileges of playing in the Football League. How do you intend to keep clear of them?"

Westward smiled, aware of where such a question was going.

"You speak as if you know well of these so called 'temptations', Miss Park-Simmons." The journalist looked down as if a spotlight had shone on an uncomfortable area. "I believe what the Bible says, Miss Park-Simmons. I presume that it is Miss Park-Simmons? Anyway, in the book of James it says that sin starts with temptation, and temptation always starts with a thought. If we can control our thought processes, we can deal with any temptation presented to us."

"There is a lot of pressure out there, Mr. Westward."

"There is a big God as well, Miss Park-Simmons. Do you know Him yet? I would encourage you to seek him with all your heart while you can. Next question, please." Westward simpered in apparent victory.

The barrage of questions continued for another fifteen minutes before Nelson bought an end to proceedings. Westward confidently winked as he pulled the shirt from the bag again to kiss the club badge before allowing Brian Chambers to hold the shirt in front of Westward's jacket again for final photos.

"Well, we'll have to wait and see the papers tomorrow to see how that all went," commented Chambers as he watched the reporters disperse.

****

The next day.

The youth and reserve squad ran through drills and casual passing and shooting exercises as Westward and Chambers stood in examination on the sidelines.

"Brian," Westward began, pointing at a group of teenage lads a few yards away casually kicking a ball between them, "what kind of investment has there been in the youth academy recently? tell me about these guys."

Westward watched each player closely to read the body language of each of the group.

"I'll be honest not much. But we have a few terrific prospects. Take the red-haired lad for example. Max Oswald," he shook his head and chuckled, "now this lad shows incredible promise. Bit of a glory hound, if you know what I mean, but a great lad on his day. He prefers wide right but he can play on the left or up front. Once he's got the ball – you've got no chance of getting it off him."

Westward's gaze followed Oswald as he nonchalantly trotted along the far touchline of the pitch weaving his feet around a moving ball. He then ran past the ball, flicked it between his feet and over his head before laying a pass off to another player who graciously stood and applauded the youngster's skilful exhibition. Oswald responded with a grin and a bow. Westward raised his eyebrows and cleared his throat as he and Chambers exchanged glances. Chambers smiled as he looked down at the ground before pointing to a tall, fair-haired, slight-framed player.

"Forrest Dane. Quiet lad. Always smiling, very likeable kid. Central defender. Always, always eating. Makes you wonder where he puts it though, eh?"

"What about the prima donna, the other tall lad?"

Chambers sniggered at Westward's description as he watched the player in question run his hands through his longish brown hair again and again as he walked towards a football with a relaxed swagger.

"Ah, Mr. Ryan Bentley. Looks like he could fit into an Italian World Cup team with all that hair, eh? Now he is an interesting character. Doesn't he just love himself! Great left foot though. Plays in between the midfield and up front, so it makes it difficult for him to be picked up. He's lost a lot of weight too. Good, strong fitness usually but you have to watch you don't over train him." He glanced at Westward before continuing, raising his leg and pointing to his knee. Westward smiled and chuckled.

"And that lad on the end – the other blond lad?"

"Patrick Swindon," Chambers accentuated.

Westward frowned inquisitively at Chambers as if he was expecting more to be said.

"Super player when he's on form as well - dribbles fantastic," he paused thoughtfully, shrugged his shoulders with resignation before continuing, "just lacks confidence some of the time. Plays defensive midfield."

"What about the big built kid? Looks like a young Rooney with that haircut."

"Ah, that would be Mr. Donze. Scots lad, so I'm naturally biased. Very strong, heck of a right boot on him too. Trying to build his confidence in the air and work on his speed. He and Mr. Oswald seem to team up well."

Chambers whistled and gestured for them all to join him and Westward who made mental notes of what he had been told. Chambers made the introductions of the players to him. Forrest Dane produced a chocolate bar which he promptly demolished with fervour before scrunching the wrapper up, smiling bashfully and forcing it into his tracksuit bottoms as if to cheekily hide it. Bentley casually chewed another piece of gum and stood, arms folded, grinning. Swindon stood, almost embarrassed, his hand fingering the hair behind his ear, his other arm hanging limply by his side. Oswald could not stand still, interspersing jogging on the spot with bouncing.

"How are we doing, boys?" Westward broke the silence, "thanks for taking time out to see me. I thought I'd run the current situation of the club by you to see how you guys feel."

They all nodded, glancing briefly at each other, seemingly to seek approval.

Chambers added, "As you are aware, Mr. Westward is now major share holder, manager and player with Woodmouth. He will be seeking confirmation from everyone currently on the club's books regarding their playing intentions."

Westward nodded his agreement before continuing.

"The situation is, technically, that you are out of contract because the business entity for whom you were committed to has ceased to exist. Consequently, as of today, you are free to leave the club if you so wish. As you know, according to league rules, as you are unattached to a club, you are free to sign with anyone outside the transfer window, which is, of course, currently closed until 1st July. That is one choice that you have." The group scanned each other's faces for any opinion before Westward continued.

"I understand that you are all on around £300 per week, yes? Well, I have watched each of you briefly and Mr. Chambers here speaks very highly of you all. You guys are the future of the club. We do not have a stash of money to spend on fancy players. We can't offer huge salaries, but I can offer a vision for the next few years. If you work hard, I see no reason that you could not be more involved in the first team. Chances are, some of the others will be leaving so a sizeable hole will appear in the squad list. If you choose to stay, which I hope you will, I'd like to offer you all a year's contract with a rise to £600 per week. You don't need to tell me right now, but I'd like to know before training tomorrow. How does everyone feel about that?"

The cluster of boys once again looked at each other, this time in amazement. They knew it was a good deal, most likely better than any from another club. A momentary silence followed, broken by Bentley.

"Hey, I'm in." He confirmed, shaking hair out of his eyes.

"Sounds good to me," added Donze, smiling broadly as he folded his arms across his ample chest.

"Me too!" nodded Dane enthusiastically.

"Well, if that's what everyone wants to do..." Patrick Swindon indecisively agreed, but in his hesitancy, he caught Westward's approving smile and wink. Swindon delved into his pocket and pulled out a tube of mints and popped three into his mouth.

Oswald grinned, hands behind his back. That was enough for the others to know he agreed too.

"You realise that we will be implementing morning and afternoon training sessions? Does that bother you? Can you take the pressure? We may not have the most skilful squad, but we'll make sure that we have the fittest." He looked around at each of them. "Any questions?"

They all shook their heads.

"Well, I wish all my business worked out as easily and as quickly as that. OK, don't let me hold you up and welcome aboard," Westward delightfully shook hands again with each boy and they began to trot off joyfully with a 'thank you, Sir,' to complete their training for the day when Westward called them back.

"Sorry fellas, one other thing. Something very important that I'll need you guys to do," he began, nodding in contemplation, "How do you fancy coming to more games? Not just as a spectator or boot cleaner. I need some of you to write reports on the first-teamers as part of a bonus system I've got in mind. I want you to keep a secret record of certain players. Forrest, for example, I would want you to make a report on the performance of one of the two guys that play alongside me. Passing, attitude, do you sense holding back in the way they play? Is their tackling fair? What about their heading? That kind of thing. Are you with me?"

Dane's face beamed at the idea.

"Jack," Westward pointed at the stocky young striker, "you'll need to check out Paul Lincoln and the guys up front. Their work rate, their shooting, team play, fitness and running off the ball, that kind of thing. What do you think?"

Donze again folded his arms, slyly smiled, slowly nodding in approval.

"What about you Patrick? You'd need to comment on Magnus Gustavsson and occasionally, depending on whom we play, there may be a second defensive midfielder alongside him. Same sort of thing. Could you do that? Watch a whole game from the point of view of one single player?"

Swindon casually shrugged his shoulders and scraped the grass with his boot as he looked down at the turf.

"Mr. Swindon," Westward raised his voice to get attention which made the young lad jump and fix eyes on him. "Do you understand?"

"Yes, Sir!" Swindon replied with a jolt.

"OK, don't let me hold you back, we'll talk again nearer the time. Reporting won't start till next season. Thanks for your time."

Chambers and Westward stood, arms folded, watching the boys chatting as they ran back to the pitch, Dane showing clenched fists of absolute achievement at his new situation with the club.

"You're in a generous mood," Chambers stated.

Westward affirmed with a nod, screwing up his lips.

"Mind you, I see what you mean about Swindon. He sure does lack confidence. We could be short of players as I just said. We may have no choice come next season to play these guys. Tell you what, tomorrow, put them in with the first team for training. Boost their self-esteem. I know that's unusual, but I want to instil an attitude that no player at this club is worth more than another. We are a team, a family. Everyone is valuable in his own right..,"

Chambers listened thoughtfully.

"You don't agree?" Westward questioned, turning his head.

Chambers smiled, shaking his head. "I totally agree, Jordan, I am just in awe of your confidence. You do realise that you could be trying to get a silk purse out of much less than a sow's ear, as they say."

"Hey, you signed them initially, they can't be that bad."

"No, they're not. To be honest with the right training, they'll do well."

"Incidentally, why do they particularly hang around together? They seem to be removed from the other kids their age."

"You mean you couldn't tell? A spiritual giant like you and you couldn't tell? Let's just say there we have five guys who are already men of war."

Westward again slowly turned his head in pleasant surprise "You mean....?"

"Uh ha. All Christian lads. You won't have any trouble with them. No clubs, no booze, so far no women trouble. Just solid kids. Tell you what, if my brood had turned out half as committed to Christ as they are, I'd be a very happy father."

Westward stood in silence, considering his fortune.

What an influence these boys could be in this new regime.

He silently prayed with thanks a blessing upon the group as they laughed together, heartily kicking the ball around again.

Westward glanced at his watch. "It's nearly twelve-thirty. Better get over to the big guys and talk to them. How do you gauge the mood amongst them?"

Chambers sighed. "There are a few I know who seriously will not be happy. Our German lad for one. Let's go."

They swiftly moved over to the first team and gathered the squad together. Chambers called everyone into the goal area nearest the changing building. Some walked, some trotted, a couple even stood still some distance away. A well-built German stood arms folded, casually chatting and laughing with Eric Page, Woodmouth's first choice goalkeeper. Westward stood, waiting to see how Chambers dealt with the pair. Chambers finally spoke, but Westward could tell he had no respectful authority. "I wish I could motivate these two, they wind me up."

"Brian, win, draw or lose, you can't relax," Westward muttered, "like I said, you've never commanded the respect that your position demanded. I told you before about Messen. He's overpaid and an underachiever. I had no idea that Page was so disinterested as well. Mind you with two years left on his contract, I suppose he's not desperate yet."

Chambers' disdained look at Westward said everything.

"Eric, Gerhard, can I borrow you for a second please?"

Westward smirked. "That sounded like a manager in control, that did," he sarcastically commented. Chambers looked sheepishly away.

The two players idly lumbered their way over as if they had all the time in the world. Westward simply shook his head and closed his eyes in abject disappointment with the apathy and attitude on show.

"Gentlemen," Chambers began, "most of you already know of Jordan Westward, the club's new owner and player/manager." There were a few casual, silent nods, many with suspicious and doubtful looks. "He wants to run through the changes that are going to be happening at the club. As you know, with the board transitions which we have just shared with the younger players, you guys are now out of contract." There were sharp intakes of breath all around and mumbles of disapproval and shock. Chambers closed his eyes and raised his hands as if to silence the squad before continuing.

"Listen, I can appreciate your concerns so I do not want to say much more, I'll leave it to Mr. Westward. He has a vision and a plan to bring a fresh vision for the club to pass. But what he does need from you is a serious elevation in commitment and enthusiasm."

Westward unfolded his arms and held them out in front of him, as if offering a surrender.

"Thanks, Brian." He paused as if to gather his thoughts for maximum impact. "I'll cut to the chase. Some of us," he hesitated, staring at Messen and Page who stood on the fringe of the group, "it seems have more important things to deal with." Messen sighed and squinted in silent, sarcastic response. "There are several options open to you all. And they are as follows: Number one, you stay with the club for the final three games. Everyone gets five grand a week with a bonus if we stay up. Nothing to lose. If we stay up, you can talk about a new contract. Number two, leave now. You're out of contract, clubs can sign you straight away if you get a better offer. We'll pay you to the end of the week. Number three, you can sign a new contract now. I will emphasize though that everyone gets five grand a week, max. If you leave the small print on your own personal details until later, bonuses will be different."

Again, there were a few low tones of mumbling disapproval. Westward held up a hand to silence the noise.

"Enough please. It is about time that each of you gets an understanding that all of you are replaceable. If you want nothing more than to play football, take your money home and be a star, then you have no place here. I don't want a bunch of what most of you have become – selfish, big-headed, over-paid wasters. I would sooner you leave now. I want a squad that appreciates the fact that they are privileged when they pull on a Woodmouth shirt. I want a squad that believes that this is a Premier League Football club, and players that believe that they are the best because you are part of a team," he halted again for effect before finishing, "I want a squad that wants to win the Champions League – and knows deep down inside that they actually could."

That was enough for Messen who roared with laughter whilst sarcastically slapping his thighs. "Who is this guy? Champions League! Ha ha!" he cynically commented, his

Bavarian cadence steaming over his English speech.

Westward stared, untouched by the comments. "Like I said," he continued, undaunted, and concluded, accentuating every syllable, "some of you are selfish, overpaid, big-headed wasters." Messen tilted his head, returning Westward's stare. "He who is not with me," Westward began, still staring, "is against me," he replied, folding his arms in indignation.

"And who will play instead of me if I leave? Who's going to get the goals then, huh? Champions League indeed! You will be in the Blue Square League before you know it. And what's in this for you? What salary are you taking?" A few of the players looked at each other, mumbling and grunting agreement with Messen's interrogation like a troop of suspicious apes. Westward once again waited a moment before replying, keeping a calm, forceful, dignified tone.

"Like I said, no one is irreplaceable. I took on board some wisdom from an old player/manager, John Gregory. He said strikers may win you games, but defenders win you championships. I would sooner put my trust in youth players, who believe me, have more heart than you do, Mr. Messen. And as a matter of fact, I inherit a massive debt and will not be taking a single penny for my work here."

"You are a joke! I am an asset to this club! I'm worth millions!" he emphasised, "and you reckon the club can really throw that kind of money away?"

Again, Westward paused before proceeding again. "You're right, this club did throw a whole bunch of money away when they bought you, and to be honest, my heart sank. Yes, it does seem a shame to see it go for no return, but that's football – or rather I should say, that's business. It's just another one of those decisions that will have to be put down as one that did not work. Not just that, but you also now cost a gargantuan amount of cash a week in wages, so if you go, so does a big chunk of our wage bill."

Messen was seething by now.

"You have a serious problem, Mr. Westward. If I leave, so will many others," he angrily erupted, his accent more pronounced the more heated he got. He pointed an accusing finger at Westward, "You won't even have enough to field a full team next weekend, you'll see!"

Westward chuckled to frustrate Messen even more. "Mr. Messen, I would sooner have my wife and kids play than someone with your attitude. Like I said," he shrugged for emphasis, "you're free to go when you want."

Messen, realising Westward's unrelenting seriousness, walked up to him, leant forward to spit on the ground, stared in contempt at Westward and walked back to the changing rooms.

The shocked squad watched in silence as he, and he alone left. When he was out of range, Westward continued. "Anyone else feel the same way as he does, leave now. You are not welcome and are a liability to this club."

None moved.

"In three years time, we will win the Champions League. This year we will stay up. Next season we will get promotion to the Premier League. The season after that we will qualify for the Champions League. The following season, we will be champions of Europe. I look at each of you and I see so much talent which is hidden under your unbelief. There is more than enough ability here to achieve incredible things. All that is needed is faith. In yourselves, in your team.........and in God. I want to get something that has been lacking here for seasons – harmony. Unity. Single heartedness!" he paused before continuing, "OK, let me ask you all a question: what is the club's motto?"

There was silence and frowns of perplexity.

"No one know?" Westward quizzed, faking a look of incredulity as if he knew something that they all should have done. "Well, it hasn't actually got one, that's probably why you didn't know it. That changes today. It is now Per Unitatem Vis!"

Paul Lincoln spoke up a few moments later, smiling. "From unity comes strength!" he stated, nodding in appreciation of the sentiment.

Westward allowed himself a brief smile. "Well done, Mr. Lincoln. Seems we have a Latin scholar in the midst!"

"No, not really boss," Lincoln humbly retorted, "it was the motto of my scout group years ago!"

The squad laughed together. For a fleeting moment, there was a unity. Whilst Westward wanted to appear to be in control, in authority, he allowed himself a brief smile. He did not want to be an overbearing tyrant.

"OK, OK! Then you'll know what I am getting at. Seriously, gentlemen, I do want to change things a lot here though. I like to play a different system to most clubs. There once was a time when 4-3-3 was the norm, but not the 4-3-3 that we know now. Back in the sixties that meant exactly that – three strikers. Now they try and kid you that two wingers and one striker in the middle is three up front. It is not, period. It is what is effectively 4-5-1 – they only have one striker. Then that changed to 4-4-2. In my humble opinion that's the only other formation worth giving thought to. Now we see 4-5-1 as most common. Or should I say 4-2-3-1. Again, they try to kid you it is four up front. It isn't. It is still playing with a lone striker. It causes stifled, unentertaining sport with a cramped midfield and defence. No, I know it is perhaps a cliché in some people's books, but I still believe the best form of defence is attack, and that is what we will do. Build from the back with quick, counter-attacking football. I like 3-5-2, but for that, we need very quick, very fit wing-backs – so several of you will have to change position.

"Craig," he nodded to Craig Halbeath, Messen's current strike partner in place of the injured Paul Lincoln, "I want you to be a third centre-back with me and Martin," he pointed to Martin Haynes. "Martin – you know you're a potential England player. I hope that you don't see that you need to move to a bigger club to realise that. I implore you to stay with us. You'll be playing at Wembley, believe me."

Halbeath looked aghast at the idea. "Craig, you are an ace in the air, you're quick and I've seen how you can read the game and anticipate others' moves so well. You'd be an excellent central defender – that is if you wish to stay at the club. Now your place up front would be taken by this man," Westward walked around slowly towards Chris Haynes, patting his shoulders. Haynes their current right-winger and younger brother to Martin looked bewildered. "Again, I want to build the club on a higher tempo game. Quick, one touch passing, prompt running off the ball into space, ready to take another pass, anticipating every move from your team-mates. It can be done.

"Rudi here," he patted Rudi Radzednic, a full eight inches shorter than himself, on the shoulder, "will be playing just behind the front two. We need him to link the defensive midfield with our front men. I see him as the perfect guy along with Clive. Also, Magnus," he nodded at the big Danish defender, "will play just in front of the defenders. I think he is made for that role."

Westward paused to take a deep breath. He once again looked at expressions on faces, wanting some further reaction. He could tell that there were already several who were doubtful of his decisions before he announced the tactical changes. Now there were even more so. During the silence, Kevin Ayres spoke up.

"Jordan..."

Westward scowled disapprovingly at the right-back.

"It's Sir, boss or Mr. Westward, son." Westward affirmed.

Shocked, Ayres continued, actually appreciating being told where he stood. "Erm, you said that if we want, we can see the season through and then look for another club if we don't like these changes?"

Westward nodded. "That's correct. I have made it as easy for you as I can. But if you do decide to stay for next season, I will need to know by say, mid-May at the latest. That gives you several weeks to find another club or confirm your commitment here. I must say though that if you do not find anywhere else, I will not take you on after that date. I have to know very soon in order to consider getting players in. I want players who want to succeed and see that success is coming to this club because of what they can offer to this team. I'm being as fair as I can, but I will not be held over a barrel."

Ayres nodded, perplexed.

Bruce Dean, the left-back, rubbed both his hands over his stubbly face, feeling the worse for wear after a late night at a club in town. Westward discerned his condition.

"Another thing," he began, "I will not tolerate anything less than 100% during training workouts. If you want to carry on drinking and womanising during the week - find another club. It is not fair on those who are prepared to do the right thing. We cannot be expected to hold up those who abuse their status as a professional footballer with this club. If one of you arrives here with so much as a hint of alcohol on your breath I will train the lot of you until you throw up. The lot of you.

That includes me."

Dean tried to avoid Westward's direct gaze. The spotlight had been shone. Ray Somerton, the thirty-three year-old veteran defender of ten years service at the club was next to speak up.

"Mr. Westward, you said that contracts can be immediately negotiated. How long do you envisage they will be offered for?"

Westward ran his hand through his hair which blew into his face in the slight breeze. "As I said before, I see us winning the Champions League in three years time. You commit to the club now, you'll get a three year contract. Maximum pay £5,000 per week, but better bonuses to top things up. I hasten to add though that bonuses will be for performance, not necessarily results. I would sooner you play well as a unit and lose than scramble a win and play poorly. That leaves it up to you to work for more money instead having it put in your hand as a matter of course. I personally am totally against today's over-inflated football wages – most of the time, it just produces over-inflated egos. You may find a better deal somewhere else, that's fine, you go where you wish. But I guarantee, if you stay here, things will be much tighter, but fairer for those who are serious about their football. Value your status and your attitude, you'll do well. Fines will increase for breaks of discipline and poor attitude. If you are late for training, you'll be fined. Do it twice, the fine trebles, do it three times, you're off the books. You need to appreciate your role here and not take it for granted.

"If you get booked for a lack of discipline, you'll be fined, no questions. If you are sent off, it will be a month's wages as a fine. I am that serious. Breaks of discipline must hurt or you will never learn. Any drug abuse, you will be immediately dismissed. That will simply not be tolerated. And just because you may be what you consider to be an immediate choice pick for the first team, it does not mean it will stay that way. Your place in the team will depend on your attitude on and off the field both as an individual and how you integrate with the team."

The squad had changed in minutes from bored party guests to children gathered around their school teacher.

"While we are on the subject of bonuses," Westward paused as he pulled a thick wad of papers from his jacket pocket and handed them out to the players, "this is how you will earn them." Players passed them around and scrutinized the contents. "As you can see, performance related bonuses have nothing to do with your ability – but everything to do with your character. You can be the most skilful player on the club's books – but unless you show me that you have achieved your potential, you will not be paid much in a bonus."

Brian Chambers slid a finger down the page as Westward continued.

Responsible.

Co-operative.

Respectful.

Dependable.

He sighed once again at what he considered was nothing more than Westward's dream world.

"Think of it like this. Imagine we are all listed in the FIFA computer game. Some of you are maybe 90% skill level, some are only 70%. If a 70% player gives a 100% he has shown more to me than a 90% player who gives 70%. Does that make sense? As you can see, gentlemen, there are twenty categories, all to do with people's character more than their ability. I emphasize a Biblical precedent here – to whom much is given, much is expected. Bottom line is we are an individual team, not a team of individuals. Each category a player will score a possible fifty points, giving a maximum one thousand. We then multiply this score by two giving a performance bonus potential of two grand. Add to that an extra five hundred for a win or two hundred for a draw and you guys could score a lot on top of your basic wage. Most clubs operate on bonuses only for wins or draws – I am not so interested in the result as I am the performance to start with. Naturally, we need to win games – but I want you guys to have the satisfaction of reward for effort, not reward for result. Believe me, gentlemen, results will come. But they will only come if we identify a vision of unity. All for one and one for all mentality. Any further questions?"

Clive Belkin raised a hand. "Boss, erm, who exactly will be doing the scoring?"

Westward smiled as he pointed directly at each player as he mentioned them. "Messrs. Swindon, Donze, Oswald and their compatriots. Anyone who is not playing that day but is making the trip to the game. I expect every member of this club to be actively involved on a very intimate basis."

Westward clicked his fingers as he pointed in response to Paul Lincoln. "So, boss, are you saying that even if we do not play, we will still be expected to travel to games?"

"That's exactly what I am saying – barring serious injury, of course. Does anyone not regularly involved in the first team have a problem with that?"

They knew that he was serious. His changes were significant and weighty. Westward remained silent for a few moments before Magnus Gustavsson spoke as the rain clouds began to drizzle their contents in fine dots. He scratched his full moustache between his thumb and forefinger and cleared his throat.

"I've been at the club three years. Three years of hard work going nowhere. What the boss has laid out may sound tough but football is a tough game at the top. You all know about my faith in Jesus. I know you may say that so far it hasn't helped me much. But Jesus can only work through people who are open and willing to do whatever it takes." A few of the players scoffed at Gustavsson's openness about his Christianity. "Listen, I've probably only got a few years left before I hang my boots up. I'm in total admiration of the boss for playing at his age. It is amazing. I believe he can do it. I'm in, I don't know about anyone else."

Westward nodded his appreciation. He scrutinized each face in the group. "I'll teach you to worship God with all your heart. You will be so aware of God's mercy and grace and presence that you will want to. God has a plan for each of your lives that He is aching to reveal to you," he paused for effect during which time Halbeath spoke.

"What if we do not believe in God, boss?" Halbeath frowned in quizzical contemplation.

Westward closed his eyes in silent prayer awaiting wisdom.

Has God ever ceased to exist just because people choose not to believe in him? Does the earth suddenly become flat just because people decide to not believe that it's round?

"Let me tell you all. Jesus Christ came into this world as God in the flesh." Westward spoke of his Saviour with a smile of love and appreciation. "He came to die in your place because all of us were born sinners, destined for hell. Yet He gave His life for us so we could have His eternal life. You may have heard it said before that we sin because we are sinners, and we are not sinners because we sin. Only God himself could pay the price and he did so at the cross of Calvary. I do not force my beliefs on any of you. God has to be real to each of you individually. But let me tell you something, worshipping God has nothing to do with church, singing hymns or bible reading. All those things are good, but are not the point. The true issue is your attitude. How you approach everything in life."

Gustavsson nodded, smiling joyfully.

Westward continued. "I want you guys to know something about the commitment that I am making to this club. Whatever you do, I will do also. And more," he paused and looked several players in the eye before continuing. "I would literally die for any of you."

A silence had fallen upon the captivated group.

"Well, I'll be here for another twenty minutes. If you intend to be available for team selection for this weekend's game at Rotherham, I need to know before I leave. I have copies of the draft contract for you to see. Please take one with you. If you want to discuss any finer details, please call me or call in at the club office this afternoon." He began to turn towards the changing building but hesitated. "One final thing," he concluded, "there will be two training sessions each weekday. If there is a match midweek, there will still be a morning session should travelling allow. I expect supreme fitness. Whatever you will do, I will be doing myself. I am committing to at least a five mile run even before I get here with you. You decide if you need to up the game a little. But as I said, your first team place at the moment is not guaranteed. I have a bunch of young lads joining you from the youth team tomorrow. I can assure you that they're very excited about their future here."

The idea of younger players training with them clearly had damaged their lofty status as they mumbled to each other.

Up until now Chambers had remained very quiet. Having managed them for several years and knowing their personalities, he could already gauge who would want to stay. He knew that putting out a team could be a problem that coming August.

"That's all I have to say. Anyone have any final questions?" He scanned the faces around him. Shock more than anything else seemed to be keeping them quiet. Westward could see that he had made his point, but began to wonder how many were with him. "OK, AM and PM training starts tomorrow. You're free to leave. Anyone wishing to speak to me in private, like I say, I'm here for twenty minutes and at the office until about four o'clock." He simply nodded and commandingly made his way to the changing building.

"Well you might want to change the ways that you try to make friends with people, Jordan," Chambers commented with a hint of sarcasm as he jogged to catch up with Westward.

"Brian," he replied, "I remember listening to an interview John Toshack gave once and it summed management up. He said in football administration you only have eleven friends – the first team that you pick to play for a game. Let's say you have a squad of twenty-four. That makes thirteen enemies straight off. Multiply that by their spouses, parents etc – you have many, many adversaries in football."

Chambers screwed his face in a sarcastic smirk. "That's enthusiastic. I also read somewhere, can't remember who said it, 'you've never really been a manager until you've been sacked.' I guess you have an advantage here – that can't happen to you."

Westward smirked at Chambers. "Well, while we're playing quote tennis, I also read some guy said that you only had eleven players to keep happy."

"Well, yeah, I guess the eleven in the first team," Chambers quickly replied in a rhetorical tone.

"No, Brian, they're already happy – they're already playing in the first team. The eleven to keep happy are the reserves."

"No wonder I've struggled in management. Good job you're here I suppose," Chambers said caustically.

"Well, better watch your step now I'm in charge then! Man, it sure must have been tough at the top for you!"

Chambers laughed and mockingly punched Westward's arm. Behind him he could hear the distant low tones of some bewildered, disorientated footballers, each with mixed feelings about their very uncertain future.

****

Later that evening.

Westward had made a call to the WestTech office to check on the day's activities and gave a list of his suggestions to be complied with in his absence. He had then spoken briefly with several of the players, not wishing to compromise from his vision, but still finding it difficult to balance his authority with the fact that he was also a player and therefore an equal. As always upon his return home, the atmosphere was quiet, how he liked it. Gentle music was playing in the background as the twins Chloe and Caleb helped to lay the table for dinner. His wife greeted him with a loving hug and assured him that his evening meal would not be too far away. The spicy aroma of chilli drifted deliciously from the kitchen to the dining room.

Westward took a brief shower, allowing the water to spray from its many angles to ease his already stressed body. As he dried himself in the bedroom, the phone rang.

"I'll get it!" he yelled, "Hello, Jordan Westward here."

"What on earth do you think you're doing, Jordan?" a gruff voice began.

"Excuse me, who is this?" Westward firmly demanded, throwing his towel on the bed.

"It's your father, here."

Westward swallowed hard in shock. "Dad?"

"Yeah. What are you doing? We just watched the news. It said some crazy story about you buying Woodmouth and you're gonna be playing for them."

Westward took a deep breath to stay calm. "Yes, that's right. God has healed my knee and I'm going to be playing."

His father let out a heavy sigh on the other end of the phone. "Who do you think you are? You're barmy, Jordan, absolutely barmy. When are you going to get a proper job instead of constantly messing about. I told you years ago to sort your life out before it was too late."

"Dad. Listen. Listen very carefully. I am director of a multi-million pound corporation and....."

"Jordan, you listen to me. I still remember that time you were rude to me years ago. I haven't forgotten. And you still live in this dream world. Well, let me tell you this: if you don't come to your senses soon, you're gonna waste your life."

Westward wanted so much to say something that would impress, but knew he was wasting his time.

Abigail then appeared in the doorway.

"Well," Westward began hesitantly, "thanks again for your encouragement, Dad. Maybe one day you might actually see that I am not the waste of space that you think I am."

Abigail shook her head and silently mouthed, "No! No!"

"Well, like I keep saying to you, go get a decent, real job before it's too late. Alright?"

The phone went dead.

Westward faked throwing the phone at the wall and fell on to the bed with his head in his hands. He looked pleadingly at his wife. "What's it going to take for him to see? What more can I do to enthuse him?"

Abigail slid next to him. "Maybe that's the problem. You'll never be able to so you might as well stop trying."

Just then, they were interrupted by the heard the sound of the front door bell. "Who's that at this time of night?" he frowned, rushing to get dressed. He ran downstairs to the front door which had been opened to reveal Magnus Gustavsson.

"Magnus," Westward frowned, a little startled at the presence of the big Dane, "what brings you here?" Westward stood back motioning for Gustavsson to come in.

"Boss, I know this is probably out of line me being here, but I could not wait any longer. We need to talk."

"Sure," he assuredly replied, waving a hand towards his study, the door of which he closed behind him. Gustavsson took a seat without asking.

A little forward, Westward pondered to himself as he sat down, *or is it the natural boldness of a leader?*

"Boss, I have read the contract, read your player appraisal forms and, well, even though I am in, there are still many who are uncertain. What do you intend to do to pick them up, you know, motivate them?"

Westward clasped his hands together on his desk.

"Magnus, the first thing that these players need is respect. Self respect and respect from their peers. I see too much multi-level activity where some players clearly think that they are more important than others because they are better than them."

Gustavsson nodded. "It is inevitable – I am sure that a while back, no offence to say, someone like Cameron Jerome who wasn't a bad player, but he was not in the same league as Messi. How do you combat that difference in skill-level?"

Westward sighed in contemplation. "Let me ask you: what good is a team of Messi's if they do not perform to their maximum effort? I studied some clips of Ronaldinho, an awesome player, but when you look at his attitude in some games and off the pitch, it stank. Players need to know they are respected – but that they also have respect for everyone else. This is paramount amongst young players. Some managers believe that young players should be left to develop themselves. I disagree. These lads are at a crucial time in their lives. They need nurturing, fathering – to keep them out of bad habits. As much as I want to improve players, we need a winning team. A team that believes in itself as a unit."

Gustavsson nodded before adding, "Kind of accepting personal responsibility – recognising our own weaknesses and not being afraid to confess them?"

Westward grinned. "Exactly. Exactly. As a manager I can accept overall responsibility for how well or how badly a team plays – but this is unique because I am one of them too. I must be open to as much scrutiny as anyone else. I can demand respect and commitment from the squad – but they must respect each other too and know that there is no place for anyone not 100% committed. Most coaches will take responsibility for their players' behaviour, which is all well and good," he paused, "but I want to install in every player personal responsibility."

Gustavsson hesitated before continuing. "What do you see yourself as? I mean, you are a Christian, a well-known businessman, but where do you fit in? OK, if I can be so bold - what's in it for you?"

A knock on the door interrupted them as Abigail slid her head behind the door.

"Oh, sorry!" she apologised, embarrassed. She was not unused to visitors to see Westward, but she did not recognise the Dane.

"That's OK, sweetheart, come in a second," Westward got up and walked around to be next to Gustavsson who also stood, "this is Magnus Gustavsson, Woodmouth's current captain. He is a fellow soldier, if you know what I mean."

Gustavsson humbly bowed briefly and shook hands with Mrs. Westward. "Pleasure to meet you, ma'am."

"Pleasure too, Mr. Gustavsson. Can I get you gentleman anything? Tea? Coffee?"

"Just water for me please, ma'am."

Westward nodded in agreement for the same for himself and Abigail left.

"To continue, I am in this for one reason, and one reason only – for God's glory. Financially, it is costing me initially, but I am convinced that God is going to use this club for great things. Revival in this town – and on a wider basis. To answer your question in more depth, I see the job of a coach going way beyond skill and knowledge of tactics. A bit like being a born again believer in Christ goes further than just knowing things from the Bible. You must become a fitness trainer, social worker, motivator, disciplinarian, friend, journalist, mentor, manager and administrator, all rolled into one. To be honest, I am really glad you are here. It is all very well getting info from Mr. Chambers – but I think you could help in a different way as you, as a player currently, could give me the pulse reading within the team. Do you understand what I mean?"

Abigail came in with two glasses of water, handed them to each of the men, to which Westward smiled his thanks. She left as quickly as she had arrived – discreetly.

"So how does Mrs. Westward feel about your venture? I would imagine that you are a busy man at the best of times and how many children do you have now? Four?"

"Actually it's five and she's awesome," Westward proudly announced before taking a sip of water. "Funny thing, well not funny I suppose, but uncanny, is that the same night God spoke to me about buying the club, He had already prepared her heart for it too. It was not an issue. Don't get me wrong, I do not underestimate what lies ahead, but it sure helps when your best friend is on your side."

Gustavsson understood. "I am sure my wife would get on well with Mrs. Westward."

"I also see that, just as in my computer business, I will need patience, a desire to learn and humility to know that I can learn from someone younger than me. I have to learn to exhibit the same high standards that I expect my players to.

And one other thing – an American Football coach once said that 'winning isn't everything: wanting to win is.' I think that needs to be our philosophy too. Concentrate on solid performances and the results will come. A firm belief developed from the confidence of improvement."

Gustavsson drained his glass and, satisfied for the time being, got up to leave.

"Boss, thank you for your time. Something else you need to know, though."

"Sure. Magnus, shoot."

"I probably only have a couple of seasons left and, well, I don't feel I have much to show for my career."

"So your point is?"

"Well, I sure would like to go out with something."

"Can you stretch that to three seasons? We might be able to help," Westward grinned.

Gustavsson held out a hand and as Westward stood, the two firmly shook hands. "May God grant us wisdom, strength and endurance to see this through."

The corners of Westward's eyes creased as he smiled and nodded to his visitor. "Amen. Let's start by giving Rotherham a going over this Saturday, shall we?"

The two heartily embraced.

"Du satse!" Gustavsson replied.

Westward pulled away with a puzzled look. "What on earth does that mean?"

Gustavsson gently punched Westward on the chest.

"You bet!" he responded and turned to leave.

As the door closed, Westward shot an arrow prayer.

Lord God, thank you for people like Magnus and thank you being my Father.

****

"I could sum up Jordan Westward in one word: enigma. He promised so much yet never consistently delivered the goods. I never could visualise where he would end up. A quiet lad - and a bit of a loner."

James Morris,
Teacher,
Woodmouth High Grammar School.

Chapter 8

Extract from the Daily Mirror, the morning of Woodmouth's trip to Rotherham:

MISSION IMPOSSIBLE!

Team	Pyd	Pts	GD
Brighton	*43*	*52*	*-13*
Chesterfield	*43*	*43*	*-12*
Oldham	*43*	*43*	*-14*
Woodmouth	*43*	*43*	*-18*
Rotherham	*43*	*39*	*-26*

After the technical rigours and mental demands of a boardroom take-over, Jordan Westward, a local Northern Midlands business entrepreneur, faces the reality of the challenges of the Football League today. He aims to save Championship side Woodmouth Albion from what many say is almost certain demise. Last Monday, Westward invested several millions of his own money, plus that of a consortium of several close compatriots into financially aiding the ailing club. Without this, the foreclosure of the club was inevitable as it has transpired that a mere coin flip separated a winding-up order and the club filing for bankruptcy just as Westward stepped in. Not only that, but he also has the tough task of redeeming morale after one of its worst seasons in the club's history. Some are questioning his decision to become a player at this level at the unimaginable age of thirty-seven. Many are wondering about his fitness and ability, when most players are already retired or seriously considering it at that age. Westward has no experience in football management and many do not realise that Westward has not so much as kicked a ball around on a park pitch for over a decade.

Woodmouth lay second to bottom in the Championship with three matches left, two of which are away to fellow-strugglers, including today's trip to bottom club Rotherham who also know that defeat today will virtually send them to League One. Woodmouth have managed just one win away from home all season. We asked Westward how he viewed the coming weeks for himself and the club:

"I am no stranger to challenges," Westward commented. "I am excited at the potential in this new era for the club. Many have expressed concern that I am too old to be playing professional football in general, let alone just starting out. This I can totally understand. I can only say that I will prove critics wrong. I believe that I can bring a lot of positive things to this club.

"Since coming here we have made a serious assessment of our current playing staff. There are some good players here who we have experimented in different positions and we believe that we now have a team that will get us the results that we need to stay up. We then intend to conduct a full-scale re-building programme using both youth and experience," Westward continued. Woodmouth are faced with a difficult home match against Champions elect Leeds next week, followed by another away game at Chesterfield who are one place above them. They need seven points from these final three games to be sure of staying up.

Brian Chambers, effectively now assistant first-team coach, only had positive comments regarding Mr Westward's arrival.

"Since Jordan Westward arrived I can only say that there has been a sense of hope instilled that has been missing for many weeks. Naturally the pressure that has been on me now moves to him but having known him personally for many years and his track record in business, I know that he has the ability to motivate people and bring the best out of them. I am looking forward to a long and illustrious time with him at the helm."

Fans on the other hand are not quite so enthusiastic and readers could be excused for their reluctance to trust such a footballing novice as Westward. Some are saying that it is "too little, too late" for a new manager to come on board and that new blood should have been sought out long before. Some are also saying that keeping Chambers is not in the best interests of the club. It does seem however that, for example, the team selection is not now in his hands. This is reflected by the dropping of key players like Gerhard Messen and also the change of position of Rudi Radzednic to central midfield.

"We feel that Gerhard has not been given the service needed to utilise his skills and that for this game we needed to look at other striking options. As for Rudi, he is a very skilful player who likes to see a lot of the ball. By dropping him deeper, he gets the chance to use his skills more effectively," Westward explained.

It is likely that there will be a recall for striker Paul Lincoln who is available again after injury. He will be accompanied by former wide-man Chris Haynes who will also be playing in a totally unconventional role for him. Westward made clear his enjoyment of watching teams that adopt what could be seen as an unconventional 3-5-2 formation. Saturday teatime will be an interesting time for Woodmouth fans when the final whistle blows at Rotherham.

With regards to the other teams around them,

Brighton, with Gary Turner back after suspension, know that two points from their last three games, starting at Coventry, will safeguard their position in the Championship while Chesterfield face a difficult task away at Derby. Oldham meanwhile will entertain Q.P.R. who still have an outside chance of a play-off place. They will offer a late fitness test on Kevin Yates who injured his calf muscle in their midweek draw at Oxford.

Woodmouth:

Page,
M. Haynes, Somerton, Westward,
Ayres, Radzednic, Gustavsson, Belkin, Dean,
C. Haynes, Lincoln

****

Westward called the squad to order as he dragged over a mobile white board with the outline of a soccer pitch clearly defined in neat, permanent, black outlines.

"OK, gentleman, we need to dissect our new system and get a better understanding of who does what and when. You need to know the strengths of the plan – and despite what many would tell you, they are there. But, weaknesses will be easily exposed if we all do not play together as a team. Per Unitatem Vis – remember?"

He picked up a handful of red and blue circular magnets, representing players.

"Now," he began placing three magnets across the outside of one goal area, "to be honest, if you are a central midfielder or a striker, your role probably will not change that drastically. But for central defenders and wingers/full-backs, your role is all about adaptation." He turned to check that his attention had been gained.

"3-5-2 or 5-3-2, it will alter according to match circumstances. But here," he pointed to each of the first magnets, "is where the game is won or lost. Being good in the air is now the minimum requirement as a quality central defender. If you are one who just sees your job as tackling and hoofing the ball upfield - you may as well leave now. You are going to have to learn skill and pace and quick, accurate passing. You'll need to be comfortable on the ball and have a sense of being in control. Two central midfielders just in front of the back three, two very wide players on the half way line, a lone player in the centre of the half way line and, against modern day practice, two strikers."

Ray Somerton was the first to speak as Westward placed the final magnets on the board to represent the rest of the team. "Boss, I am a bit confused. With four at the back, the full backs are always allowed to push forward to support the wingers. How does this work with 3-5-2?"

Westward pointed at Somerton. "Excellent question, Mr. Somerton. OK, what is important with three at the back is the rigidity and getting used to all doing man for man marking. These guys," Westward pointed out the outside pair of the three at the back, "must never be drawn inside. If they are, huge gaps will be left out wide because obviously you won't have full-backs to mop up after you. You mess up and you will give a decent winger every chance of getting to the by-line to get his crosses in and expose the potentially weak goal area."

A few players whispered and nodded in acknowledgement.

"What also is key," Westward turned to again point at the two players in front of the defence, "is counter attack. Get the ball to one of these guys who will ping the ball out to one of the wing-backs and hopefully there will be acres of space for them to maraud up the wing to support the attack. Strikers – you will need to be quick and agile. The old fashioned big guy up front I don't believe is conducive with this system. You will need to sprint away from your marker with probably a second or two to decide what your next course of action needs to be. You are going to have to learn to anticipate where your partner is at any one time. It is not impossible, but it will take effort. To be honest, 3-5-2 will either work impeccably or fail miserably. Do it well, it is unbeatable. Do it wrong, well, you will simply self-destruct."

Kevin Ayres, the cockney-sounding right full-back spoke next.

"So, are you saying that me and Bruce are going to be up

and down the whole pitch all game? We are going to be hammered within the first twenty minutes!"

Westward again folded his arms and nodded.

"Actually, wing-backs are simply deep-seated attackers. If your central defenders all do their job, you will only need to come back to just inside your own half. You need to be further upfield so you can charge off when you get the ball. You stay as wide as you can, stretch the pitch to its limits. That way these guys and this guy in the hole," he pointed to the central midfielders in front of the defence and the man in the middle of the centre circle, "can control the game in the middle."

"But, to be honest, Boss, we have never been encouraged to get forward too much. It isn't our natural game. We're defenders primarily," Ayres added scratching his head as he shuffled in his seat.

Westward nodded sympathetically. "I do understand, Kevin. What you say is absolutely true. But, clearly, there are lessons to be learned. Woodmouth are on the brink of relegation. We either have to adapt and develop something new or accept that Woodmouth may not be a Championship club in a few weeks. In short, I know it maybe a bit trite, but it's my way or the byway, I'm afraid."

Ayres shook his head and sighed.

Westward scanned the faces of the squad. He noticed Clive Belkin frowning. "Clive – a problem?"

"Aye, man," the friendly Geordie began as he pointed to the lone magnet in the middle, "you said 'the hole'. Can you explain that, please?"

Westward smiled, tapping the area just behind the two strikers. "The hole. A crucial role – as all are to be honest, but this role can be used to devastating effect. The question is – is he a midfielder, or is he a striker? That's why it is called 'the hole' – it's an area that a lot of teams do not know how to deal with. If he is an attacker, who covers him? There's no one spare at the back. If he's a midfielder, again, who tracks him? He's not really a 'number ten' like we have seen of late so we are going to use this to our advantage. Messrs Belkin and Radzednic, I see, will fit the role perfectly. And having seen how Mr. Bentley here is coming on, he is going to be able to do the same."

Martin Haynes raised a hand. "Boss – we've noticed a few teams still playing the long ball game down the middle – how do you work with that?"

Westward turned and pointed to the three defenders.

"With these guys, if they are good in the air, the long ball is fruitless. With the added strength of good aerial ability from the holding guys in front, the long ball game is easily dealt with. The holding guys, the play-makers, however, must never be drawn wide. They press any space, not players. Defensively, this system works a treat – provided your central defenders are happy on the ball and willing sometimes to go forward as well. With Magnus' knowledge of defence, he is the ideal holding guy as well. Also, if we press – we press as a team. Fitness is paramount and quality, short, quick passing needs to be developed. Any other questions?"

A brief silence was broken by a quickly raised hand from Forrest Dane.

"Mr. Westward, erm, with only potentially one striker on an opponent's team and three central defenders, how do we know who marks him and in what areas?"

Westward nodded in appreciation at Dane's astute observation. "I am so glad that you have brought that up – this is crucial, absolutely crucial." He turned once again to the board and added magnets to represent an opposing team. "4-2-3-1. One striker and two wide men. As I have said before, we have been fooled into thinking that this is 4-3-3. It isn't. So, we have no full-backs – so who marks who and where? Any ideas? They are marked by...." Westward left his statement hanging, awaiting the answer.

Forrest Dane, quiet as ever, nervously voiced his thoughts.

"Well, I thought that the middle defender would pick up the striker and the other two guys would have the wingers. Is that how it works?"

"Absolutely! Breathtakingly simple isn't it? Then, the attacking midfielder should easily get picked out by one of your holding men," he paused and moved magnets around.

"Now imagine a line here, about a third of the pitch up – that is as far as you track your man. Do not go any further. Let him go. One of the midfielders will pick him up then, but stay with him everywhere until then but do not break your line -

let him go. We must all learn to hold our positions. If we can perfect this, we end up with spare men all over the pitch."

Westward again swept a glance around the room. Some had caught on, others still looked puzzled.

"Alright, gentlemen, we have a match in a few days – let's go train and put this plan into action."

Within a short space of time of running drills, passing practice and running scenarios of various match possibilities, Westward became very aware of the inadequacies of this squad – not least of all in himself. Theories, he reasoned were one thing but the execution of those theories was an altogether different story.

I gotta shape up, he thought to himself.

****

Rotherham v Woodmouth, the following Saturday.

Westward's fitful sleep was shattered that morning at seven-thirty by the shrill, mind-disturbing, high-pitched squeal of his alarm. Immediately, before he had raised his head from the pillow, he was wound up. His children had once again been meddling with his alarm clock. He reached out for the noise, and without opening his eyes, fumbled and found the clock. He threw it with the small amount of strength that he could find against the wall next to him. It had the desired effect and the noise at once ceased.

He tried to refocus his thoughts:

What day is it?

What am I supposed to be doing?

God, my head hurts.

He tried lifting his head but it felt like two sledgehammers had hit each side of it and a dagger had been stabbed into his forehead, so he allowed it to fall heavily back to its rest. He closed his eyes momentarily and then tried to focus on the chest of drawers on the opposite side of his bedroom. He was aware that he was alone.

Bless Abigail, he thought to himself.

Having been very aware of his terrorised night, she had gotten the children up early and left him in the hope that he could rest for longer.

He wearily sat up, slumped on the edge of the bed. That was as far as he could get for several minutes. If he did not know better, he would have thought that he had drunk an excessive amount of alcohol the night before and was now paying the price. He slid his toes in circles on the softness of the beige coloured carpeted floor and squinted again to focus his blurred vision. He rubbed his hands through his hair and over his face. His stomach rumbled, but he could not tell if he was actually able to eat or not. He stood up and immediately knew that he had moved too fast as his head pounded so sat down again, slowly, and tried to compose himself. He tried to convince himself that it was just a headache and that everybody gets headaches. But he conceded that this was far more than a simple headache.

A few moments later, he once again stood up, this time more gradually, almost listlessly. He stood and leant against the window-sill as he surveyed the Spring scenery around him. He had to look down to take away the pain of the daylight on his eyes, even though it was overcast.

Help me, God, he thought, *this is no headache. What a day to get a migraine!*

He gently shook his head and closed his eyes as he put a hand to his forehead desperately hoping that it would alleviate the pain.

From downstairs, he heard the laughter of a happy family at breakfast. The warm, mouthwatering smell of toast would usually have attracted him but his original wonderment of hunger was fully dispelled as he staggered his way around the bed, leaning on the wall. He just got into the ensuite bathroom in time as he vomited the contents of his stomach into the toilet. After retching until he was spent, he knelt and rested his head on the toilet seat, closed his eyes and concentrated on breathing.

Slowly, slowly.

He swallowed painfully and remembered that it was Saturday. He was now a professional football player and club manager and was playing in a crucial game that day. A wave of foreboding, fear and nervousness ran through his body at the recalling of these facts. What was left in his body had worked its way to his bowels. Despite his head's total objection, he sat quickly on the toilet just in time to allow his body to go through its function as he held his stomach tightly and slowly rocked backwards and forwards with his eyes closed.

Then, he remembered God. He smiled as he focused on a gentle, loving, comforting vision of Jesus. His eyes still closed, he imagined Christ himself reaching out his hand and touching his head. His mind went back to a message that his Pastor had preached a few weeks before.

"God wants you well!" he had begun, enthusiastically. "He does not inflict you with sickness. God has a plan for you and does not add pain to his blessing. Proverbs 10:22 says this! God is our healer! Christ died and took our pains on the cross! Just put your faith in Him and what he has already done. Faith requires action to perfect it though. Action. Act on your faith. God is there to give you all that you need to get through whatever trial that has beset you. There is a difference between a miracle, and a healing, though. Miracles happen instantly. God can do this. Healings can take a little longer though. Believe, hold fast - and trust in Christ!"

Westward crossed his arms over his legs and rested his head on them. He prayed a simple prayer.

"Jesus, I need you right now. I need healing, a miracle, whatever. I need your grace to get me through this day. Grant me the strength like you did Samson. We need a win today and I need to play. Your will be done, Lord. Amen."

He slowly raised his head as Abigail appeared with a horrific look on her face upon finding him. The cup and plate that she had bought up was quickly placed by the bed as she rushed in and knelt by him, comforting him. She had seen this so many times before. For a few silent moments, she stroked his head and he wept, tired, exhausted tears.

"Jordan, you need to rest. You are doing too much. I wondered if this would happen." She spoke gently and lovingly kissed his forehead.

He tried to focus his fatigued, half-closed eyes on her.

"What am I supposed to do?" he groaned between sobs. "In six hours time I am supposed to be playing football."

She smiled compassionately and continued. "How long will it take to Rotherham from the ground?"

"Er..." he thought as he squinted and swallowed heavily, "about an hour and a half. Probably go south on the A50 and up the M1. That should avoid getting close to Manchester."

"Goodness me. You and your details. OK, so what time is the coach leaving?"

"About twelve. I've told everyone to be there at twelve."

She tenderly patted his broad shoulders and said, "go back to bed. It's eight o'clock. You can get another few hours rest."

He lifted himself and shuffled, bent over, both hands on his head, back to the comfort of his bed. He tossed and turned, each movement an arduous activity, until eleven-thirty.

****

It was a dull, breezeless spring day as the Woodmouth team made their short journey north east to Rotherham. Westward sat in silent prayer for the journey, strong painkillers having somewhat alleviated his suffering. He listened to conversations around him to learn of the characters in the squad. Gustavsson, the leader, Belkin, the skilful joker, Radzednic, the tactician. The journey passed otherwise with little incident but Westward felt his stomach flip in nervousness as the coach pulled in to a spot outside the tiny ground of Millmoor. Peeling away on the side of the building in red paint was italically blazen, 'Welcome to Rotherham United'.

As Westward stepped gingerly down from the coach, Chris Haynes whispered to him as they walked along.

"Welcome to the Championship, boss. Not exactly Wembley is it? Do you know Millmoor holds less than 8,000 people? Still, Bernabau to look forward to, eh?"

Westward stopped in his tracks, pulled Haynes back and stared harshly through half-closed eyes. "I will not tolerate any joking about any opponent or their ground or players. I don't care whether we play Inter Milan or Interflora, it's all the same to me. One of the reasons for the lack of success at our club is because of this sort of cavalier attitude and casualness. Today, this club stands between us and survival, Mr. Haynes. Let us remember that. Our joy should be when we pick up three points at the end." With Haynes standing open mouthed in shock at his bosses unexpected harshness, Westward continued towards the changing room.

"I heard all that," Magnus Gustavsson commented as he stopped to briefly speak to a shell-shocked Haynes, "couldn't have imagined Mr. Chambers speaking like that. Perhaps some respect is in order, Chris." Haynes sighed, took a deep breath and walked on.

Childhood excitement returned to Westward as he walked around the wood panelled walls which made up the small opponent's changing room at Millmoor. He thought it seemed a far cry from the crisp, clean, modern sleekness of the counterpart at the Santiago Bernabau stadium in Madrid that Chris Haynes had mentioned earlier. He had seen them in a TV documentary a couple of weeks earlier. He remembered also the wisdom he had heard in a church message once: *Despise not the day of small beginnings.* King David, he considered, killed a lion and then a bear before he conquered Goliath. And so it is in football, he reasoned. He knew he could not expect his team to beat major European teams without first getting results at grounds such as this.

As he changed into his kit and took in the mesmerising odour of the muscle rub from around him, he held up his blue shirt, the club's away strip, and stared through his pain at the back. He nodded to himself and grinned, almost arrogantly, as he enjoyed the moment of reading his name sown above the number thirty-five. He had made a decision that from the beginning of the following season he would wear the number five in the squad, the number currently held by Magnus Gustavsson. His wife had made comments about what she considered to be his obsessive compulsion disorder. "What was wrong," she demanded, "and did it really matter if a central midfielder wore number five?" He had reminded her of the comments that an old Liverpool manager had once voiced: "Football isn't about life and death – it is much more important than that."

The second moment of memories flooding back for Westward was as he led his team down the narrow tunnel towards the outside. The low ceilinged, plain painted brick wall area led to two red doors, separating them from the pitch outside. For a brief moment he was transported in his mind to a gladiatorial entrance at the Colosseum. As the doors were opened, the ground's colour, noise and spectacle was opened up, the daylight, meagre though it was, caused Westward to squint through the intense torture of his ongoing distress. The ground Westward estimated was around three-quarters full, but to him, it was a spectacle. Six thousand, Westward reasoned was still several thousand more than what he had been used to when playing in previous games. From the pitch, even for a small ground, it seemed like a major, international stadium to him, even though a few of the die-hard home supporters booed as he and his team jogged onto the pitch.

Woodmouth's opponents had never played in the League's top division. They seemed to have flipped between what was the third and fourth division and once again, it looked like after a single season in the Championship, they would be back down. A brief flutter of anticipation back in the fifties saw them miss out on top league football on goal difference, but limited finances, low capacity crowds and player morale which seemed to ebb and flow had held tight shackles on the club through recent decades. This afternoon, like their opponents, they would be scrapping for survival once again. Westward momentarily now had the all too familiar sensation of being totally out of his depth and how we wished he was back at home in the security and familiarity of his family home and in the arms of his beloved Abigail.

****

At three-thirty that afternoon, back in Woodmouth, Matt Westward turned the radio on in the kitchen of the Westward house to catch up on the latest scores. His heart sank as he listened to the report of the match so far.

"We now go over to Millmoor for the big relegation battle, Rotherham against Woodmouth, John Sykes has the news."

"Yes, Mike, and it's not good if you're a Woodmouth fan. Rotherham lead by two goals to nil. It's been a disastrous start for new player/manager Jordan Westward. On fourteen minutes he gave away a free kick on the edge of the box from which Rotherham scored their opener through Colin Robertson and he got booked for arguing over the referee's decision. Then three minutes later, he miscued a clearance of a corner and the ball sliced backwards past a helpless Eric Page in the Woodmouth goal. To be honest, for all the hype of the last week or so, there seems little change in the Woodmouth side. They still can't seem to string a series of passes together and haven't had a serious shot on target. Rotherham on the other hand look the more likely to take the points as Woodmouth look a long way away from making what would be only their second away win of the season. Both teams need the win but so far it's all Rotherham, they lead two-nothing."

Matt turned the radio off, with his arms folded and stared into space forlornly. In the lounge he could hear his brothers and sisters playing. As he slowly walked back to the noise of his siblings, he prayed.

Come on Dad, he willed.

****

The home side were totally in control and the same old demons began eating at Westward's heart, mind and confidence.

What do you honestly think that you're doing?

Who do you think that you are?

What makes you think that you are that special to God that you can turn this team around?

He began to take on the vacant, distracted look that he had had all too often in the past when he was in a position of self-inflicted stress – and the migraine was not helping.

"Hey boss!" Gustavsson yelled as he picked himself up from a tackle to clear a Rotherham attack, "You OK?"

Westward nodded briefly without making eye contact and slowly got up from the turf after his mistimed tackle had put pressure on the Dane. He shook his head to clear his mind and to focus back on the game. "You playing or what?" Gustavsson roared. At any other time he would have not tolerated such talk from a player but Westward knew his error and actually appreciated the rebuke.

He began to stay out of tackles that years ago he would have done without hesitation. His confidence with his passes began to fade. A forward pass changed to a side pass. A side pass turned to a back pass.

Then, the other voice spoke.

You can do all things through Christ.
You are more than a conqueror through Him who loves you.

Within a few minutes he was built up again. He so much wanted to take the man on top from Westward Technologies and bring him here to the football pitch, to be the motivator. The real Jordan Westward needed to take over. Many, many eyes were watching him, some whose hope had been instilled in him. Some, however, really wanted to see him fall.

Westward tried to rally his team but the defeated attitude prevailed as the referee blew the whistle for half time. The usual frustration showed on striker Paul Lincoln as he kicked the ball high into the crowd behind the goal and swore under his breath. He earned himself a booking for the waste of time and unsportsmanlike conduct.

Where is this new era that this guy promises? he thought to himself.

Lincoln had spent most of the first half having to come deep to be involved and had only had a couple of shots on goal, and those from distance. He had made up his mind that as the team was going to be demoted, he would leave the club. He felt that at 27 years old, he could still have a chance to prove himself at top flight football.

Westward was the first one off the pitch as he and the rest of the team faced the boos from the small band of supporters who had made the trip. The familiar sound of heavily trodden studs echoed as they entered the changing room. Each player sank, heavy-heartedly on to the bench where he had gotten changed earlier.

Westward stood in silence, back against the wall next to the door. Magnus Gustavsson was the first to speak.

"Do not be discouraged, guys. We may be behind, they may be creating more chances but I have a quiet confidence that we can do this thing. What do you say?"

"Also, well, I owe you all an apology because I have been a poor example," Westward prompted after a few seconds silence, as he looked around the room and wiped his mouth on his sleeve. "I have shown completely the wrong attitude and I'm sorry. I've got at least one player on my side. What about the rest of you?" He continued as he swigged from a paper cup of diluted orange squash. "You just gonna roll over, sulk and die?" He closed his eyes, the pain-killers beginning to wear off.

"Hey, Boss, you don't have a wife that you've got to go home and tell that you're getting a pay cut and next season you're taking her to the away games at Darlington and Rochdale," joked Clive Belkin exhibiting his sarcastic mood, "You know, I told my missus one day I'd fractured me ankle, man. All she said was 'oh, lame excuse'. Then one day, we was walking round that big Swedish furniture shop. I happened to pick up this odd looking draining board thing while she had her back to me. All I said was 'what do you reckon to this Rationnel Variera?' She turns round with this filthy look and says to me 'is that the guy that's just signed for Chelsea?' and then questions if I think about anything other than football?'

Several sniggered at the usual humour of the comical Geordie and this seemed to lighten the atmosphere but Westward was all too aware of his midfielder's disposition. Even Westward forced a smile as each player moved past him to take his turn at the drinks table.

"Honestly, boys, I really feel that this team are for the taking. All you must do is believe. Have you seen how weak their left-back is? Kevin," Westward pointed at the young right wing-back, "you can roast him! And perhaps then you can give Clive here a chance to do his job. Provided he hasn't gone walkabout to do Magnus' job." A couple of Ayres' team-mates nodded in agreement at Clive Belkin's nigh-on non-presence behind the strikers.

"And Rudi," Westward nodded towards Rudi Radzednic who looked up from his drink, "there is a huge space in the midfield where their left sided guys are committing themselves too much in attack. Get in there and push forward. We are not dead yet."

Westward stood in thought for a few minutes as he listened to the rest of the team in conversation before he broke in. "I know that you lot are not religious. Neither am I. But I love God and know that He has not led me to invest millions of pounds of my money to see this club go down. What do you say that we pray? Hmm?" A few of the players looked up with reluctant frowns on their faces, others simply shrugged their shoulders.

Then they turned their attention towards Brian Chambers who had just appeared in the doorway.

"I'm with you Jordan even if this bunch aren't. By the way, both Chesterfield and Oldham are 0-0 in their games," he smiled. Westward nodded and began as each man bowed his head in silence.

"Almighty God, we come before you as a team. We come before you with hearts uncertain of the future. We cannot even ask that you be on our side. Our prayer is that we are on your side. Impart to us a spirit of unity. One mind, one heart, one accord. Whatever the result, Lord, may we at least know that we gave it our all. Amen."

There was a tentative, mumbled amen as each man opened his eyes.

"Gentlemen, the others are coming out. Better go," Chambers swung a glance at the tunnel leading to the pitch. The players replaced their shin-guards and trudged outside. As they ambled to their positions, again they faced the ridicule from their supporters as the Rotherham fans began to chant with whole-hearted intimidation.

"You're going down! How does it feel?"

"Come on!" Westward roared as he scanned the team and clapped his hands and shook his fist with a gritted face of determination. The whistle was blown and Woodmouth kicked off. Rotherham at first seemed to be content to sit deep and protect their two goal advantage but ten minutes into the half, Woodmouth at last began to click. Chris Haynes played a square ball to Kevin Ayres on the right. Straight away he took a chance and sprinted past the Rotherham left-back. He got to the by-line just as a central-defender came sliding in. He dummied back, crossed with his weaker left foot, and watched as the ball arched to the far post where Paul Lincoln rose above his marker only to see his header cannon off the post and out of play. Lincoln and Ayres caught eye contact, nodded and applauded their mutual appreciation.

Rotherham began an attack only to see a pass go astray into the path of Clive Belkin who, with a quick glance, put Ayres away once more, wide on the right. This time his first time cross was low, cleared by a defender out to the oncoming Radzednic whose half-volley was only inches over the crossbar.

Woodmouth were soaring and confidence began to flow through them. For the opening fifteen minutes, the ball was 70% in the Rotherham half.

Then it happened. The breakthrough.

Belkin, Radzednic and Chris Haynes played some neat one touch passes before Bruce Dean found space on the left. He slotted a square ball for Lincoln to latch on to just inside the Rotherham goal area but just as he brought his right foot back to shoot, Rotherham central-Defender Xavier Blanc clumsily made a tackle which immediately prompted the referee to blow the whistle and point to the penalty spot. The small band of Woodmouth fans behind the goal joyfully jumped up and down and frantically waved their scarves.

Several Rotherham players made a fruitless attempt in protest but eventually the area was cleared allowing Rudi Radzednic, Woodmouth's usual penalty taker to go through the motions of preparing. He placed the ball a few inches to the left of the small hole that had appeared during the course of the season, twelve yards from the goal. He paid careful attention not to look at the goalkeeper at all, remembering what Westward had explained about penalty-taking.

Radzednic, out of the corner of his eye noticed the giant six foot three Rotherham keeper, who stood, legs apart, arms wide open. He was the only thing between him and pulling a goal back. Radzednic looked down at the ball and drew a few steps back, keeping his eye on the ball all the time. He noticed the goalkeeper shuffling around, bouncing on the spot. Westward turned away, not wishing to look. Radzednic began his run, eyes on the ball, head down. He hit the ball perfectly, it remained two feet off the ground as it travelled several inches out of the reach of the despairing dive of the goalkeeper. A few seconds later, the cheers and quiet song amongst the silence of the Rotherham fans behind the goal indicated to Westward that Radzednic had scored.

Joy. Hope. A chance.

Five minutes later, Woodmouth were level. Given a free-kick, just to the right of the goal area, twenty five yards out was perfect position for long range specialist Kevin Ayres. Westward and Martin Haynes moved up to add height to the Woodmouth attack, but Ayres' free-kick was perfectly placed over everybody, including the unsuspecting Rotherham goalkeeper. The ball hit the post, bounced back into play only to deflect straight over the line off an unfortunately placed defender's back. As the players ran back to their half for the re-take, smiles began to break out. Westward looked around, punched the air as if to say *we can do this*.

With sixteen minutes left, Westward brought off Belkin who in the second half had given his all, but knew his strength was ebbing away. David Somerby, a more defensively minded midfielder came on to add steel next to Gustavsson. Westward was more than fatigued himself but he knew that if he was to go off at this stage, it would have meant a whole team re-shuffle when they were beginning to show the connectivity that he had hoped for.

Somerby was immediately in the thick of things. Once again, Kevin Ayres was the target for a long, low pass. He took the ball in his stride, ran forward twenty yards. His low cross caught everyone out as it went behind the defenders, a few yards from goal at the far post. Westward himself, to the absolute shock of everyone, including his own players, arrived like a baseball player sliding into first base and connected with the ball with his outstretched left foot.

The keeper was totally wrong-footed as he could only stand and watch the ball hit the back of the net. Westward jogged back, hand raised in salute to the fans who were by now nothing short of ecstatic. It seemed the impossible had happened. Just minutes later, the final whistle was blown as every Woodmouth player jumped, arms aloft in recognition of the result.

That was all but Westward.

He simply bent over and took a deep breath in the hope that we would not vomit the contents of his stomach onto the pitch. Those near enough to a team mate hugged each other before the entire team jogged towards their supporters behind the goal where they had scored three times, more than they had done in their last five matches together. They stood in line and clapped raised hands in thanks for their loyalty.

Westward, through half-closed eyes, allowed himself a quiet smile as he glanced through exhaustion and pain at Radzednic next to him. He himself nodded and beamed in delight.

"We can do this boss, we can do this!"

The Rotherham players meanwhile stood a while, hands on hips, staring at the ground, wondering how they had let a two goal lead disappear. A few minutes past before taking their dejected hearts towards the tunnel encompassed by boos.

Woodmouth eventually left the pitch with the tinny strains of a currently charted pop song straining out over the public address system. Magnus Gustavsson strode over to his manager. All he did was pat his manager's back as he past. Westward looked ahead, squinting through the migraine as Gustavsson just looked back and winked. Gustavsson, although four years Westward's junior, with no words but a minor physical contact, kept him afloat in a sea of momentary doubt. Westward knew that here was a leader.

Later, as the coach pulled out of the Millmoor ground and made the way back to Woodmouth there was a joy that had not been around for many weeks. Westward put his head back against a headrest and closed his eyes, he silently spoke a prayer of thanks to God. He once again took in the conversations around him and the laughter. There was still a chance. But he could really do without another headache like this on a match day. And he knew that he had to get much, much fitter than he was.

****

The following Monday afternoon, Westward sat and read the report prepared by an anonymous person on his own performance.

Overall team work 90%.
Boldness and confidence 90%.
Creativity 70%.
Alertness 55%.
Care 60%.
Decisiveness 75%.
Dependability 70%.
Efficiency 65%.
Energy 40%.
Industry 60%.
Leadership 70%.

Responsibility 90%.
Skill-level 50%.
Discipline 50%.
Adaptability 65%.
Co-operation 80%.
Enthusiasm 85%.
Fairness/honesty 80%.
Respect 80%.

He was well aware of his weaknesses and had to work out a plan to combat them. The last thing he wanted was for fingers to be pointed at him regarding the very things that he was trying to instil in the other players.

****

"Of all the guys I have played with, Jordan Westward has to be the most enthusiastic. He never let his age or ability get in the way. Despite being ten, fifteen years older than most of us, he gave everything. A true professional."

Max Oswald,
Wing-back,
Woodmouth Albion.

Chapter 9

Prior to home match vs Leeds United, the following Saturday.

SAM KINDRED, A FEW MONTHS past his sixteenth birthday, once again trudged heavily homeward from yet another failed interview for employment. As he made his way despondently to the convenience store on the corner of Alpine Drive, a few neighbours made sarcastic and cutting comments about his vain attempt to look smart, his hidden brokenness exhibited in the foul language in response. He had tried, he had reasoned with himself. His mother had not been present at home for several days, therefore his clothes had not been washed. His best attempt for the interview was a blue shirt with a red and yellow diagonally striped tie borrowed from his mother's new partner's pile of clothes in their bedroom.

His appearance had not been aided by cream trousers from the dirty washing basket, still arrayed with stains from a chinese take-away. The fact that he had the mother of all hang-overs from the night before and therefore was not adequately mentally prepared for the questions, had not helped his situation.

He thought back to having been dismissed from his first position with a local insurance company six weeks previous.

Maybe, he thought to himself, *I shouldn't have been such a jerk.*

He had since found it very difficult to find worthwhile work in the local area. Even though buses from his housing estate were regularly ferrying residents to the centre of Woodmouth, he now had to deal with the ban from travelling with the bus company for sparking a fight on the number twenty-six coming home from his previous job. He was therefore restricted to walking or hitch-hiking the three or so miles to town's central business hub.

He stubbed his cigarette out under his scuffed black boots and entered the shop, pushing open the door and belligerently and angrily shoving his way past a hunched, short lady in her seventies. The lady simply tutted and continued her pained journey home.

"Hiya Sam," an over made-up skinny girl in her late teens greeted as she counted out change for the customer ahead of him. The tall, thick moustached man in a red and black lumberjack shirt and baseball cap nodded in acknowledgement and departed.

"You alright, Chas?" he gloomily responded.

Charlotte Simmons leaned over the pile of magazines waiting to be sorted, her immodest vest a distraction that Kindred was not slow to notice. She blew her straightened brown fringe out of her eyes as she turned to pull down Kindred's brand of cigarettes.

"So whose funeral you been to today?" she derided, sensing his unhappy state of mind.

He tried a smile. "Another interview. No good though," he replied, slapping a five pound note onto the counter.

"Something'll turn up, don't worry."

He sighed, taking the cigarettes. "It sure needs to. I'm one of the line that stretches from London to Edinburgh. That's how many young people are out of a job. And I need some money for Big Stu."

Charlotte's eyes widened in horror. "You never borrowed from him, did you?"

"Yep."

"Why? He's an absolute crook! If you don't pay him, he can get really nasty, so I've heard."

"That's what worries me."

"What do you owe him?"

Kindred turned away to cough coarsely before grimacing at the chest pain. "Two hundred quid," he wheezed.

Charlotte noticed a middle aged woman down the centre aisle. "If you're looking for bread, it's not in yet. Try this afternoon." The woman waved and moved on. Charlotte moved in close to whisper. "Two hundred? Are you totally insane or just well on the way?"

"Makes you wonder, doesn't it?" he responded with a resigned grin.

"So, how you gonna pay him back and when do you have to?"

"He wants fifty this weekend. You due a fag break?"

"Yeah, can do. I'll just tell Ahmed," she replied, glancing behind at the clock above the doorway to the back of the shop.

She shortly returned, grabbed her thin, pink cardigan and followed Kindred out of the shop. The sun caused a brief squint as they adjusted to its presence as a brief breeze blew past them, the lighting of a cigarettes taking several attempts of Charlotte's lighter.

Kindred took a long draw from the cigarette and blew the smoke straight up, watching it dissipate in the air. A young mother, no more than Charlotte's age pushed her two year-old child in a buggy, pushed it into the shop as Charlotte held the door open.

"You seen your Mum at all?" Charlotte enquired kindly.

Kindred took another drag, shaking his head. "No, she seems to appear for a few days with this new bloke of hers then I don't see her for ages. Probably round his place, I suppose."

Charlotte could sense the loneliness of the young man. Should she tell him now of her new life? Could she risk the potential rejection?

"You ever been to church, Sam?"

He looked at her in disbelief. "You what?"

"I mean, have you ever thought about God and stuff?"

"You're not going all religious on me are you?" he scoffed.

She smiled. "No, not really, it's just that.....well....last Sunday

I went to that new church opposite the park in the Community Hall. It was really different. People seemed different. No old people just singing along to an organ, you know, it was quite fun. They had a real band. I'm going back next week. Do you fancy coming? They have a special meeting on Sunday afternoons for young people especially." Knowing Sam's love for football, she added, "Funnily enough, guess who the speaker was?"

Kindred lowered his head and pulled a face as he rubbed his aching head. "The Prime Minister for all I care." He looked down at the chewing gum marks on the pavement and scraped his heels. "Who?"

"That new Woodmouth manager? Jordan Westward?"

"You what?" he smirked with clear unkindness. "Listen, I can't see him saving the club from relegation, let alone saving your soul. No thanks. I'm hoping to get a ticket for the football, for what it's worth though. Home to Leeds. A Sunday game for a change. Must be on TV."

Charlotte sighed inwardly. She wanted to reach out to him with the new found love from God that she herself was becoming accustomed to. "Maybe next week, eh? Maybe God can help you."

Kindred scoffed, shaking his head. "Don't think so. Why should God care about me? No, its not for me," he replied disinterestedly. He dropped his cigarette butt and twisted his boot to extinguish it. "Chip shop's open. I'm hungry. Anyway, when do you finish?" He stretched and yawned.

"What did you have in mind?"

Kindred raised his eyebrows, the impertinence of his grin not lost on his companion. "Well, haven't seen you for a while, how about some time together – if you know what I mean?"

Charlotte shuffled uncomfortably, unable to now look Kindred in the eye.

She stubbed her cigarette out against the wall of the shop and allowed it to drop to the floor, smoke still faintly rising.

"Man, I've got to stop those things." She sighed and folded her arms defensively. "Look, listen Sam, I don't know how to tell you this but I'm not the person I used to be. I mean, I don't do some of the things that I used to do. What I mean is, well, you know, what you meant about this afternoon, but, well, I -"

Kindred turned in anger. "Well listen to you, Miss all-high-and-mighty," he growled, his antipathy for her all of a sudden like that of an unkind King passing a tramp. "Since when did you become all self-righteous? You're a tart, Chas, a tart, and you always will be. You can't change. You never will."

Charlotte managed to hold back her tears as she bit her lip.

"Sam – I met with God last week. He is real."

"Well if he is, why does He not sort my life out, eh?" he derided.

"Sam, He will – you just won't let Him."

"What – give up booze, fags, football, girls and all that for someone who you can't see and who doesn't care anyway? Sounds a fun life to me," he retorted sarcastically.

"It's not like that!" she pleaded. "Jesus is a real person and He rose from the dead. He died for me and you. We have to invite Him into our lives!"

"Jesus - wow, you really have flipped," he gibed, turning his back to walk away.

"Sam, I -"

Charlotte allowed him to get to the end of the road before screaming at the top of her voice. "JESUS LOVES YOU, SAM!"

All she received in return was an obscene hand gesture.

****

League Table:
Bottom of Championship

Team	Pyd	Pts	GD
Brighton	44	53	-13
Chesterfield	44	46	-11
Woodmouth	44	46	-17
Oldham	44	44	-14
Rotherham	44	39	-27

Westward once again re-ran the final ten minutes of the first half of Leeds' 3-1 win at home to Hull the previous weekend. He had noticed that they rarely used the wings and tried to keep possession in the centre of the pitch. That gave him an idea.

He would drop Clive Belkin back alongside Magnus Gust-avsson to block the central attacks. He would hold the wing-backs more defensively, and attack on the break. If Leeds do not score, Woodmouth would not lose. He would hope for a goal on the breakaway. It would not be exciting football, but at this stage of proceedings, he reasoned that the result was more important than the performance.

He scribbled down his final team as the tape ran:

Page,
Haynes, Westward, Somerton,
Ayres, Gustavsson, Belkin, Dean,
Radzednic,
Haynes, Lincoln.

Hull, safe in mid-table, had offered little in midfield, where Leeds gratefully dominated the game from start to finish. Westward reasoned that Hull's line-up was predictable: Flat back four, two wide players who rarely tried to push past the full-backs, two attacking midfielders and two strikers, one a standard, big, hulking centre-forward in the traditional style, the other a skinny but quick guy who played alongside him.

From the moment the second Leeds goal went in just before half-time, the match as a contest was over.

Westward pressed the stop button on the remote control and leaned backwards, running his hands through his hair. It was the ultimate make or break game. He also had to prepare another message for the new church on the Chartwell Estate for the following Monday evening. It had been awesome to see troubled young people respond to the Gospel. Despite the pressure upon him, the club and his family, life was good. He felt slightly fitter, albeit fatigued.

There was a long way to go to the Premier League though.

****

Friday evening arrived and Kindred was in a foul mood. Despite Charlotte's rejection, he had found nearly a hundred pounds in cash hidden underneath his Mum's bed mattress. He paid Big

Stu and had enough for a few beers after the Woodmouth game for which he could now pay for a ticket.

He stuffed the remaining money into his back pocket and walked through the rain to the run down pub on the corner of his road. He glanced at his watch. Eight o'clock. He had money for beer and football and a smoke for later. Who needed a job?

And who certainly needed God?

****

National press, Sunday morning, following the game.

WOODMOUTH PAY THE PENALTY.

Woodmouth Albion 1 Leeds United 1

Just sixty seconds stood between Jordan Westward's new look team taking a giant leap towards Championship survival. Sixty seconds that saw a cruel blow to their efforts when for the previous 89 minutes they had played with the hearts of a team that believed in themselves. Disparaged, ridiculed and, from this performance, unfairly labelled as a villain, Westward led from the back with steel with the prospect of their first clean sheet for seven games and that against the Champions elect Leeds. Sadly, no one could have expected the cruel sting in the tail that came in the guise of a dubious penalty which gave Leeds what most would have said was an undeserved point. Coupled with the violent run-ins between the rival supporters after the game, player/manager Westward will now have more than just the last game of the season on his mind. Fortunately, the police presence during the game was enough to keep the supporters apart but the ugly scenes outside the ground and up and down the Woodmouth high street, could signal long-term repercussions for this already troubled club. It is likely that the Football Association will ban all Wood-mouth supporters from at least next week's final game of the season at Chesterfield and a substantial fine for failing to control their supporters would be added to their woes.

Woodmouth were unchanged from the week before, so once again no Gerhard Messen, but showed that they have the foundation for future entertaining, attacking football along with the balance of a much more solid defence than they had showed for many months.

Leeds started brightly forcing a number of shots on target in the first fifteen minutes from ace strike force James Hutton and David Hartley, who were both eager to add to their collective tally of over forty goals between themselves this season. Hutton himself was denied as early as third minute as he slipped past Martin Haynes to fire straight at the approaching Eric Page's knees. Woodmouth however showed resourcefulness and withstood the early storm. Magnus Gustavsson looked confident and composed in his new holding midfield role for Woodmouth, Chris Haynes looked bright up front and Rudi Radzednic looks like he has a new lease of life in his new central midfield role. In fact, the little Pole carved Woodmouth's first chance after twenty minutes. His neat one-two with Clive Belkin left him with enough time and room to pick out Paul Lincoln at the far post, but his header was only marginally wide as Leeds defender Alan Milton did enough to put him off balance. It served to build confidence into the home side and for the rest of the first half, they maintained the upper hand. Chris Haynes and Paul Lincoln proved a handful for the Leeds defence and they were given tremendous support from the attacking attitude taken by the Woodmouth midfielders.

The second half began as the first did - all Leeds - but the Woodmouth defence, marshalled well by Gustavsson, withstood everything that was thrown at them. Then after sixty-five minutes, Radzednic, once again the play-maker, produced one delightful moment of magic to put Woodmouth deservedly ahead. Having shuffled one way, then the other in front of Leeds hard man Paul Taylor, thirty yards from goal, Radzednic got half a yard from his marker, scooped a mesmerising chip with his left foot over the top of the Leeds defence which all ran forward in effort to catch the Woodmouth strikers offside. Radzednic continued his run, rounded Graham

Fraser in the Leeds goal and scored a truly memorable, and for Woodmouth, priceless goal.

Leeds, champions bar a mathematical disaster, had no real need to put themselves out, apart from pride, took Hartley off with ten minutes left and put Philip Young on as an extra midfielder. With the Woodmouth contingent of the near 16,000 crowd cheering in delight at the potential three points, Westward in his own area was adjudged to have handled the ball when he was in the way from a shot by Taylor. Westward showed once again the volatile side of his cause for justice in remonstrating his opinion to referee Dennis Whitworth of his decision and was booked for the second successive match as was Martin Haynes. James Hutton stepped up and despite guessing the correct way, Eric Page in the Woodmouth goal was inches short of pulling off what would have been a memorable save.

Woodmouth can take great heart from this performance, but with an away victory required at fellow strugglers Chesterfield next Saturday, it may be too little too late, especially with the possibility of playing with no supporters present.

✳✳✳✳✳✳✳✳✳✳✳✳✳✳✳✳

The previous afternoon

Sam Kindred, along with two other inadequate youths, Paul Weston and Nick Rogers, filed their way with the throng exiting the stadium towards the main road.

"Man, I am so gutted. I can't believe we were that close to winning!" Weston demonstrated.

Kindred lit a cigarette as his attention was caught by a group of Leeds supporters a number of yards to his left. Between them a larger than average contingent of police, albeit still inadequate, along with several rows of parked cars, made a wall. The group began chanting their songs in an effort to rile the home supporters. Almost immediately, a crowd of angry fans ran at the police, pushed through and began attacking the Leeds fans. The police who did manage to stand on their feet began clubbing anyone in the vicinity with batons. Several fans fell to the ground clutching their heads, arms or legs or whatever the police were able to make contact with. Kindred, Weston and Rogers stopped and stared, aghast. Nearest to them, but still a way off, they saw the anger in the faces of the Woodmouth fans as they smashed their way with all their strength through to the Leeds fans. A further group of home supporters stopped and looked on in disbelief while others chose to ignore the fracas and swiftly continued on their journey home.

Kindred smirked at his two friends, dropping the cigarette. "What do you reckon? Fancy a ruck?"

Weston and Rogers' eye contact was less than enthusiastic.

"Come on, you wimps!" Kindred screamed as he ran off, hoping for them to follow. Within seconds, he was lost in the crowd, the police dogs' barking not dispelling Kindred's courage. The first person he made contact with was a policeman, several inches taller than himself. He knocked off his helmet and laid as hard a punch to the officer's nose as he could. The officer, caught off guard, spun as blood began to pour. Kindred followed up with a kick to the back of the officer's knee, albeit in a limited space. It still caused the uniformed man to buckle and fall to the floor. Kindred added two forceful kicks to the man's head and, satisfied that he was one less to stop him, lunged headlong into the melee. He was unfortunately hit by accident by a flying fist from a Leeds fan which further enraged him. He went in, all fists and legs, making contact with anyone - it didn't matter. It was just the thrill of the fight that spurred him on. Within minutes he was a blooded and bruised mess, out of breath and hobbling away.

Two police officers, newly on the scene ran towards him lashing out with their batons momentarily before moving on to the crowd. He held the back of his head in pain as he fell to his knees. As fast as he could scramble away, he left the scene and sat on the wall, well away from the disturbance. Within a few minutes, a few other Woodmouth fans joined him.

"Flipping heck!" one exclaimed, laughing heartily, despite his injuries.

Another swore several times within the space of two sentences.

"I know several of the Leeds blokes are not making their way to the train station – they're heading for town. It's not over yet."

"What shall we do?"

Kindred closed his eyes in an effort to appease the pain rampaging through his head. "I'm in. What you gonna do?"

"I saw some of them with knives and all sorts – it might be a bit nasty. Are you sure we should?" another fearfully questioned.

"Don't wimp out now – where's your loyalty?"

"Look, my life is actually worth something at the moment. I'm going home."

"I got nothing to lose," Kindred shrugged, "when you going, where you meeting?"

"Big Stu is coming down. Said he's bringing some bottles for cocktails."

Kindred's eyes widened. "Big Stu? From the Estate?"

"Yeah – do you know him?"

"Yeah, I do. How do you know him?" Kindred replied, excitedly.

The stranger shook his head. "Never met him, I just know he likes a good ruck."

That fired Kindred up.

This would really impress Big Stu.

The small group made their way as discreetly as they could, despite their blooded countenance. They chose a longer but quieter way away from the scene which, as time went on, the police seemed to have under control. Two hours later, it was a different story in Woodmouth's town centre. For the most, a totally inadequate band of police officers could only watch on at the running battle between rival fans. Molotov cocktails were swapped from the protection between over-turned cars, some of which now burned ferociously. Shop windows smashed and the odour of burning petrol hung heavy in the air as flames rose higher to complete the almost dystopian environment.

Like the promise of a cavalry on a bygone battlefield, riot police with shields were drafted in to separate the fans. The whirling of squad cars and ambulances completed the scene as they screeched to a halt close by.

As the shielded and helmeted police slowly moved in an orderly line towards the Leeds fans, those fortunate enough to have been served in Woodmouth's pubs in the locality threw their glasses, full or otherwise, each smashing against the shields. A unison of voices began to chant "if you hate the Old Bill, clap your hands," followed by a huge cheer as one individual, full of alcohol and bravado, ran and high kicked one of the shielded police to be instantly set upon by three officers as the rest continued on. The individual had both his arms roughly driven behind his back to be cuffed and dragged away, kicking and screaming as best as he could. A tazer to his neck stopped any further resistance.

Kindred, crouched and hid behind a large refuse bin next to the department store in the pedestrian precinct, long since alone having lost contact with those whom he followed to the town centre. He took his hand away from the wound in his right side and was shocked at the huge stain on his shirt caused by the still flowing blood which covered his hand. He was no longer interested in the battle, his bravado long gone – he just wanted to get away. He was continuously shivering, the drop in the spring temperature more than his thin jacket could protect him from. The loss of blood was certainly not helping.

He watched as the air was filled with chanting, crude singing, glass breaking and the explosion of yet another car bursting into flames. The supply of beer glasses for ammunition had now been replaced by ashtrays, the police shields still more than a match for the implements. Within a few minutes, the mob became aware that their time of offence was coming to an end. They regrouped and began to run towards the bottom of the high street and along the waterfront. The police followed in hot pursuit.

As the Leeds fans charged away towards the other train station at the East end of town to catch the late Football Express, the violence eventually dissipated, but the final statistics told a horrific story. Twenty-nine arrests, sixty injuries, thousands of pounds worth of damage to shops and pubs. But worst of all, three deaths. Kindred escaped being the fourth as he was discovered, unconscious, purely by chance, an hour later.

****

Later that evening, back in the comfort of his home several

miles away, Westward watched in horror as the news captured the drama of the night's battles. He shook his head in disbelief and wondered about the backlash that the club could expect.He, like the rest of the country, had long believed that football hooliganism had long since left the United Kingdom. The Football Association, he thought to himself, was not concerned with who started the fight, who ended it or indeed how it started or ended – all they would want is retribution in some way to satisfy the public and make them look like they were in charge.

Westward considered how the F A had handled similar events in the past. Always, in recent years, it seemed that in their own inimitable way of being unable to control this behaviour, a fine administered to the home team was the answer and to clearly dump the blame on them. Claim a large amount of money and tell the club 'you fix the problem'.

That's never going to work, he resigned.

The next day it was confirmed that Woodmouth would play at Chesterfield the following Saturday with none of their own supporters present and be subject to a fine of a hundred thousand pounds for failing to control their supporters. Leeds United had been fined a mere fifty thousand pounds.

****

Final match of the season, away vs Chesterfield.

Westward sighed as he once again took a sideways glance at the clock on his bedside table once again. Two-fifteen. An hour had passed and he was still unable to break the present, consuming curse of insomnia. He turned to his wife, blissfully at peace, small breaths visible from her mouth every now and then. He carefully sat up, trying not to disturb her, blinked several times and rubbed his eyes. He took his dressing gown from the back of the bedroom door as the light from the landing filled the bedroom momentarily as he quietly made his way towards the staircase.

As he slipped into the eerie quiet of the lounge, he flicked on a standard lamp behind one of the couches, flopped down and reached for his Bible. He closed his eyes and silently prayed.

"Heavenly Father, right now I cry out to you for assurance. I am afraid. No one else knows. I confess that I share nothing of my concerns with any other person. Only you know and only you need to know. I know you have called me to this task and I feel so inadequate. Right now, the players need leadership. Lord, I feel like Joshua must have done when he took over from Moses. I am overwhelmed. My resources seem not enough and our task virtually impossible. But Lord, I know that nothing is impossible with you. All things are possible to those who believe. Help my unbelief, Lord. Grant me your assurance in this situation. In Christ's name, amen."

Westward simply sat in silence, his face in his hands for a few moments as he waited on the presence of God. Then a simple word came into his spirit.

Isaiah.

He opened his eyes with a start. It was clear - he knew the voice of God, but how could a single word be the answer to his prayer? He looked at his Bible and noticed a piece of paper that was not normally there. He frowned and opened the Bible where the piece of paper poked over the top of the pages. It was Isaiah 41. He examined the slither of paper, an inch or so wide, six inches long, torn carelessly at the top and bottom. On the paper was simply hand-written text in writing he did not recognise. It said "Isaiah 41:10. Thanks from John."

How could that piece of paper have gotten in my Bible at that exact place?

He already knew the verse, but ran his finger down the text in his Bible until he found the verse. "Fear thou not; for I am with thee: be not dismayed; for I am thy God: I will strengthen thee; yea, I will help thee; yea, I will uphold thee with the right hand of my righteousness".

As Westward closed his eyes, he felt the peace of God's Spirit flood his soul. A solitary tear made its salty journey down his cheek as he once again was taken aback by the love of God.

I will uphold thee.

Some people had judged and condemned him for reading the Bible like he did. 'The Bible isn't a magic book!' they would say, 'You can't just make it say things that it really doesn't say just to suit your circumstances.'

But he was reminded once again by the Holy Spirit that in Romans 8 there is now no condemnation and that if he was led by the Spirit of God, he was His son.

He sat in silent thanks as he wiped his cheek. He was still amazed that of all the places that he could have slipped the piece of paper, it would have been in the exact place of the text. John, Westward remembered, had been a worker in the local supermarket with whom he had had an encouraging conversation. He had scribbled the words and since the visit, Westward had completely forgotten to check the note. Until now – when it had given the ultimate in confirmation that he had needed.

He returned momentarily to his thankful prayer and praise. When his fears had been appeased he returned to his bed. The clock turned, as he watched, to three o'clock. Within minutes of resting his head on his pillow, he slipped peacefully into deep, restful sleep.

God was in control.

****

Pre-match article by Jamie Southport, football reporter, Woodmouth Gazette.

JORDAN'S CRUNCH

Team	Pyd	Pts	GD
Brighton	45	56	-11
Chesterfield	45	47	-12
Woodmouth	45	47	-17
Oldham	45	44	-15 **
Rotherham	45	39	-29 **

(** Already relegated.)

Three weeks ago, no-one including this writer, would have ventured their money on a bet in favour of Wood-mouth surviving for another season in the Champion-ship, but how time can prove sceptics wrong. The club have gone from the edge of extinction to a very real possibility of continuing their enjoyment of that particular League status for another season. Their task is clear, but far from simple: take all three points at Chesterfield on Saturday afternoon. A draw will be inadequate. Defeat, unthinkable.

There is no doubt that new coach Jordan Westward has instilled new life and hope in an ailing side, but even he recognises that their task is an uphill one. A lucky 3-2 win at Rotherham, after being 2-0 down was perhaps worthy of greater reward than a mere three points and an extra goal off of their negative goal difference, despite the fact that even their own players will admit that their defensive frailties still need attention. The club have conceded a record 68 goals this season – only Rotherham at the bottom have picked the ball from their own net more times.

"Three points from the match at Rotherham was our goal and I am delighted with the hope that Jordan has injected into the club," assistant coach Brian Chambers enthused with a rare smile. "Jordan is a man used to getting results and he has proved that whether he is in a business deal or on a football pitch, he is much the same man. Naturally, everyone was disappointed with events on and off the field against Leeds."

"Some fans have made it clear that they felt that Jordan was not going to be up to the rigours of a Championship level football. As for Jordan's performances, taking into account his age and recent experience, he has shown his potential to do his job."

"The lads have shown great character over the last couple of weeks. There is still belief here. We recognise that scoring goals is also an issue but we must more than anything tighten up on our defence," Westward commented yesterday at the club's ground. "It was tough on us all to concede the late goal last week against Leeds and to make it even harder, Chesterfield's late winner was also a harshly awarded penalty. If things had gone our way, we could now be sitting two points ahead of Chesterfield with just a draw needed. But, it seems God wants to take things to the wire. We will simply just have to give it

everything we have next weekend."

It is true to say that there were many critics a few weeks ago when Westward announced his first side. Messen dropped, Haynes, Gustavsson and Radzednic having to get used to new positions and the entire team adjusting to a whole new playing system sounded like too tall an order to take on board but four points out of six shows that there is potential, albeit late in the season.

Woodmouth are likely to be unchanged for the third successive match since Westward took over. This means that Gerhard Messen, Woodmouth's record signing ago, will once again be left out of the squad. There have been rumours that he has had a number of run-ins with Westward and that their relationship is potentially beyond repair. It is certain that he, along with several of the Woodmouth key players will depart from the club at the end of the season. Westward remains confident despite this eventuality.

"Gerhard knows that his skills are not consistent with the style of play that we wish to adopt here. We have spoken at length and Brian (Chambers) and I respect that he wants first team football. With this in mind, we wish him every success in whatever direction he chooses to take."

Chesterfield welcome back captain Michael Willis to the heart of their midfield. He replaces Gary Turner who drops to the bench. Winger Tony Hampton failed a fitness test yesterday on his Achilles injury. His place is taken by youngster Wayne Carter. Striker James Hurley keeps his place despite having gone 11 games without finding the net and he will be partnered by Lee Vincent, playing the penultimate game of his loan from Gillingham. He has found his name on the score sheet two games on the trot, scoring the winners at Derby and at home to Sheffield Wednesday last week. Let us not forget the wealth of experience on offer from former Egyptian international Coshi and ex-England midfielder Andy Crawford. Between them this season they have scored plenty of goals and assisted in more than half that they have not netted personally.

Ninety minutes stand between ultimately success or

failure for Jordan Westward's efforts. Any further ambitions that he may have for the club will certainly be weighed in the balance according to their result on Saturday afternoon.

Woodmouth:

Page
Haynes, Westward, Somerton
Ayres, Gustavsson, Belkin, Dean
Radzednic
Haynes, Lincoln

Chesterfield:

Gordon
Lea, Shaw, Bradbury, Pearson
Carter, Coshi, Willis, Crawford
Hurley, Vincent.

****

Westward called in the squad. He remained standing as the rest sat on season-thinned grass at the training ground beneath the warm caress of a late morning spring sun. He read the comments from the Gazette, highlighting a few words that he himself had been quoted. He folded the paper, tossed it on the ground in front of him.

"Well, listen up. We have ninety minutes to score more goals than they do to see phase one of this club's revival coming to pass. I know that several weeks ago, a draw from this game, away from home, would have been a point gained. Tomorrow is very different – one point will not be enough. Now, I am not going to kid you into thinking that you are a better team than Chesterfield – to be honest, at the moment, you are not. In twelve months time, it may be a different story but whatever happens tomorrow, we will not be playing this team next season. If we win, they go down. If we draw or lose, we go down, it's that simple."

He paused, folded his arms and looked around at the squad before continuing.

"Last week, we lost two points because of my stupidity in

giving away that penalty. I totally screwed up. If we had gained all three points against Leeds, all we would have needed tomorrow was avoid defeat. I am sorry. But I will re-iterate this – you all played well. You showed character – that is what we are after. Giving your best. Now I was praying last night -,"

A few groans once again arose from the squad to which he paused, sighed deeply and sternly looked around.

"As I was saying," he steadfastly confirmed, "I was praying last night. I believe God spoke to me. Isaiah 41 verse 10. Understand this – if we do not stay up, God is a liar. If we do, He needs to be glorified. Do you all understand? It is not a matter of luck. If you give glory to God, like I will, and some of you others as well, He will take care of you." He paused again, waiting for any comment. It came from Ray Somerton, veteran central defender.

"Boss, how can you be so sure about this? I don't believe in God. Never have done, never will."

Westward looked around, as if for inspiration to gain allegiance from his fellow defender. "Let me offer you something, even more than what was offered when I first took over. Can I ask one thing from you all? One thing. That you pour your heart and soul into this game as if your very lives – and those of your families – depend on it. If you give less than that, we do not deserve to be in any division on a professional basis. Please, give it your all, leave the rest to God. Do you know that my Saviour Jesus said that he did great things, but greater things we - that's Christians - will do, because He went to be with the Father."

Paul Lincoln raised a hand to which Westward nodded.

"Boss, you talk about God, but isn't this Egyptian guy, what's his name?"

"Coshi."

"Yeah, that's him. Isn't he praying to his god for favour as well?"

Westward smiled. "Does his god offer eternal life, free of charge, to those who have faith in him? Does he uncond-itionally love people, even when they still fall short? Did his god make a decision to open his arms to anyone that would trust him – even when they were unworthy of his attention? is he compassionate, loving, caring and has a heart to bless people and have a living relationship with them?"

Lincoln shrugged. "Well, no, not from what I have seen, no. Look around the world, it just seems religion causes more wars than solves them."

"Who here," Westward asked as he slowly circled the group, "has heard of the story of Elijah and the Prophets of Baal?"

A few nodded, a few looked at each other and shrugged, confused.

"Well, let me tell you. Elijah was the prophet of God during a time in Israel's history when God's people had gone into idolatry and began shambolic sacrifices. What was worse was that some people were doing them to God Himself and others were doing them to the false gods. Elijah offered a challenge to them at a place called Mount Carmel. He invited a whole bunch of these false prophets and said that both they and himself would make an altar and put an offering on it. He said to the Israelites, basically, it was time to stop messing about and sitting on what was in fact a very shaky fence. They needed to make a decision. Either show allegiance to the God of Israel or to Baal. He said that they should call out to Baal, and he would call out to God. Whoever showed up with fire, then they would be the one true God. He sure put himself on the spot a bit. Anyway, the false prophets went about their dealings and nothing happened. In the end, Elijah said it was his turn. He stuck his beast on the altar, but, just to make sure that a miracle was going to happen, he absolutely soaked the animal with buckets of water – must have met with a few horrified comments seeing as it was a time of drought. Then, he prays from his heart for God to glorify His own name. You can guess what happens – flames from Heaven consume the sacrifice and God was proven to be the Lord."

Amongst the squad, murmurs of 'Wow, never head that before' went around.

Westward concluded, before sitting down again. "All I am asking is for you to give it your all. But, we still have practicalities to deal with. My main concern is that we are still giving the ball away too much. With a 3-5-2 formation, we must, must, must keep possession. Short, quick passes, running off the ball. No long balls down the middle hoping some big man is going to get the ball. That way of playing will no longer work. Now, we also must look at the dangers that Chesterfield have. Coshi is one of them, as we have mentioned. He may now be thirty-five, but who remembers him two World Cups ago? He got Egypt to the semi-finals. They won all three of their group games, including one against Holland which was no mean feat. 0-0 against Italy wasn't bad and, OK, a penalty shoot out is not a sure display of a team's potential for ninety minutes, but nevertheless, they got through. Then they beat Belgium 2-0 and only lost to Germany in the semi-finals because of a disputed offside decision. Coshi still has a lot of skill. He may not be as quick as he once was, but he is still the beating heart of the team. Also, don't forget Andy Crawford on the wing. He played for England thirty-odd times and knocked in a dozen goals if I remember rightly. Again, he is not the fastest man on the pitch anymore, but he still has a footballing brain."

Westward continued to outline the strategy for the game before dismissing the squad for an afternoon of rest ahead of the game the next day.

Do they believe enough? he pondered as he watched cars depart one by one?

Come to think of it, do I?

****

The team gathered at Wiltshire Park at 10:00am and fifteen minutes later they were on the road for the journey to the opponents. As always, Westward looked into the club's history, having never visited the stadium. On his mobile phone, he checked Wikipedia for any nuggets of information that would stand out.

'Stadium is called B2NET stadium...... capacity just under 11,000...... cost £13 million...... nickname 'The Spireites'...... club formed originally as offshoot of their cricket club...... great cup run in 1997...... scandal surrounding former manager Darren Brown in 2000...... club didn't win for 21 games...... debts amounted up...... hopped between League One and Two for most of the time...... revival under Geoff Lambert who bought in Coshi and Crawford...... club in Championship for last four seasons...... highest placing eighth two years ago.

To him it sounded like every other second string club who, despite every effort, would never make it any further than their current status. He felt such empathy, having seen Woodmouth suffer the same fate for so many years. He only hoped that he had given his players a vision strong enough to change theirs.

****

Woodmouth started brightly, and, as per their manager's instructions, concentrated on keeping possession. Gustavsson was expected to do a man-on-man marking job on Coshi and, as expected, despite his age and mere five-feet, five-inch frame, the little Egyptian still had an enormous amount of skill. Twenty minutes passed and neither side had produced a worthwhile shot on goal. Crawford on the left wing was stopped more than once by excellent tackles by Kevin Ayres.

On twenty-five minutes, Woodmouth won a corner on their left. Rudi Radzednic chipped over a full length, in-swinger, which Paul Lincoln glanced goalward only for Chesterfield defender Steve Bradbury to clear desperately off the line. Chris Haynes' desperate follow up was inches past the post. Haynes held his head in his hands as he knew that he should have had the ball in the net from that distance. Westward still applauded his team-mates and encouraged them to keep things going. Bruce Dean began to forage further down the left and, after interchanging two passes with Belkin and Gustavsson let fly an opportunist effort from thirty yards which clipped the post. He turned in frustration, hands on his head. He caught his manager's attention. Westward gritted his teeth and clenched a fist in appreciation of the wing-back's effort.

Chesterfield's central attacking options were all successfully dampened by Gustavsson and Clive Belkin, the latter once again playing a much deeper role. Crawford's frustrations began to show and he was booked just before half-time as once again Ayres dispossessed him and cleared his attacking wing-play. Half-time arrived and neither side had managed to break the deadlock in another afternoon caged with hesitant nervousness.

Westward had no negative comments regarding his team's performance in the dressing room at half-time. He felt that defensively they had held firm, the midfield was showing some creativity, the only challenge had been the lack of chances for Lincoln and Haynes up front.

The second half began with Chesterfield having made a substitution. Striker Lee Vincent was taken off and Neil Barnes, a central defender came on. They began a very cautious approach, knowing that they only needed a draw to guarantee their safety for another season. More and more Chesterfield players stayed behind the ball and it seemed once again that only a moment of skill or fortune would change the scoreline. For fifteen minutes, events continued as they had done – both sides unable to offer anything in the final third of the field. Woodmouth pushed but the final pass always seemed just out of reach of their strikers. Westward once again encouraged them to build from the back and keep possession. On seventy-three minutes, their patience was rewarded. Rudi Radzednic ran slowly, unchallenged to the halfway line. As Coshi approached from the left, he quickly saw a run in front of him made by Clive Belkin. He took the ball to the right. With this move, he also took with him the attention of two Chesterfield players. This left a big gap where Radzednic surged on to take Belkin's back-heel. Radzednic continued his run, fed a through ball, perfectly timed into the path of oncoming Bruce Dean on the left. His first time cross was leapt for by two defenders along with Paul Lincoln who, even though a couple of inches short of his markers, still made contact and the ball looped its way over the approaching goalkeeper. The ball however, did not have enough momentum to cross the line, but Chris Haynes was a split second ahead of his marker to stab the ball home from very close range. He turned and ran back to his team-mates, arms aloft in triumph. Chesterfield players looked on in despair, hands on hips.

Woodmouth now had their chance.

"Let's hold on now! We can do this!" Westward roared.

Chesterfield's tactics immediately changed as they sieged the Woodmouth goal area. Coshi became much more involved, Crawford and he interlacing passes but again, Ayres, Dean and the three central defenders held firm. Until the eighty-fifth minute. Five minutes from victory. Coshi ran at

Gustavsson who was by now spent. The Egyptian with every ounce of his remaining energy nipped past the big Dane and released a right foot shot from the edge of the box. It curled away and bounced off the crossbar, Page in the Woodmouth goal beaten. Westward attempted to clear the ball, but his clearance, instead of finding Martin Haynes, clipped off Ray Somerton's leg right into the path of James Hurley who had time to pick his spot to make it 1-1. Woodmouth were devastated. Westward screamed at them. "This is not the end! It does not finish here! We are not beaten yet! Get your heads up!"

With one minute of normal time left, the fourth official held up the electronic board to show three minutes of added time. Chesterfield took a short goal-kick and attempted to keep possession to run down the clock. Every pass was pressured by a Woodmouth player. The referee looked at his watch. Westward's heart beat with dread.

You promised me, Lord! You promised!

At last the Chesterfield goalkeeper, having been warned by the referee for time-wasting, took a long goal-kick which Westward himself chested down. Aware that he had just seconds remaining looked up and chipped a ball down the centre of the park. Every Chesterfield player ran towards the halfway line and screamed for an offside decision. It never came. Chris Haynes remembered his boss's constant words in training.

Play to the whistle.

Westward had wondered how the tiny pocket of Woodmouth supporters had snuck in behind the goal to which Haynes ran but their meagre encouragement frantically urged him on. He sprinted and caught up with the ball with the keeper running at him. He took a shot from twenty-five yards which skimmed the diving body of the keeper and bounced over him. Haynes kept running and saw an open goal. He knew there were players catching him up. He was out of breath but still ran. He took a shot but screamed inside in frustration as it cannoned off the post, but back into his path.

Again, he shot, this time it hit the underside of the crossbar, but bounced in front of the line. He launched himself at the ball, a final effort knowing that the encroaching players would probably have beaten him to it otherwise.

Somehow, his chest made contact with the ball, instead of his head, which was the intention. As the ball was about to cross the line, the boot of a defender caught Haynes on the side of the head and a split second later, managed to stop a certain goal. Haynes collapsed in agony as the referee blew the whistle. He had tried. He had given his all. But, still he had not made it. Then a shout arose from the Woodmouth fans behind the goal. He looked up, wincing. The whistle was not the end.

Woodmouth had been awarded a penalty.

He laid his head down again.

Will it always be a knife edge like this? He thought to himself as was besieged by team-mates.

The referee, as expected was also surrounded by demonstrating Chesterfield players. Two were booked, one sent off for aiming a kick at Rudi Radzednic. Wisely, as his manager had endorsed, he walked away and said nothing. A few moments later, having regained the control of the game, there was yet another hold up. A linesman was waving frantically to get the referee's attention.

Oh no, Westward thought, *surely he is not questioning the penalty?*

The referee trotted over to the byline and the two men in black had a very animated conversation. Westward stood, staring at the sky, almost begging God for favour. The referee turned and pointed to the penalty spot. Westward, even though he tried to remain calm and assured, jumped with arms aloft.

By now, even though shaken, Haynes was on his feet.

"You want the kick, Chris?" Westward offered.

Haynes, still short of breath, squinted. "Boss, I've got blurred vision, give it to someone else."

Westward looked around at his team. "I'll take it. I could not ask for any more from you guys. I would hate for one of you lot to be responsible for a missed penalty. If I miss, that's my fault. I'll take it."

Westward placed the ball on the spot and did his best to avoid looking at the goalkeeper. He turned, walked a few paces. The referee blew the whistle.

You won't make it.

Everyone will laugh at you.

Go back to computers.

The old demons of doubt demonstrated.

Watch for the rebound if he saves it or it hits the post. Don't worry. Just hit the ball, he told himself, his heart racing.

He turned back, ran eyes closed as he shot low to the left.

The keeper got a finger to it.

Westward somehow tripped as he did continue his run, along with a number of other players. As he twisted and fell, he somehow managed to make contact with the ball and from the ground watched it trickle three inches over the line. He got up and ran and ran and ran, his team chasing him all over the pitch. Those on the bench, Brian Chambers included in a rare moment of seeming foolishness, joined the circus parade, forgetting that the match had not yet reached its conclusion.

The handful of Woodmouth supporters raced past the few policemen on duty onto the pitch and embraced whoever on the Woodmouth side that they could reach. The referee tried desperately to gain some order once again. Eventually the police did escort the fans away and the teams lined up for the restart. Crawford passed the ball to Coshi, ran three yards forward and attempted a shot from what would have been forty-odd yards. The ball nestled safely into Eric Page's hands. He held the ball and casually waved a gesture of 'calm down, I have it.'

As he rolled the ball short to Kevin Ayres, the final whistle blew. While the rest of the team jumped in the air, Westward fell to his knees and dropped his face to the turf. His body convulsed as he began to weep tears not of joy but of simple relief. Beaming team-mates mobbed him, hugged him, and in the end protected him from well-meaning but foolish supporters. Westward eventually dragged his exhausted body up and raised his tired arms in triumph with a roar of sheer satisfaction. Questions began to bombard him in his enervated state. Could they really achieve anything greater than this? Did he have the fortitude to carry on? Could he sustain motivation in the team?

One thing was certain: Woodmouth had achieved the almost impossible.

They had survived.

Just as God Himself had promised.

****

Jordan Westward
will return in:

Three More Minutes.